Counting the Stars

TRACY McJAMES

Heart on Paper LLC

Dear Reader,

Due to the overtones of grief/loss and a small (not overly descriptive) violent scene, I've decided to add a trigger warning to this book. I do guarantee lots of laughs and a happily ever after, but completely understand if you choose to skip this one.

This book is dedicated to my ARC readers of When Our Stars Aligned. You took a chance on an unknown author and have shown me so much love. For that, I am forever grateful!

Contents

1. Alex — 1

2. Gabby — 7

3. Alex — 17

4. Gabby — 25

5. Alex — 30

6. Gabby — 34

7. Alex — 38

8. Gabby — 43

9. Alex — 49

10. Gabby — 57

11. Alex — 63

12. Gabby — 67

13. Alex   76

14. Gabby   79

15. Alex   87

16. Gabby   92

17. Alex   97

18. Gabby   103

19. Alex   111

20. Gabby   117

21. Gabby   124

22. Alex   133

23. Gabby   138

24. Alex   147

25. Gabby   155

26. Alex   165

27. Gabby   169

28. Alex   176

29. Gabby   182

30. Alex   190

31. Gabby   194

32. Gabby   204

33. Alex	209
34. Gabby	216
35. Alex	219
36. Alex	223
37. Gabby	229
38. Gabby	233
39. Alex	237
40. Gabby	244
41. Alex	250
42. Gabby	254
43. Epilogue	260
44. Bonus Epilogue	264
Acknowledgements	268
About the author	270

1

Alex

"Drop your drawers and bend over, princess," the burly nurse orders.

"Oh, come on, Hilda, don't you think we're moving a little fast? I mean, you haven't even bought me dinner." I flash my megawatt smile that's always a favorite of the ladies. Of course it does nothing for Hilda. She might as well be a troll that lives in the swamp and eats her young.

Figures I'd get the worst of the worst assigned to me. I know almost every worker in the Emergency Department of Starboard Beach Community Hospital. I've been working right next door at the firehouse for several years. Sometimes I even moonlight as a paramedic with the first aid squad, which is conveniently attached to the firehouse. As a matter of fact, our police station is directly across the street from the hospital. Basically, this section of Starboard Beach is a one-stop shop for all your emergency needs. Unfortunately, today, I'm the one in need.

The troll nurse pumps the syringe, letting a string of liquid spew onto the floor.

"Don't tetanus shots go in the upper arm?"

"Not when you do something stupid and cut both shoulders," she replies gruffly, nodding in the direction of my bandages. My scrapes aren't too bad, but the gauze currently covering up my wounds does block access to where the needle would typically go. At least I didn't require stitches.

"I was trying to save a kitten!" Okay, it wasn't my smartest move. I cut my arms sticking my hands down a rusty drainpipe. I could barely reach the kitten's whiskers, so I tried using my other arm...like that would be any longer. Not my finest moment. In the end, my buddy Mickelson was able to coax the little furball out and even offered to adopt it for his two daughters. He got the kitten. I got several scrapes and a trip to the ER for a tetanus booster.

"Survival of the fittest." Hilda shrugs. "The kitten shouldn't have been exploring in a drainpipe."

"It was probably trying to seek shelter from the rain and—" I look at her stone-cold face. "Why am I even bothering explaining this to you?"

"Beats the hell out of me." She grunts. "Now drop your drawers and bend over."

Not wanting to offend the troll nurse, I do as she says. As I unbuckle my belt, I hear a small gasp and a shhh from behind the curtain. It's then I notice several sets of shoes poking out from underneath. I smile and scan the shoes disappointedly. No purple Sketchers, a telltale sign that Gabby would be one of the nurses trying to catch a glimpse of my ass. It's not like she needs to sneak around to see me half naked anyway. I parade around both of our condos in a lot less than what I'm wearing now, which happens to be my usual outfit of jeans and a dark blue SBFD T-shirt.

More muffled sounds come from behind the curtain as I pull down my pants along with just a bit of my boxers. I don't feel like mooning half of the hospital staff, although privacy is not my strongpoint. I've always been a bit of an exhibitionist.

I'm also a bit of a genetic phenomenon. My mom is from Mexico and my dad is from Canada. They met while in college and decided to settle in the US. I inherited my mom's tan skin and dark hair but have my dad's blue eyes and stand at just about six-foot-two. I am the youngest of seven children. Half of my siblings look like my mom and the other half look like my dad. I am the only one who is a true combination. It's the running joke that my parents stopped after me because why mess with perfection?

The cold sensation of an alcohol wipe on my skin makes me do a little jump. I don't have a fear of needles, but I'm really not fond of Nurse Ratched anywhere near my nether regions.

"Is Gabby here today?" I ask.

"Haven't seen Ms. Ramirez."

Gabriella Ramirez will one day become Mrs. Gabriella Ramirez Jones. She just doesn't know it yet. I, on the other hand, have known it from the moment we met.

It was a dark and stormy night (no, seriously, it was winter and the rain was coming down in buckets).

I had just finished up my shift when I pulled into the parking lot of the condo I share with my buddy, Carter. The wind was whipping so hard it was difficult to see a hand in front of me, but somehow, I noticed a small figure hovering over a light blue sedan.

"Do you need some help?" I asked the figure.

She turned to face me and at that moment, I swear the sky cleared and the clouds parted to reveal the most stunning woman I had ever seen. The streetlight shone down, giving her the look of an angelic halo. She was drenched from head to toe; her dark hair clung to her face. I never really believed in love at first sight, but when she looked up at me with those beautiful brown eyes, I knew at that moment, I was looking into my future.

"I locked my keys in my car," she said, trying to brush back her hair.

"Ah! Well, it's your lucky day because I have just the thing to help." I ran back to my SUV to grab my Slim Jim. I don't get to use this tool much since many newer car models have an electronic system you can bypass, but fortunately for this mystery woman, she was driving an older vehicle. I grabbed the tool from my car and in no time was able to pop her door open.

"Thank you," she said quietly as I retrieved her keys from the driver's seat. "I'm no damsel in distress, by the way."

"I didn't think you were. It happens to the best of us." I placed the keys in her palm, noticing that her hand was absent of a ring. Perfect. I may have enjoyed the company of women, but I was no homewrecker.

"I do this all the time." She shook her head, seemingly mad at herself. "I usually have a hide-a-key under my bumper, but I guess I forgot to put it back the last time I did this."

"Well, lucky for you, I was here to help." I stuck my hand out to shake hers. "I'm Alex."

"Gabriella." She reached out and shook my hand. "But you can call me Gabby."

"It's nice to meet you, Gabby. Are you visiting?" I noticed her license plates were from Arizona. I hoped her stay wasn't temporary. That could put a damper on the whole meeting-my-future-wife thing.

"No, I just moved in yesterday."

"Yesterday," I repeated. "Are you Michelle's new roommate?" Michelle lived in the condo adjacent to mine. She mentioned she was interviewing potential roommates, but I hadn't been around much to know if she found anyone.

"Yes. You know Michelle?" She cocked her head to the side in curiosity.

"I live right next door in 310."

"Oh, wow!" she stammered. "Are you roommates with Carter? I met him last night."

Of course she'd met Carter already. He was like the damn welcome wagon for all of us on 3rd East. If it wasn't for him, I probably wouldn't have met Michelle or Jax, who lived across the hall.

An icy gust of wind blew, making her visibly shiver. The rain might've stopped, but we were both soaked to the bone. "You must be freezing. Come on, let's get inside."

"Yeah, I'm not used to the cold like this." She wrapped her arms around herself and followed me through the doors of the lobby. We had a nice little setup here at the Woodland Condominiums. The building was basically a square with each side named after the direction it faces. The main floor had a pool, small gym, laundry room, and mailroom; the condos started on the second floor. We lived on the 3rd floor on the east side, hence the 3rd East name.

"So what brings you to Oregon?" I casually asked as we stepped onto the elevator.

"Job relocation," she replied, with nothing more.

"What do you do?"

"I'm a nurse."

"No shit! Will you be working at the hospital?"

She nodded while staring at the numbers over the elevator door. "I start next week in the Emergency Department."

"Well, I guess we'll be seeing a lot of each other. I'm at the firehouse next door." I gave her a flirty wink, but her face seemed to wash over with sadness. I brushed it off. Maybe she was just tired from her move and getting caught in the rain.

"I guess so," she replied noncommittally and practically jumped out of the elevator when it reached our floor.

I followed behind her like a lost puppy.

"Umm, what are you doing?" She turned when we stopped at the door of 312. I hadn't realized I walked right past my place.

"Just making sure you get home safely." I smiled and hoped that would save my blunder. I was usually much smoother with the ladies.

"Oh, okay, well...thanks again for helping me with my keys."

"Anytime, and I know you're no damsel in distress, but if you ever need help with anything, just remember I'm right next door." I pointed in the direction of my place just as she slipped through the door of hers.

I stayed standing in the hallway until her door was completely shut. I couldn't believe my luck. My future bride not only just moved in next door, but she would be working right beside me as well. This was going to be so easy.

"OW!" A sharp burning sensation pulls me out of my thoughts. I swivel my head to glare at Hilda. "You just stabbed me in the ass!"

"It was one little prick," she says, holding up her weapon of choice. I swear there's a drop of blood on it. Hilda disposes of the needle and stomps away, muttering something to herself just as a familiar face pops her head through the curtain.

"Now you show up?"

2

Gabby

Gripping my extra-large caramel coconut cold brew from Portside Perks, I head into work, ready to start my shift at Starboard Beach's Emergency Department, only to discover a small crowd hovering around the curtain of Room 2.

"What's everyone doing?" I ask Dr. Cody, one of the attending physicians who doesn't seem to care about the commotion behind him.

"Mr. February's getting a tetanus shot." He rolls his eyes and walks away.

Mr. Feb—Ah! He's talking about Alex! That's been his unofficial nickname since he posed for a firefighter calendar last year. I run toward the crowd as I hear a yelp and a "That's what you get," from Hilda.

"Man, I didn't get to see anything," Rebecca, a nursing assistant, whines as she and the crowd disperse.

I pull back the curtain to see Alex rubbing his right butt cheek while Hilda disposes of the syringe and walks away with a scowl.

"Now you show up?" Alex looks at me with disappointment as he zips up his pants.

"I just got here and haven't even started my shift yet. What in the world did you do to earn yourself a tetanus shot?"

"I was trying to save a kitten from a rusty drainpipe and got scratched." He lifts up the sleeves of his T-shirt to show me his bandages. "I'm pretty sure she used sandpaper and lemon juice to clean my scrapes."

"Oh, *pobrecito*." I feign sadness as I walk up to him and place my arms around his waist. My hand rubs along the spot of his injection. "Does this feel better?"

"A little." Alex dramatically pouts. He places his hands on my hips. "But I think the pain is traveling a little bit around to the front." A mischievous smile plays on his lips, and I know he's about to bring out those dimples of his that make me swoon.

"Not happening." I playfully smack his chest. I usually don't get this touchy-feely with Alex, but I didn't like how there was an audience trying to get a glimpse of him with his pants down. My roommates and I see him in his underwear all the time, but somehow, that's different.

"Fine." His grasp on my waist gets tighter. "I know something else that will help me feel better."

"I'm also not going out on a date with you."

"That's not what I was going to say."

"No?" I raise a brow.

"Nope. I was going to say you should marry me."

"Alex!" I groan. If he's not asking me out on a date, he's proposing. The man is incorrigible.

"What?" He pulls back to look at me. "Let's just skip the whole dating thing and go straight to marriage. We can date each other once we are betrothed."

"Betrothed?" I chuckle.

"It's a good word." He shrugs.

A voice clearing has both of our heads whipping around to meet the sound. My nurse manager, Gail, stands near the curtain. "When you're done with whatever this is, Ms. Ramirez, I'd like to see you in my office." Her gaze shifts from me to Alex for a minute, but she says nothing more before walking away.

"Oh God! That was my supervisor!" My eyes go wide. "I can't lose my job!"

"Relax. You're not going to lose your job for grabbing my ass. I know Gail. You'll be fine," Alex says matter-of-factly. I'm convinced he knows everyone who lives in Starboard Beach. As for me, I just moved here a little over a year ago and I'm not as gregarious as Alex. "Gail is a good one. Unlike Nurse Nightmare over there." We step out of the room and walk down the hallway in comfortable silence until we reach Gail's door.

"Want me to wait out here for you?" Alex leans against the wall.

"No, I don't know how long I'll be and I'm sure you have to get back to the firehouse."

"Nah, I'm done for the day. I guess since you're just starting your shift, I won't see you later."

"Nope, but Michelle told me if I saw you to let you know that she's making some type of stir-fry tonight and pineapple upside down cake for dessert."

My roommate, Michelle, is the youngest out of all of us on 3rd East. She's in law school, but I have a feeling she'd rather focus on her culinary skills. She's constantly trying new recipes and loves to feed all of us. On days when she's too busy to cook, Aly or I pick up the slack. Aly was our roommate for a while, but she ended up marrying Jax, who lives across the hall. Thankfully, she didn't have to move too far and our 3rd East crew is still tight-knit.

"Best neighbors ever!" Alex does a little happy dance. "But you know you're still my favorite."

"I know." Secretly, he's my favorite too. I give Alex a little wave as he walks down the hall. I turn toward Gail's door, take a deep breath, and knock.

"Come in!" Gail says in a pleasant tone. Well, that's a good sign, I hope. Still, I'm nervous as hell, wondering what she wants to talk about.

"I'm so sorry, ma'am!" The words spill out as soon as I step into the office. "I know that looked extremely unprofessional. I wasn't on the clock yet, not that it matters. I mean, I still shouldn't have been messing around with Alex. It's just that I know him. I mean, we're neighbors...and friends—"

"Gabriella!" Gail holds up her hand to silence my rant. "You're not in trouble."

"I-I'm not?" Air refills my lungs.

"No, not at all." She shuffles around some papers on her desk and motions for me to take a seat.

"I thought when you called me back here—" My voice trails off as I sit down.

"I called you back here for something completely unrelated to whatever that was I walked in on." She waves her hand nonchalantly in the air. "I wanted to catch you before your shift started. How would you feel about a change in departments?"

"A change?"

"Mm-hmm." Gail nods. "One of the nurses from Pediatrics will be going on maternity leave soon. We need someone to fill her spot, and I think you would be the perfect person for the position."

"Peds?" I never thought about working on the pediatric floor, but I know I can't be an emergency room nurse forever. I can handle the fast-paced environment, but sometimes the stress of certain cases keeps me up at night. Some hit too close to home.

"I've seen how you are with young patients. You have a gift, you know. Kids feel comfortable with you. I hate to lose you here, but I know you will be a perfect fit for them. If you want the job, of course."

"Yes! Thank you! Thank you so much!" I pause. "Are you sure you're okay with what you saw between Alex and me?"

"You mean Mr. February?" She flips her calendar back three months to the picture of Alex posing shirtless in front of a fire truck with a hose wrapped around his broad shoulders. "Honey, if I were twenty years younger and single, I'd be all over that man."

I laugh as she stands up from behind her desk. We walk out of the office together and cross paths with Hilda pushing a code cart.

As soon as the world's grumpiest nurse is out of earshot, Gail leans into me and whispers, "The moment an opening becomes available in the ICU, I'm sending Hilda there. That way most of her patients will be comatose or too drugged to remember her."

I laugh again and my shoulders relax. I can't wait to tell Alex and my friends about my new position. As I head toward my station to finally start my day, Dr. Cody taps me on the shoulder.

"Miss Ruby is back," he says when I spin around to look at him. "Room 5."

Miss Ruby is what we like to call one of our frequent fliers. She's here several times a month but not for your typical ailments. At eighty-eight years young, she's a woman who has an affinity for living life on the edge. In the short time I've worked here, I've treated her for minor burns from setting off fireworks and whiplash from a ziplining adventure gone wrong. As crazy as she may seem, she's a delight to work with.

"Hello, Miss Ruby! What did you do to earn yourself a trip to the ER today?" I step into the room and notice an extra person standing in the corner. "Alex? What are you still doing here?"

"I was getting ready to leave when I heard the familiar voice of the beautiful and vivacious Miss Ruby. I just had to check on her."

"Oh, you are one of my favorites." Miss Ruby's hazel eyes twinkle as she turns to look at the tall, dark, and handsome man beside her.

I don't even need to ask how Alex knows Miss Ruby. He's brought her in several times since I've been here.

"I was out watering my garden when a few of the neighborhood kids came by on those things that look like a skateboard, but you don't push them," Miss Ruby starts to explain.

"Hoverboards," Alex answers.

"Yes, that's it." Miss Ruby nods. "It looked like fun, so I asked if I could go for a ride."

"And you fell?" I assume.

"One of the kids tried to catch me." She lifts up her bedsheet to reveal a nasty bruise on her upper thigh. "It was a soft fall and I landed in a grassy area, but the neighbors insisted on calling an ambulance so I could get checked out."

"I understand," I say, stepping a little closer to her bed. Typically, elderly patients have brittle bones, but not Miss Ruby. She's stronger than most.

"I'm fine," Miss Ruby continues. "But that doctor with the poor bedside manner insisted I need these things." She points to the heart monitor. "I hate these wires."

"I get it, Miss Ruby, but while your bones are as tough as nails, you do have a history of heart disease. Dr. Cody just wants to make sure you're in tip-top shape before sending you home." I grab a pair of gloves to inspect the hematoma closer.

"Do you think this bruise will heal by next Thursday? I volunteered to be a nude model for a sculpture class at the art institute."

"Oh! Umm..." I snap my head up and immediately regret making eye contact with Alex, who has gone pale. It's not often he's stunned silent. I chew on the inside of my cheek to hold back my amusement. "It might not be entirely gone by then, but I'm sure a good concealer will take care of that."

"Well, I think I've overstayed my time. I don't want to be late for dinner." Alex finds his voice and an excuse for a quick exit. "Miss Ruby, as always, it was a pleasure to see you." He does a little bow, then turns to me. "And you have a wonderful and hopefully uneventful night." He places a chaste kiss on my temple before sauntering away. My eyes can't help but follow him as he walks out of sight.

"If I were younger, I'd be all over that man," Miss Ruby says, pulling me out of thoughts I should not be having.

"Funny, you're not the first person to say that to me today." I turn back to my patient.

"It's the truth. Alex is quite the catch and I'm not just saying that because of his charming good looks. He is always the kindest when it comes to helping out. About two years ago, before you moved here, I twisted my ankle while rollerblading. Alex came over every week with bags of groceries. I told him I had neighbors and friends to help, but he insisted it was no trouble at all."

"That's so nice. I didn't know that." Although I'm not surprised. While Alex is probably one of the most sarcastic people I've ever met, there's another side of him that's as sweet as can be.

"I know he's a lot of talk—acts boastful and such—but there's a heart of gold underneath all those muscles...those big, rippling—"

"Miss Ruby, your heart rate is spiking!" I run over to silence the beeping monitor.

"Ah." She brushes me off. "Sometimes it's good for this old ticker to get the blood pumping. So tell me, why don't you go out with him? He seems to have taken a liking to you."

"Yeah, well, you know Alex has a bit of a reputation." I keep my tone casual. It's my go-to excuse whenever the topic of why I don't take Alex up on his numerous offers comes up. Since he is Starboard Beach's biggest flirt, no one ever challenges me on my explanation. In truth, I couldn't care less about his history. My reasoning goes much deeper than that.

"Hmm...that excuse sounds good. But I've been around a long time, Gabby. You can't fool me. There's something else. Isn't there?"

"I-I," I stumble on my words. "It's just that... Things have happened in my life that make me hesitate to get into any relationship..." My voice trails off and I hope what I've said is enough to appease the woman.

"I see." She solemnly shakes her head. "You know, you remind me a lot of my younger self in many ways." She pats the side of bed for me to sit down.

"I do?"

"Oh yes, always working and tends to keep to herself. I was a telephone operator for the county back before they had all this new technology." She waves her hand around the room with a wistful look on her face. "Oh, I loved my job. I worked every chance I could get...nights, weekends, holidays. I took every extra shift so my coworkers could spend time with their families."

The typical light in Miss Ruby's eyes begins to dim. "Everyone assumed I was just a strong, single, independent woman who loved to work. The real reason I worked so much was that I hated coming home to an empty house."

I adjust my position on the bed to face Miss Ruby as she continues. "I was only a year old when I lost my mother. She passed away shortly after the birth of my little brother. My father couldn't handle the stress and drank himself to death by the time I was five. I went to live with relatives for a while, but then my brother fell ill and passed away. The grief of losing my family was too much. I acted out a lot and was sent to live with other relatives until they got tired of me and passed me off to an orphanage."

I gasp and place my hand over my heart. "I'm so sorry."

"It's okay, Gabriella. I'm telling you this for a reason." The creases surrounding her eyes grow deeper. "I shied away from relationships for a long time. I had a lot of acquaintances but never any true friends. I was afraid to get attached to anyone because I figured I would eventually lose them. That fear was paralyzing.

"But then something happened to me on my eighty-third birthday. I woke up and realized that not many people make it to my age. What did I have to show for it? Not much. I was eighty-three years old and never really lived...or loved."

"So that's why you skydive and go streaking?" I nervously fidget with the hem of my scrubs.

"I never would've gotten injured streaking had that sprinkler not popped up. But yes, and I'm happier than I have ever been. I'm finally experiencing life the way it should be lived. The way it was intended to be enjoyed. I may not have any blood relatives left, but I've surrounded myself with wonderful people. They are my found family and bring me so much joy. Don't wait until you're eighty-three to start living your life."

"How do you know I'm not?" I tilt my chin up.

"Like I said before, you remind me of my younger self. I can see it in your eyes. Those are the eyes of someone who has experienced a lot of loss. So tell me, dear, who did you lose?"

I look down at the floor, wondering how to answer the question. There's no sense in lying. She'll see right through me. I finally respond, "Everyone."

3

Alex

"That's going to be a tight fit. It might be better if we go through the back." Jax looks between the large stainless-steel refrigerator and the front door of his future home.

"That's what she said." I can't help myself.

"Alex, I'm in no mood for this," Jax grumbles.

"Sadly, that's also what she said."

"Why the hell is he here?" Travis, Jax's best friend and business partner, smacks the side of the box. I don't know him too well. He seems like an okay guy, a bit high-strung at times, but I know he's been through a lot of shit. Shit I can't even imagine.

"We've been through this." Jax looks at Travis, clearly getting agitated. "This house had more issues than expected. In order to keep us afloat, the crew needs to work on the house on Anchor while we put in as much effort as possible into this one. It needs to be move-in ready before Aly has the baby. Plus, Alex is cheap labor."

"Thanks," I huff. I actually don't mind helping Jax out. I admit I'm here more for muscle than to actually fix something.

I'm not much of a handyman, but I'd like to learn a few things for when I eventually settle down and have a place of my own.

This house has been a bear to work on. The entire electrical system needed updating as well as the plumbing. Jax and Travis also replaced the roof, siding, and windows. And did I mention there was also one room covered in floor-to-ceiling mirrors? I was tasked with the job of taking all of them down. Getting to see myself from every angle is not as much fun as I thought.

Jax has been working on this house for months, even before he and Legs, aka Aly, got together. Once they realized their relationship was a match made in Heaven (literally), they eloped and immediately started planning a family. I'm happy for them. Jax is much less of a grump nowadays, and Legs has become a great friend.

"Aly isn't due for months," Travis grumbles. "There's still plenty of time to get this done."

"I want everything as perfect as possible," Jax argues.

"How about we take a lunch break and order a pizza?" Carter, forever the peacemaker, whips out his phone.

"I think that's a great idea." I study the fridge currently sitting in the driveway. "We can figure out a game plan for this monstrosity while we eat."

Everyone agrees and we head toward the almost completed kitchen to get some drinks and wait for our food.

"Have you decided what you'll do with your condo once you move in here?" Carter places a large cooler on the kitchen counter.

"Aly gets all emotional when I bring up the subject. She's excited to move in here, but she doesn't want to leave all of you either." Jax waves his hand between Carter and me. I know he's also referring to Gabby and Michelle, who were Aly's original roommates. "I think we'll stay at the condo for the duration of her pregnancy so she has everyone around her, and then we'll move in once J.J. is born."

"I'm sure we'll be over all the time. You know, since you have so much space here. That wraparound porch of yours gets some great light. It would be the perfect place to sunbathe." I grab a bottle of water from the cooler.

"Note to self: add an awning to the porch." Jax swings around and points a finger at me. "And I'm establishing a new rule. Every guest in our house must be fully clothed at all times."

"Fine," I huff. I have an issue when it comes to wearing clothes... I don't like them. I'm okay in my heavy gear when I'm fighting fires 'cause you need to protect the goods and all. But when I'm at home? Everything comes off. Well, almost everything. I keep my boxers on when I'm around Carter because that would be weird. I'm also required to wear clothes when I eat with the girls. They claim it's too distracting or whatever.

"Pizza is here," Travis says, tilting his head toward the window. An older model Volkswagen pulls up to the curb.

"I'll get it." I run over to the front door and swing it wide open. "Well, hello." I smile at the sight of a young, college-aged blonde holding our delivery.

"Hi." Her face flushes. "I, umm...I have two large pizzas—one meat lovers, one pepperoni with extra cheese."

"That's us." I take our order and hand her some cash. "Keep the change."

"Are you sure?" Her eyes widen when she adds up the tip I just gave her. It's more than I usually give, but her tires look pretty worn.

"Absolutely. I appreciate the prompt, friendly, and might I say beautiful service." I wink.

"Thank you." Her face turns an even deeper shade of red.

"Have a wonderful day!" I call out as she makes her way back down the driveway. I close the door and turn back to the guys, who are all giving me a look.

"What?" I place the pizzas on the counter.

"You just can't help yourself." Carter shakes his head.

"I was being polite."

"Your polite and my polite are two different things." Carter grabs a slice of meat lovers. "You flirt with anything on two legs."

"Glad I only have one." Travis snorts, referring to the fact that he has a prosthetic. I don't know much, but I know he and Jax were injured overseas during their time in the Navy. Jax is able to cover the majority of his scars with tattoos, but Travis's are too numerous and severe to hide.

"See, this is why Gabby won't go out with you," Jax chimes in, grabbing a slice of pepperoni and mumbling something about it lacking pineapple.

"Oh, like you're the relationship expert now?"

"Of course not, but it doesn't take a genius to figure out that Gabby doesn't want to go out with a guy who has slept with half the population of Starboard Beach." Jax takes a bite of his pizza.

"This coming from the guy who has slept with the other half," I counter. It's true. Jax and I are not known for our celibate ways, although he's cleaned up his act since Aly came into his life. I, too, have calmed down significantly. I haven't been with anyone since I met Gabby. Oh, there have been opportunities, but the thought of being intimate with anyone else makes me ill. It's funny. For most of my life, I was against long-term relationships, but everything changed once I met her. I just wish the feeling were reciprocated.

"I'm reformed now!" Jax says defensively.

"So am I. I just don't have a way to prove it."

"I will admit," Carter pipes up, "Alex spends a lot more time at home now compared to when I first moved in."

"See!" I point to my roommate. I've always liked this guy.

"I don't think it's just the excessive flirting." Carter shakes his head. "She doesn't take you seriously. How many times have you asked her to marry you?"

I throw my head back and think. "Counting today?"

The guys let out a collective groan.

"How much do you really know about her?" Carter presses.

"I know that her favorite coffee order is caramel coconut cold brew, she hates flowers, and she's petrified of spiders. She loves the color purple and reading romance novels and has the best sense of humor because she always laughs at my jokes." I pause. "And the way her ass looks in those leggings she wears—"

"Dude!" Jax cuts me off. "Quit it! I feel like you're talking about my little sister."

"Agreed." Carter rubs his chin. "So you know some basic things about her, but you need to get to know her on a deeper level. Why doesn't she like flowers?"

"I'm not sure. She mentioned it to me one time when a patient brought in a huge arrangement as a thank you to everyone who took care of her in the ED."

"That's kind of odd," Travis chimes in. "Is she allergic to them?"

"No." I shrug. "She just doesn't seem to like them."

"If you are really serious about her, I think you need to get your shit together and come up with some sort of plan." Carter grabs a piece of paper from a notebook on the counter.

"A plan for what?"

"To win Gabby's heart because right now, you are stuck in the friend zone and trust me, I know all about that." He mumbles the last part under his breath.

"I'm not stuck in the friend zone." I brush him off.

"Really?" He gives a sarcastic smirk. "How are the wedding preparations going?"

"Okay, fine. I guess I could use a little help in the dating department." Geez, I never thought I'd say those words.

All of us watch intently as Carter scribbles down a list. He hands it to me a moment later and I read it aloud.

Operation Ms. to Mrs.

Step 1: Stop proposing every five seconds.

Step 2: Spend more time with Gabby alone and get to know her on a deeper level.

Step 3: Show her you're beginning to take life more seriously.

Step 4: Find out why she doesn't like flowers.

"Okay, not bad. I agree I should probably simmer down on the proposal stuff. Spending time alone could be difficult considering our schedules, but it's not impossible. What do you mean about taking life more seriously?"

"For starters, you act like a thirty-year-old man-child," Travis interjects.

"I'm still twenty-nine, thank you very much. And I can be serious when I need to be." I turn to Jax. "Remember when you fell off the roof and were all doped up on pain meds? I helped look after you."

"You tried to extort government secrets out of me," Jax deadpans.

"Oh yeah, I forgot about that." I play with the paper in my hands.

"I was thinking somewhere along the lines of keeping your clothes on or taking on more responsibilities." Carter mindlessly doodles on a clean sheet of paper.

"Like what? I already have a full-time job and volunteer when I can."

A panting sound comes from beside me.

"Where'd you come from?" I look down at Travis's three-legged dog, Gus. I didn't even realize he was here today, but it makes sense. Travis rarely leaves home without the scruffy hound mix.

"He loves pizza crust," Travis says, giving his trusty sidekick some scraps. Gus eats them in one bite.

A thought occurs to me. "Oh! I know! I could get a dog! That would show Gabby I'm responsible."

"And who would take care of this dog when you're at the firehouse?" Travis asks.

I look over at Carter, who puts both hands up in the air. "Don't look at me! I have enough responsibilities as it is." Carter is an electrician and owns his own business, but on top of that, he helps out his mom and much younger siblings. The man is a saint.

"All right, no dog." I frown. It would be cool to have a dog of my own, but once again, my roommate is right. I'm not home enough to take care of one. I look over at Travis. "Maybe I could borrow Gus sometime? You know, pup sit or something?"

"I take him everywhere with me. When would I need you to pup sit?"

"I don't know." I shrug. "Is there any place he isn't permitted?" Even though Gus is Travis's shadow, he is not a certified service animal. We're lucky to live in a town where most businesses are still locally owned. Many places allow Gus to come inside, but there are a few places that are off-limits.

"We could go to the movies!" Jax says excitedly. "You did mention you wanted to see the new Marvel movie with me."

"I did say that." Travis ponders. "And I hate to leave him home alone."

"Well, now Uncle Alex can watch him while you go to the movies." I stand a little taller, feeling proud of myself for thinking of this. It really is a win-win situation.

"I'll think about it." Travis looks down at his dog and back up to me. "But he's not calling you Uncle Alex."

"Then he can call me Tio Alex," I suggest.

"Oh, for heaven's sake." Carter throws his hands in the air. "He's a dog. He's not calling anyone anything."

"Not with that attitude." I cross my arms over my chest, giving my roommate a stern look.

"I don't know why I even offered advice." Carter shakes his head. "This could be a disaster."

"It might, but I have to give it a shot." I fold up the list and place it in the back pocket of my jeans. I have to for both of us because deep down, I know Gabby cares about me as much as I care about her. I just have to find a way for her to let me in.

4

Gabby

*G**rief*. How can a five-letter word pack so much power? There are days when I go about living my new normal like everything is okay. And to be honest, my new normal is pretty sweet. I adore the people in my life. I love my job and my shared condo, and even though the winter can be brutal, Starboard Beach is a beautiful place to live. Sometimes, I can't believe a place like this exists.

Along the main road that borders the beach side of town, there are many lookout spots to pull off to the side and embrace the majestic scenery. Some of these sites have benches that face the rocky landscape and ocean. Today, instead of going straight home after work, I decide to visit one. I need some time to just be.

The waves crash against the rocks and recede back. I think I like watching the ocean because I can relate to its moods. There are days when the sea is calm and the sun shines down, making the water glisten like diamonds from the heavens above. These are the days that bring me hope. The days when I feel like everything is going to be all right with the world. Then there are times when the waves crash irately against the shore, pounding the rocks with such intense anger. After its fury has been spent, the water withdraws almost apologetically, with sadness for its turbulent behavior. Sadness: that's my mood today.

Earlier during my shift, I was listening to a patient's lungs. It was nothing out of the ordinary, but when she moved her hair to the side, I got a whiff of her perfume. The musky vanilla scent instantly transported me back in time to days spent at home with my mom. I miss my family so much. I'd give anything to go back to our cramped two-bedroom apartment. We may not have had much in the form of material things, but we had a ton of love.

"Mind if I join you?" A familiar voice scares the hell out of me and I let out a scream.

"Alex! What are you doing here?" I clutch my chest, trying to regulate my breathing. I'm relieved it's him and not some random stranger who snuck up on me, but I still wasn't expecting any company.

"Sorry, baby girl, I figured you would've heard me driving up." He hooks his thumb over his shoulder, pointing to his black SUV.

"I was so lost in my thoughts that I didn't hear anything. What are you doing here?" I scoot over on the bench, giving him room to sit next to me. As he sits, he puts his arm around the back of the bench, and without thinking, I lean into his side. The comforting warmth of his body against mine makes my racing heart calm instantly.

"I was coming back from a doctor's appointment and saw your car parked on the side of the road. I swung back around to see what you were up to."

"Doctor's appointment?" My mind immediately jumps to the worst conclusions.

"Just my annual physical for the fire department." His arm comes around closer. "Good news. I'm healthy as a horse, which is funny because I'm also hung like a—"

"Alex!" I elbow him in his side. How this man can turn any normal conversation into something sexual is truly a gift.

"You know I can't help it." He shifts a little. The smell of his cologne combined with the fresh saltwater air is intoxicating.

"I know." I rest my head in the crook of his arm. It's funny how natural this feels.

"So, what are you doing out here?"

"Oh, umm…" I stiffen. "I had a rough shift and just needed some time to unwind before heading home."

"I get that." He nods. "You know, if you ever want to talk, I'm here for you."

This. This is the Alex I adore. Yes, he's goofy and has an aversion toward clothes, but underneath that silliness is one of the kindest souls I've ever met. He will make an amazing husband and father one day.

"I think I'd rather like a distraction."

"Okay then. Any word on when you'll start in Peds?"

After I took care of Miss Ruby, I remembered that I forgot to tell Alex about my meeting with Gail. I called him on my lunch break to tell him the news. He was elated for me, of course. Once the call ended, I realized I haven't had a person to do that with in such a long time. Years ago, if I had something to share, like getting a solo in the choir or my high school boyfriend breaking up with me, I would debate on who to tell first: my mom or my sister. It feels like forever since I've had someone to call.

At the end of your nursing school journey, there's a pinning ceremony. It's a symbolic way to celebrate your accomplishments and transition from student to nurse. During this rite of passage, students choose a family member or close friend to pin them. It's a beautiful and emotional time, although for me, there wasn't much beauty in it. I had no one to pin me. I had no one to look for in the audience. I had no one to give me a hug and tell me they were proud of me. In the end, a faculty member pinned me. Afterwards, I went home and cried myself to sleep. For most, the ceremony symbolized success and new beginnings. For me, it was a reminder that I'm all alone.

"I'm not sure yet," I respond, swallowing down the heartbreaking memory. "The nurse going on maternity leave is having some blood pressure problems. She may need to go on bedrest, which means I could start soon. Marissa, the charge nurse, gave me a tour the other day. I think I'll like it there. It's much calmer than the Emergency Department."

"It is, and I know Marissa. She's terrific. I'm sure you two will get along well."

"Please don't tell me you dated her," I groan. I've heard all sorts of stories about Alex's promiscuous ways. With his charm and looks, I'm sure there's some truth to it. Though, honestly, I've never seen him with a woman.

"I did not." His tone is icy. "I know several of the nurses on that floor because I volunteer for the station's community outreach program. You know, the one where we visit the kids and hand out stuffed animals, firefighter hats, stickers—that kind of stuff?"

"Oh, I didn't think of that." My heart sinks, and I hope I didn't insult him.

The sound of the station's fire alarm blasts in the distance, alerting those nearby to clear the way for the trucks coming through. You can't hear it from inside the hospital because the thick brick walls and other noises drown it out. But outside on a clear day? You can hear that thing for miles.

"I better go," Alex says, pulling out his phone and checking the time. "My shift doesn't start for another half hour, but the guys might need some help."

"Hopefully, it's just a glitchy smoke detector," I say, trying to calm my nerves. The thought of him headed into danger eats away at me.

"Maybe." He stands and pulls his keys out of his pocket. "Did I tell you the ladies at the nursing home pulled the fire alarm last week? It was Mrs. Donaldson's ninetieth birthday and they wanted a show."

"Please tell me you didn't dance for them." I laugh. The older generation in this town is something else.

"I was off that day." He shakes his head. "Good thing too 'cause a bunch of those ladies would've been popping some nitro pills after they saw my moves." He shimmies his hips provocatively.

"Well, thank heaven for small miracles." I'm sure he's not wrong with his assumption considering Miss Ruby's heart rate spiked just from the mere mention of him.

"It was probably for the best," he agrees and starts walking toward his car. "I'll see you soon."

"Yup, see you soon."

Alex's SUV pulls out onto the highway to head to God knows what type of emergency.

"Please be safe," I whisper as his vehicle fades out of view.

This is why I can't be with him.

5

Alex

Steam rises up and over the shower curtain as I rinse the shampoo out of my hair. The warm water hits a spot on the back of my shoulder, easing the tension in my muscles. Last night, we helped the neighboring town of Midway battle a four-alarm structure fire. It was an abandoned warehouse that's a popular spot for the local homeless. There was a concern that victims may be trapped inside, but thankfully, we got everyone out. Unfortunately, there were a few close calls and two firefighters were treated for smoke inhalation. Needless to say, I'm exhausted.

"Allllleeeexxxx!" I hear Gabby's voice and the sound of the bathroom door swinging open. My fatigue immediately dissipates knowing she's nearby.

"Hey, baby girl!" I pull back a bit of the shower curtain to look at her. "Are you here to join me?"

She grabs it and pulls it back. "No! And how did I not scare you?"

"I admit, it's not every day a beautiful woman storms into my bathroom, but I heard your voice through the door. What's up?" I peek through the tiny space between the curtain and the rod, thankful for my height.

"I locked my keys in my car. Michelle is at school, so our door is locked. Jax and Aly aren't home, and I need to pee so bad!" She hops from one foot to the other like a toddler doing the potty dance.

"You know we have two bathrooms."

"Carter is in the other one and judging from the sounds coming from it, I'm not going within a ten-foot radius of it."

"Man, I told him not to eat the food from the taco truck on 4th Street." I shake my head.

"What? Why would he go there? Everyone knows they're not authentic. You have to go up to 9th street for the good stuff."

"You're preaching to the choir, baby girl."

"Oh my God, I'm about to pee my pants!" she yells.

"Go!" I'm not about to stop someone from answering the call of nature. To give her some privacy, I focus on the task at hand. I load up my loofah with some bodywash and begin scrubbing. I don't hear anything from Gabby, so I assume she's doing her business.

"Umm...can I have some help?" Her voice sounds smaller than usual.

"You need help peeing?" I call out from behind the curtain.

"No. It's just that I have a bashful bladder. I can't pee knowing that someone could hear me."

"The sound of the shower isn't enough?"

"Not when I know you're in it. Could you like...sing or something?"

"You can't be serious." I nearly drop my loofah at her crazy request.

"Pleeeeeaaase? I swear, urine is going to spring out of my eyeballs if I don't go soon."

"You know that can't happen."

"You know what I mean!" she snaps.

"Why don't you sing?" I suggest.

"I can't sing and pee at the same time!" she shrieks like *that's* the most outlandish thing she's ever heard.

"Maybe I can't sing and shower at the same time."

"Of course you can! I hear you through the walls of my bathroom all the time."

Huh. Our bedrooms share a wall, but it never occurred to me that our bathrooms do too. I wonder how many times we've taken a shower at the same time with just a few inches separating us.

"Okay, okay, let me think." Despite my magnetic personality and dashing good looks, I actually can't sing that well, so I opt to hum a tune instead.

"Are you humming the song to Final Jeopardy?"

"Umm...yes?"

"I can't pee to that!"

"Why not?"

"Because it's like a timer. I would feel like I have to finish when the song is up, and I don't know if I can do that."

"I'll hum it on repeat," I offer.

"Can't you just sing 'Twinkle Twinkle Little Star' or something?"

"Like that's any longer?! Good God, woman! You know I'd do anything for you, but this is getting a little out of hand. It's one thing to offer my toilet to you while I'm a mere foot away all soapy and naked as the day I was born. It's another to make me sing so you can pee. I'm not taking requests from your bashful bladder."

For a moment, Gabby is silent and I worry that my rant scared her off. Then the toilet flushes and the shower turns to molten lava. Without thinking, I jump out of the steamy torture chamber and come face-to-face with my tormentor.

"Oh, I'm so sorry." She gasps. "I wasn't thinking when I flushed the toilet. But good news! Your yelling was at the perfect volume, so I was finally able to go...and, umm..." Her voice trails off as she scans me from top to bottom.

It's at that moment I realize I have nothing on. I bite back a smile because I know she likes what she sees.

"Ahem. My eyes are up here."

She snaps her head up and her face flushes. "Uh...yeah...right...sorry...I wasn't thinking. You should probably get a towel," she stumbles on her words.

"I would," I say calmly, "but it's behind you."

"Whoops." She spins and grabs the towel off the hook. "Here you go. I'm sorry about that. I guess I'll be leaving now."

"Wait." I quickly wipe myself down and wrap the towel around my waist as she tries to make a getaway. "Where are you going?"

"Back home."

"Really? With what keys?" I walk out of the bathroom and head to my dresser to grab some clothes.

"Oh yeah. Ha-ha. That's why I was here in the first place."

"How quickly you forgot." I drop my towel to put on my underwear and jeans. Could I have changed in private? Yes. But what would be the fun in that? Because right now, Gabby is standing in my doorway with her mouth gaping open, watching me intently as I throw on one of my many SBFD T-shirts. Once fully clothed, I approach her, place my hand under her chin, and lift it up to close her mouth. "Come on, let's go get your car unlocked."

6

Gabby

"Thank you," I say sheepishly as Alex unlocks my car and hands me my keys for what feels like the millionth time. I'm not sure what I'm more embarrassed about, the fact that I locked my keys in my car again or that I was caught drooling over a naked Alex. My face still feels hot from seeing him fly out of the shower...and then drop his towel in his room. That man has no shame, though I wouldn't either if I were him. Now I don't know how to react the next time he cracks a joke about his size because the hung-like-a-horse joke he made recently was not too far off from the truth.

"I know I sound like a broken record, but when are you going to get a new car with—"

"Keyless entry," I finish his sentence. "I know. I know, but I love Stinky."

I purchased Stinky shortly before I began nursing school, which I paid for with my family's small life insurance policy and the class action lawsuit. It wasn't a ton of money, and I'd give every cent back to have my family whole again.

Even though I came into a bit of money at a young age, I still chose to be conservative with my spending. The settlement wouldn't keep me afloat for long. So I stayed in a small one-bedroom apartment furnished with items from a local thrift shop, cooked meals at home, and bought a used car, also known as Stinky.

Stinky is a Honda Civic from the early 2000s and has seen better days. When I first purchased the sedan, it had a strong scent of pine, but within a week, I discovered that was just a cover-up. There were little tree-shaped air fresheners tucked into every nook and cranny of the interior. Once those began to fade, the real reason the car was such a good deal became clear. Stinky has a permanent smell of garlic and despite the many washes and shampoos, it just won't go away. Luckily, the smell stays within the vehicle and doesn't transfer to my clothes or anything I keep in it. Despite the odor and normal wear and tear, Stinky is a solid car and has gotten me safely from point A to point B for years.

"It still blows my mind that you drove from Arizona to Oregon all by yourself." Alex leans against Stinky, shaking his head.

"It really wasn't that bad," I reason. "I only drove during daylight hours and made sure I stopped frequently and in well-lit public places."

"It never would have happened if I knew you then. I would've gone with you just to make sure you were safe."

I smile to myself, knowing Alex definitely would have been my copilot if we knew each other back then. The total drive was a little over a thousand miles and took about three days. It may have seemed like a drastic move, but I needed a fresh start. My mental health was beginning to take a toll on me whenever I drove past places that brought up memories, no matter how happy they were.

Having no specific destination in mind, I applied to hospitals all over the United States. Starboard Beach was the first to get back to me, and I jumped at the opportunity. I found Michelle through a wanted ad and interviewed with her over a video chat. Since her condo was fully furnished, I got rid of most of my belongings and only took the essentials, which fit into Stinky's trunk and back seat.

I wasn't even nervous about starting over. I figured if I didn't like my job or the town, I'd just pack up Stinky and go somewhere else. I never expected to fall in love with all things Starboard Beach.

"I'm glad I didn't know you then," I tease. "You are the worst back-seat driver I've ever met."

"I do not back-seat drive. I simply offer my expertise and wisdom that no one seems to appreciate. Also, I'm mad at you." His tone holds no anger.

"For what? Interrupting your shower, or making you break into my car again?"

"I don't care about those things. I'm more upset that I saw a napkin from Whips in your cupholder. Why did you go without me?"

"First, you tell me you wouldn't have allowed me to drive up here alone and now you're upset that I went to Whips without you. You're getting a little bossy there, huh?" I cross my arms over my chest and try to look stern. It's hard to act serious around a man who basically has the same personality as a golden retriever.

"Well, excuse me for caring about your safety." Alex dramatically throws his hands up in the air. "Honestly, I'm a little more upset about missing out on Whips."

Whips is Starboard Beach's favorite place to grab a sweet treat. They are famous for their unique flavors of whipped cream piled high on top of a scoop of ice cream.

"You weren't around and Aly had a craving for mint chocolate chip ice cream with strawberry whipped cream." The truth is, I did feel a little guilty about going to one of Alex's favorite places without him, but he was at work and it would've been a melty mess if I had brought something back for him. I know because I've tried it before.

"That...does not sound appetizing." He pushes off my car door and begins walking back toward our building.

"She swore it was the best thing she's ever eaten." I shrug and follow him. "Although the other day I caught her dipping pickles into a jar of peanut butter, so you might want to take her opinion with a grain of salt."

"Will do. It's so crazy to think that a year ago, Jax and Aly were arguing over who got the one lane in the pool and now they're married and having a baby."

"Yeah, I'm so happy for them. They're going to be amazing parents."

"Does seeing them together make you think about settling down and having a family of your own one day?" We reach the front of our building and Alex holds the door open for me.

"Umm..." I hesitate. "I don't think that's in the future for me."

If you had asked me this question over a decade ago, my answer would've been completely different. I wanted to grow up and have the type of life my parents had, the type of love they shared with my sister and me. My heart longs for the holidays, movie nights, and family dinners. But opening myself up to love also exposes me to the possibility of more tragedy. I just can't take that risk, especially with someone as incredible as Alex.

7

Alex

Tossing and turning, I throw my blanket back and grab my phone to check the time...nearly 3:00 a.m.—great. I've been lying here for hours trying to sleep. Sometimes I'm so physically tired after a shift that I don't even remember crawling into bed. Other times, I can't turn my mind off no matter how much energy I expend.

Today, I received a call from my mom. My parents' forty-fifth wedding anniversary is coming up and they want to celebrate with the entire family, which means I'll need to make an appearance. I haven't been back to my hometown since the holidays, so I'm definitely overdue for a visit. And truly, a forty-five-year marriage that produced seven children and nine grandchildren is something to honor.

I love my family. They're good people who are respected among the community, but there has been a rift between us ever since I moved away. All my siblings and their families live within a twenty-mile radius of each other. I'm the only one who moved three hours away. Far enough for people not to know me, yet close enough to visit for special occasions. I just couldn't stand living my life in a fishbowl.

Through the wall, I hear the sounds of shuffling and a bed angrily squeaking. I guess Gabby is having a rough night too. I grab my phone and type out a text.

Me: Are you fighting off an alligator over there?

Gabby: What?

Me: Alligators—they do that death roll thing when they catch their prey. All I hear is rumbling and rocking noises.

Gabby: Sorry. I didn't realize you could hear me, and how do you know that? We don't have any alligators here.

Me: I love watching Discovery when I'm bored. Shark Week is life! I try to convince Carter to watch it with me, but it makes him all jittery cause sharks and surfers don't mix.

Gabby: LOL! Well, I'm with Carter on that one. I'm sorry for bothering you. I'm having trouble sleeping.

Me: Me too, but I think I have a solution for that.

Gabby: We're not having sex.

Me: That is not what I was thinking, but I like where your mind went <winking face emoji> Meet me in the hallway in five minutes. Wear something warm.

I jump out of bed and rummage through my closet, looking for some supplies. As luck would have it, I find one of my large duffle bags and quickly fill it with some blankets and pillows. I don't know why I didn't think of this earlier, but I'm glad I didn't because now I can show Gabby one of my favorite places. After I pull on a pair of gray sweatpants (yes, I know what I'm doing), a T-shirt, and a hoodie over that, I step out into the hallway to wait for Gabby.

The door to 312 opens slowly and Gabby takes a peek into the hallway.

"Hi," I whisper.

She jumps back and gasps as if she wasn't expecting to see anyone.

"Seriously?" I chuckle. "You knew I was going to be out here."

"I know. It just feels weird. I was trying to tiptoe around because I didn't want to wake Michelle. I feel like I'm sneaking out of my parents' place to go to a party." A wave of sadness flashes over her face, but she immediately schools her features. "Where are we going?"

"That's for me to know and for you to find out." I adjust the duffle bag on my shoulder and proceed to walk toward the elevator.

A few minutes later, Gabby is sitting in my passenger seat, gazing out the window. She's bundled up in a pair of black leggings and an oversized purple hoodie. I'm sure she has a few layers on under there. The days might be getting warmer, but the nights can still be cold. Even though she's been living up here for about a year and a half, she still isn't used to the chillier weather. Sometimes I worry the cooler climate will eventually get to her and she'll want to leave. It would break my heart if she did.

We drive in comfortable silence until we turn off the main road, onto a side street, and then a dirt road.

"Umm...where exactly are you taking me?" she asks, still looking out the window.

With no streetlights on this road, the only thing illuminating the path are the headlights from my SUV.

"There's a clearing up here just past this house." I tilt my head to the right. An outline of a log cabin comes into view. All the windows are dark, but there's smoke rising from the chimney.

"Are we allowed to be here?"

I decide to have a bit of fun.

"No, so you have to be super quiet. The guy who lives over there is nuts. Last time I was here, he came out of his house wearing a silver sequined leotard and furry cowboy boots. He chased me away with a tire iron in one hand and a ceramic owl in the other. I didn't know whether to laugh or run."

"Are you serious?!" she squeals and grabs onto the dashboard.

"So much spandex," I whisper under my breath as I continue driving down the path.

"Turn around!" Gabby immediately begins scanning the area for the nonexistent crazed man.

"I'm kidding!" I laugh, but when I turn to look at her, there's panic written all over her face. My heart sinks. "I'm sorry, baby girl, I didn't think you'd take me seriously. I know the guy who lives in the cabin. This is his property and he allows me to come out here whenever I feel like it."

"Really?"

"Really."

"And you're sure we're not going to end up as someone's next meal?" She relaxes back into her seat.

"Not from the guy in the house. Occasionally, a bear strolls by." Even in the dimly lit space, I can see her roll her eyes.

"Do you come out here often?"

"Not as much as I'd like to." We reach the clearing and park. "Stay here for a minute. I want to get everything set up."

8

Gabby

Should I be concerned that Alex has taken me to some desolate woodsy area in the middle of the night and no one knows we even left our building? Maybe. But this is Alex, and I trust him with all my heart.

"Do you need any help with whatever you're doing?" I study him as he gets out of the SUV.

"Nope." He presses a button on his key fob and the hatchback opens. He grabs a bag and pulls a lever to push down the seats in the back. I hear some random shuffling before he calls, "Okay, all ready."

I hop out of the vehicle and walk around to the back to see the cutest little setup. In no time, Alex has created a makeshift bed/sitting area complete with blankets and pillows. It looks pretty cozy, but... "How is this supposed to help me sleep?" I ask.

"We're going to count stars." A boyish grin spreads across his face. He motions for me to get in. "Make yourself comfortable."

"We're going to—what?" I jump up and rest my back against a pillow. "There are millions of stars in the sky."

"More like two hundred billion-trillion, give or take fifty." He takes a seat next to me. It's a little cramped, but I'm not complaining. "It's something I've done for years to help me relax."

"This helps you relax?"

"Have you even looked up yet?" He reaches and manually shuts off the overhead light.

"No, I—wow!" I stare in awe as the night sky comes into focus. "This looks like it came out of a movie or poster I would've had hanging in my bedroom." The longer I look, the more stars seem to appear.

"I hate that we can't see this from our condos, but there's just too much light pollution over there, ya know?"

"No, I get it now." I continue to keep my focus on the heavens above. The glowing orbs illuminating the sky are mesmerizing. "This is so peaceful. I can see why you come out here to relax."

"And count stars," he chimes in.

"You can't be serious." I take my attention off the wonderous sky to study Alex's face, but my eyes are still trying to adjust to the darkness.

"Yup. Let me tell you a story. When I was a kid, like eight or so, I went through a severe case of insomnia. It was awful. I would lie awake all night and be like a zombie the next day. My mom tried everything to get me to sleep—a sound machine, room-darkening curtains, and warm baths. One time, she doused my room with lavender. I went to school smelling like a cheap-scented candle the next day.

"Huh." I think back to times I've had trouble sleeping. I don't think I ever had any issues as a kid, but the weight of being an adult is a different story. I know my sister went through a night terror phase for a while. "What do you think was the cause? Did you have nightmares or think monsters were under your bed?"

"No, nothing like that. Believe it or not, I was a really angry child."

"You?" My voice is louder than expected. Alex is always such a happy-go-lucky guy. I don't think I've ever seen him angry.

"Yup. How much do you know about my family?"

"Hmm…" I chew on my fingernail. "I know your mom is from Mexico and your dad is from Canada and they settled in the States. You're the youngest of seven and the best looking out of the bunch."

"So you know all the important information." He chuckles.

The vibration from his laugh travels through my shoulder and down my body. I slowly slide up closer to him so our sides are flush against each other. Alex never says anything about the little ways I find to touch him, and I like it that way.

"Other than that, I don't think I know much," I say once I'm comfy and cozy.

"My parents are local celebrities."

"You're kidding." I swing my head around so fast that my hair smacks him in the face.

"I'm not." He brushes my hair away but then takes a few rogue curls and gently wraps them around his finger. "My parents both work for our town's local TV station. My mom is a news anchor, and my dad is a meteorologist."

"Wow! Would I recognize them?" I try to avoid news and media coverage, but sometimes it's inevitable. Especially when patients have it on in their rooms. That is definitely something I'm looking forward to when I switch to Pediatrics. Instead of hearing doom and gloom in the background, I'll hear Sesame Street or Paw Patrol or something.

"Not unless you've traveled to Elmwood Grove or any of the surrounding areas. I purposely moved to a town where no one would recognize me. My family was constantly under a microscope and I couldn't stand that. Have you ever heard the phrase, 'Keeping up with the Joneses'?"

"Of course."

"Well, everyone was literally trying to keep up with us. If my mom wore a nice dress on air, the local stores would sell out of it. We couldn't go anywhere without being recognized. I hated going to restaurants because everyone would stare at us, and of course, I had to be on my best behavior."

"That had to be hard, especially as a little kid." It's nice to see people you recognize here and there, but I don't think I'd want everyone up in my business all the time.

"It was, and I wasn't a bad kid or anything. But I was the youngest and had a lot of energy. School was the worst. Try going to school after six of your siblings have already passed through. The teachers already had predispositions about me. They expected more of me because I was the brother of Roberto, the crowd pleaser, or Isabella, the math genius. I didn't get a chance to just be me."

"That's so sad." I attempt to imagine Alex as a little boy. Trying to subdue his larger-than-life personality for the sake of his family's reputation must've been a heavy weight to bear.

"Anyway, back to the insomnia thing. I was under so much pressure to act perfect during the day, I would be a total mess by nighttime."

"That's understandable. You were just a child trying to process a bunch of big emotions."

"Yeah, and I guess my parents tried to understand. I could tell my mom was getting frustrated with me being up all hours of the night. One time, on a particularly rough night, she told me to count sheep. I thought that was ridiculous. I couldn't picture sheep in my head. But it gave me an idea. I needed something physical to count and I needed a lot of it.

"I think it was sometime in the fall because I remember putting on my coat and grabbing a blanket," Alex continues. "I went out back and sat in one of our Adirondack chairs. I decided I was going to count every star in the sky."

"You do realize that's impossible."

"I realize that now. But as a little kid? I had no clue. Anyway, it worked. I have no idea what number I got up to. I doubt it was high since I was so young, but I eventually fell asleep because the next thing I remembered was waking up in my bed. My dad must've carried me in. I woke up feeling very refreshed. Being alone outside in the middle of the night was incredibly peaceful. From then on, whenever I couldn't sleep or just needed to calm down, I would go outside and count the stars."

"That's so sweet. I'm glad you found something that worked for you. But...what did you do in the winter?"

"I will admit, there were a few times I went out dressed in my snow gear." He chuckles. "But enough about me. You have a job to do. Start counting."

"Wait, that's crazy. You can't expect me to—"

"I'd start with that cluster over there." He grabs my hand and points it upward and to the left.

"Are you serious?"

"Like Hilda giving a tetanus shot. Start counting and if one of those stars blinks, it's an aircraft and you have to start all over again."

"But—"

"Those are the rules."

"Okay, fine." I begin counting in my head.

"Out loud, please."

"Oh my God! One, two, three. I can't believe you're making me do this. Four, five, six. This is crazy. Seven, eight, nine. Only you, Alex." My gaze moves over to a large cluster of stars and I keep counting. By the time I'm somewhere in the nineties, my eyes start to feel heavy. "Ninety-ninety."

"Ready to go home?" Alex says in a hushed tone.

"Mmm...not yet." I yawn. The tense feeling in my muscles has eased, and the thought of leaving the cozy warmth of the vehicle saddens me. "How do you drive home after doing this?"

"I don't. I usually just sleep in the car with the windows cracked open to let some fresh air in."

"That sounds nice."

"Do you have work in the morning?" He shuffles some things around and leans back, allowing me to lay my head on his chest.

"Nope." He makes the best pillow ever.

"Me neither." He wraps his arms around me. "Get some rest. The sunrise will wake us up."

9

Alex

*B**est. Night. Ever.* I try to stretch out my legs to no avail. I've slept in my car many times before. I love the serenity and fresh air. But this is the first time I've had to share this space with someone and it's a little cramped. I'm not complaining. I had Gabby all to myself for the entire night.

Oddly enough, this isn't the first time Gabby and I have slept together, and I do mean slept, nothing else. About a year ago, when Aly was still living in 312, the girls' condo flooded. It took weeks for Gabby's and Aly's rooms to be repaired. Aly stayed with Jax while Gabby and I shared my bed. For the first few weeks, we worked on opposite schedules. We barely saw each other, only passing by on our way in and out of work. But then the final week happened and we ended up in bed together for three days. Gabby was horrified when she realized she had to sleep with me. She even tried putting a barrier of pillows between us. I was a total gentleman the whole time, but Gabby? Let's just say she woke me up in a compromising position. She swears she was asleep and not aware of what was going on, but I still like to bring up the topic every now and then. She's so cute when she blushes.

Tilting my head, I try to get a better look at Gabby, who's currently bundled up in a blanket and still sleeping soundly on my chest. I hope she remembers where she is when she wakes up or this could get awkward. I know she won't be asleep for much longer. The sun is starting to peek up over the trees.

"Rise and shine," I whisper into her ear.

"Five more minutes," she mumbles into my chest.

God, I could get used to this.

"But then you'll miss the sunrise."

That gets her going. She lifts her head and rubs her eyes. "It's morning already?"

"Mm-hmm." I'm relieved she didn't freak out after realizing she wasn't in her bed.

"I feel like I slept for days." She sits up and scoots back to look at me.

"I told you I had a remedy."

"That you did." She tilts her head up with wide eyes. "It's beautiful."

I swivel around just in time to see a kaleidoscope of yellow and orange hues swirling over the treetops. The view never gets old.

"I like watching the sunrise. It's a reminder that each day has a new beginning."

"I never thought of it like that," she says softly while keeping her focus on the sky. We stay quiet as the sun continues to rise. When nature's show is over, she turns to me. "What do we do now?"

"Hmm." I hop out of the back of my car and begin cleaning up the blankets. "I was thinking we could go to Portside Perks for a caramel coconut cold brew. Oof!" I take a step back as

Gabby catches me off guard by leaping and throwing her arms around my neck. "I take that as a yes?"

"Yes!" She beams and unhooks her arms from around me. I study her for a moment. Something looks different about her. There's a lightness to her features, and I realize that until today, I've never seen her genuinely happy.

***

I head down the hallway to our condo's laundry room, balancing my overflowing basket of dirty clothes and trying not to leave a trail of socks and underwear in my wake. Work has been brutal lately. Talk of our captain leaving and who's up for the job has been nonstop. I'm not too concerned about the change in hierarchy. What I'm more focused on is the potential opportunity for me to move up in the ranks. If a new captain is hired internally, then a lieutenant position will be up for grabs. Is that something I'm ready for? I'm sure my parents would scoff at the idea, but I can't make life decisions based on what makes them happy. I tried and nearly lost myself in the process.

I let out a sigh and look down at the basket of laundry I'm holding. One thing I do know for sure is that if I don't get these washed, I'll be walking around in my birthday suit pretty soon. I don't mind much, but apparently there are rules about public nudity and stuff.

The scent of detergent and dryer sheets hits my nose as I push through the door of our condo's laundry room. It's funny how I can still wrack up a pile of dirty clothes when I avoid wearing them so much. As I lift open the lid to the washer, I see Gabby hauling a netted bag of laundry.

"Hey, baby girl!" I jog to hold the door open for her. "Looks like we had the same idea."

"Oof." She heaves a large bag of laundry onto a table. "How is it possible that we work the wackiest hours and yet still manage to be off at the same time?"

"Must be fate." I wink. I've wondered that myself. Lately, our schedules seem to be in sync with each other.

"I don't believe in fate." She begins throwing a heap of dark clothes into one of the washers.

"Why not? It worked for Aly and Jax."

"Yeah, but that's their story. A one-in-a-billion chance." She measures a capful of detergent.

"Which means it could happen again. I think your pessimistic outlook on life could use a little more of my optimistic influence."

"I'm not a pessimist. I'm a realist."

"To-may-to, to-mah-to. I believe if you keep a positive attitude, good things will come your way." I take all the clothes from my basket and smush them down into the drum of the washer.

"Alex!" Gabby squeals. "What are you doing?"

"Laundry. What does it look like I'm doing?"

"You're overfilling the washer."

"Nah, it's all good." I use my fist to punch down the pile. "Once the water starts going, it will shrink down...it's kind of like spinach."

"You have got to be kidding me." She puts her hands on her hips. "You didn't even sort your lights from your darks."

I take a few steps closer to her, lean down, and whisper in her ear, "I hate to tell you this, but I've never sorted my laundry and everything has always turned out fine."

She takes a step back and looks up at me with an amused grin on her face. "You are one of a kind, Alejandro Jones."

"And don't you forget it." I playfully tap her on the nose. I turn back to my wash, remembering my plan. I need to get to know Gabby on a deeper level and I missed out on an opportunity when we sat under the stars. I realized too late that I talked about myself the majority of the time. "I was planning to go to the gym to pass the time, but do you mind if I hang out here with you?"

"Umm, yeah, I guess that's okay." She bites down on the bottom of her lip.

"Did you have other plans?"

"No. I did bring a book with me, though." She holds up a book that must've been with her laundry bag.

"Another romance novel?"

"Of course. That's all I read." She shrugs one shoulder.

"I don't get it. You don't date, but you read love story after love story."

"Yes." She takes her book and sits on one of the blue plastic chairs lining the wall. "The books I read guarantee a happily ever after. I know real life isn't like that, but for at least a little while, I can escape into a world without sadness."

"I don't think this world is that sad." I take a seat next to her and rest my arm around the back of her chair. Without fail, Gabby scootches closer into my side. I don't even think she's aware of how many times she cuddles up next to me when we're together. "I mean, sure, tragic things happen, but there's also a lot of good out there. I guess it really depends on what you choose to focus on."

"I guess so," she says noncommittally and then perks up. "I looked up your parents the other day."

"Oh? And what did you find out about them?" It doesn't surprise me that she looked them up. If Gabby told me her parents were local celebrities, I would search for them too. It's also super easy to find information about them. A quick search of Jones and Elmwood Grove, Oregon, will provide you with that.

"Well, first of all, your dad's name is Bob Jones? That's the most generic-sounding name I've heard." She laughs.

"Yeah." I sigh. "His professors in college told him he would be better off with a stage name. You know, something more memorable, but he was set on using his real one. That's why my mom insisted that all the kids have Hispanic names. She hoped it would counteract the plainness of our surname."

"Speaking of your mom, she is gorgeous."

"I do get some of my best features from her," I agree. My mom is in her mid-sixties but doesn't look a day over thirty-five. Despite rumors, she has never had any plastic surgery. She chalks it up to a healthy lifestyle and good genes.

"They also seem to do a lot of charity work," Gabby continues.

"They do. Their presence at events brings in a lot of people," I agree, and an idea pops into my head. "Would you like to meet them?"

"Umm...excuse me?"

"My parents' anniversary is coming up in a few weeks and they're going to have a little dinner celebration. I'll be traveling home for it. I'd love to take you as my plus-one." I hop out of my seat and begin pacing with a surge of energy. I don't know why I never thought of this before. Having Gabby by my side will make the trip so much more enjoyable.

"Well, I'd have to check my schedule." She fidgets with her hands.

"Of course." Hope blooms in my chest. The more I think about Gabby coming with me, the more excited I am to go.

"And this is strictly just as friends, right? No strings attached? You're not going to say we need to get married because you introduced me to your family?"

"Nope." I shove my hands in my pockets and rock back on the heel of my sneakers. "It has come to my attention that I've been a little too...persistent and I need to tone it down on the proposals."

"You're just realizing this?" She crosses her arms across her chest.

"In case you haven't noticed, I'm a little thick-headed." I grin. "Interpret that however you want."

"I appreciate you leaving that up to my imagination." Her washing machine buzzes, signaling the end of the cycle. She stands and walks over to it.

"So what do you say? The three-hour drive is so boring alone. We can load up on snacks, and I'll even let you be in charge of the music for the whole ride." I flash my signature smile, hoping to win her over.

"Quit it." She fights to keep a straight face. "You know those dimples have no power over me."

"If they have no power over you, why do you want me to stop?" I ham it up even more.

"Okay, fine. I'll go with you." Her face flushes ever so slightly. "As long as I can fit it into my schedule."

"Absolutely. I understand that." I try not to act overly excited.

She gets up and begins switching her wet laundry over to the dryer and lets out a sigh. "This is one thing on my wish list if I ever get a place of my own."

"Your own washer and dryer?"

"Mm-hmm. When I was little, I thought owning your own washer and dryer was a symbol of being rich."

"When I was little, I thought having a refrigerator with your own ice maker made you rich." I chuckle. "I thought we won the lottery when we finally got one. My parents had to put a limit on how many times a day I used it. I had cups of ice everywhere."

"That's cute." She presses some settings on the dryer.

"So tell me, what else is on this wish list of yours?" I lean myself against a large table used for folding and sorting.

"Umm..." She hesitates for a moment. "I don't need much. I'm not one for fancy things. But eventually, I'd like to save up some money for a little house, preferably with a cozy reading nook and shelves for all my books. I'd also love to have a yard for some gardening."

"You like to garden?"

"Yup. But not flowers, like herbs and vegetables."

There's that no-flowers thing again. Interesting.

"Have you ever had a meal made with fresh herbs and vegetables picked straight from the garden?" she asks before I can question about her aversion to flowers.

"I don't think I have."

"Oh, it's so much better than the stuff you get at the grocery store." Her face lights up with joy. "Growing up, my parents had a little garden on our balcony. We—" She abruptly stops, and the brief sense of happiness fades.

"You what?" I prod, realizing that she's never really talked to me about her past.

"Nothing." She shakes her head vigorously. "So, what date do I need to have off for this party?"

And just like that, Gabby shuts me down and changes the subject...like always, and I am dying to find out why.

10

Gabby

"Ladies, I need your help." I intently make eye contact with Michelle and Aly, who are sitting across from me at our booth at The Local. With its beachy theme and extensive menu, it's one of our favorite places to eat. Plus, for some reason, it always smells like funnel cake.

We try to have a girls' night at least once a month. It's something I always look forward to, but the guys hate it. Alex and Carter typically end up pouting that they have to find their own food and Jax has gotten extra overprotective of Aly now that she's pregnant. I swear, that man would put her in bubble wrap if he could. Not that she needs it; the girl can hold her own.

"What's wrong?" Aly asks with a look of concern. She brushes back a lock of her dirty-blond hair. All three of us look so vastly different from one another. Alex likes to refer to Michelle and me as fun-sized since we're both a smidge over five feet, while Aly towers over us at five eight. Michelle and Aly have light hair and blue eyes, while I'm the opposite with dark curly hair and brown eyes. Even our body types are all over the place. Michelle is the petite one, Aly is the athletic one, and me? I have curves for days.

"I need to talk to you about Alex."

"Ugh," Michelle groans. "Did he propose to you with an onion ring again?"

"No, the last time was with one of those plastic rings that come off a water bottle cap."

"Well, at least that's more durable." Aly takes a sip of her chocolate milkshake and throws her head back. "My God, that's the best thing I've ever tasted."

"Didn't you just say the same thing about the nachos?" Michelle points a french fry at Aly.

"I can't help it. My taste buds are heightened or something. I'm telling you, food tastes amazing when you're pregnant."

"I'll take your word for it." Michelle looks back at me. "Let's get back to the task at hand. What did Alex do this time?"

"He didn't do anything specifically, but we were doing laundry at the same time the other day and I found this on the floor near the washing machine he was using." I pull out a crumpled piece of paper. "At first, I thought it was just a piece of garbage, but when I went to throw it out, I noticed my name written on it. It must've fallen out of his pocket."

Aly snatches the paper out of my hand. "'Operation Ms. to Mrs.,'" she reads. "Oh boy, he's upping his game."

"That looks like Carter's handwriting." Michelle looks over Aly's shoulder. "If that's the case, he's called in reinforcements."

"Ugh!" I groan, sinking low into my seat. "This can't happen."

"Why not?" Michelle asks while studying the list. "I mean, yeah, he's goofy and all, but that's just part of his charm. Alex is such a wonderful guy, not to mention good-looking. Also, why don't you like flowers?"

"It's just not my thing." I yank the paper back out of Aly's hands.

"I think it's great!" Aly ignores my actions and swirls the straw around in her milkshake. "I like that Alex has a plan. It reminds me of my life list and…" A blank expression washes over her face. "I can't remember what else I was going to say."

"That baby brain is hitting you hard, isn't it?"

"The other day Jax asked me when I was going to start using big words again." She frowns. "And that was before he found my purse in the fridge."

"So what are you going to do?" Michelle asks.

"I'm not sure." I sit up a little straighter. "But I know I need to prove to him that I'm not the one for him."

My friends share a sad look.

"What?"

"Why are you so hard-set on not dating Alex?" Michelle asks gently.

"We've both kind of wondered why you push him away," Aly adds. "Is it because of his dating history? I've heard rumors, but I haven't seen him with anyone since you moved here."

"He's very well-known at the hospital." I dramatically roll my eyes, hoping to convince my friends. I know he's had flings with a few of the nurses. I heard a group of them talking about him once when he brought in a patient while working as a paramedic. The general consensus is that while Alex is a huge lover of women, he's respectful and always clear that there are no strings attached.

"I wouldn't be too concerned about that." Aly dips a fry into some honey mustard. "If Jax can mend his playboy ways, I have no doubt Alex can too."

"I get what you're saying, but I can't be with him. It's just... I can't explain it. But he needs to let this go. To let me go. Will you help?"

"If this is what you really want, we'll support you," Michelle says. "But I'm not sure what we can do to help."

"I've been thinking about this. I need to figure out ways to make me unattractive to him."

"That's going to be hard." Aly snorts. "You're gorgeous!"

"Thanks." My cheeks heat. "What are some things that have immediately turned you off to someone?"

The girls sit quietly for a moment until Aly pipes up. "I once went on a date with a guy who pronounced the 'L' in salmon. That did it for me."

"Eww." Michelle cringes. "I don't have much dating experience, but—oh!" She does a little jump in her seat. "I know he doesn't like the smell of rosemary. I was cooking one day and he asked why I was using a citronella candle indoors."

"Huh? Rosemary doesn't smell like citronella." I scrunch up my nose and wonder if I ever used that particular spice in my food.

"Everyone can taste and smell differently." Aly shrugs. "Like the rest of you think cilantro tastes like mint, but Jax and I think it tastes like soap."

"Good point." I nod.

"You could always tell him that you decided to go vegetarian. You know how much that man likes to eat meat," Michelle suggests.

"That would break him!" Aly chuckles. "I tried to establish Meatless Monday and Jax lost his mind." She drops her voice, attempting to sound like her husband. "Do I look like a bunny to you?"

"Well, I guess this is a start." I pick at my burger. I don't have much of an appetite right now. The thought of pushing

Alex away makes me queasy, but I need to protect my heart. That night when we counted the stars, I let myself imagine what it would be like to be in a relationship with him. I could picture having a little place of our own where we could cook meals together and relax by a cozy fireplace after a long day of work. We could take vacations to someplace tropical during the colder months to help chase away the winter blues. It would be so much fun to lie next to him on a sandy beach with tropical drinks in our hands.

It's incredibly easy to envision a life with Alex because we work so well together. Yet it's also easy to envision losing him. Picture a solemn face knocking on my door in the middle of the night and telling me he succumbed to a fire. I have no doubt he would use his dying breath to save a stranger. That's just the kind of man he is. It's also why I can't fully give my heart to him. I used all my strength rebuilding my life the last time. I'm not strong enough to go through something like that again.

"Earth to Gabby." Aly waves her hand in front of me. "Where'd you go?"

To a place that can only exist in my dreams.

"Oh, nowhere." I try to act casual and realize it's time for a subject change. If we continue to discuss Alex, I know the girls will innocently press for more information, and doing so will force me to relive my worst nightmare. I don't have the strength for that, so instead, I turn my attention to Aly. "Have you chosen a theme for the baby's nursery yet?"

"We're thinking of going with a nautical theme." Aly looks radiant as she takes the bait with ease. "You know, with Jax's history in the Navy, it just feels right. I found some bedding with little anchors on it." She claps her hands together. "It's so cute."

As Aly continues to go over the décor of baby J.J.'s room, I can't help but feel eyes on me. I take a risk and glance over at Michelle, who's silently studying me. Aly is too distracted with baby on the brain to realize the motive behind my subject change, but it doesn't get past the future lawyer.

My heart sinks at the thought of withholding my past from them. I never had friends like this before and didn't plan on building close relationships with anyone. Yet it happened anyway. I swear, there's something magical about this town, and I'm not sure what to do about it.

11

Alex

"The tapping noise is driving me crazy," Carter says from his spot on the couch.

"Oops, sorry." I put my pen down on the table. I didn't even realize I was using it as a drumstick.

"You've been sitting over there staring at something for the past twenty minutes. What's going on?" He stands and walks over to me.

"There's a spot open for lieutenant." I show him the papers I've been mulling over. So all the talk that'd been going on the last few weeks did come true. I figured it would. The guys I work with aren't much for gossip.

"Wow! Is that something you want?" He takes the application from me and scans it.

"Oh yeah. I've always wanted to move up in the ranks. I didn't think a position would open up this quickly, though." I pick up my pen and begin tapping again. "I thought I had a few more years, but our captain is moving out of state and one of our lieutenants is taking his place."

"Leaving a spot open." Carter grabs the pen out of my hand. "How many guys are applying for the job?"

"I'm not sure." I shake my head. "Mickelson, Smitty, and I all started around the same time, so we cancel each other out on experience. Mickelson is going through some tough times at home, so I don't think he'll apply. Smitty definitely wants to move up. Then there's the possibility someone from outside the department could be hired. They don't have to choose one of us."

I'm excited for this opportunity, but I'm also worried how my family would deal with the news if I do get the position. In their heads, firefighting is more of a hobby than a real job. My occupation doesn't count because I don't go to work in a suit and tie every day. Instead of having the hands of a pencil pusher, I have calloused ones that are often tinged with various oils, soot, and ash. I don't have assistants to dote on me every minute of the day, and did I mention I dropped out of college? Yeah, that went over like a lead balloon. At least while I was still in college, there was hope for me to get a white-collar job. The day I announced I dropped out and signed up for firefighting school was basically the start of a family war.

"Well, I say go for it," Carter says, pulling me out of my thoughts...or potential nightmare. "You can't be considered if you don't apply."

"You are so wise." I snatch the pen back out of his hand. My roommate makes a valid point. I at least have to give it a shot. I also have to do what makes me happy. I love being a firefighter and helping others in my community. I'm proud that I can make an impact on other people's lives. And I don't need a fancy degree or career to do that. "Just don't tell anyone about this yet. I don't want to make this into a big deal, especially if there's a good chance nothing might come of it."

"Your secret is safe with me. But I'm not sure how wise I am." Carter shakes his head. "I still can't believe you convinced Travis to let you borrow Gus."

We both turn our heads to the three-legged snoring lump of fur on our couch. Gabby asked me over for dinner tonight. I'm not sure why I'm surprised. All of us at 3rd East eat together frequently, but it seems like she asked me and no one else. When I found out I was the only one invited, I immediately called Travis and arranged to pick up Gus.

"Are you sure about this?" Carter asks as I stand up and stretch.

"Absolutely. Gabby will see that Travis has entrusted me with his precious furry family member. Which, in turn, will show that I am becoming a responsible adult."

"Yeah, about that." Carter winces. "I was pretty grumpy that day. I think I was wrong to add that to your plan. You do have the ability to take life seriously when you need to, and you are pretty responsible. Give me the list and I will cross that out."

I stare at my roommate for a moment.

"You lost the list, didn't you?" He pinches the bridge of his nose.

"I'm sure I'll find it...eventually."

"Well, I hope like hell that you do because if one of the girls finds it, they'll know my handwriting and—"

"Chill, bro! No need to get all crazy on me. It's around here somewhere. I just haven't taken the time to look for it." Carter can be a killjoy sometimes. And though I haven't looked for it since he wrote it, I'm sure it's around here somewhere.

"Well, when you find it, destroy it. You're not going to follow it anyway. I'm not sure why we bothered."

"Yes, sir!" I salute him as I turn to grab a gift bag off the counter. "What are your plans tonight?"

"I'm headed over to help my mom with some things around the house. Her oven is on the fritz and I'm hoping it's something easy to fix. I just used the money from my emergency fund to buy my brother new glasses."

"You really are one hell of a guy." I look at my friend. He's as loyal as they come. "Let me know if there's anything I can help with."

"Thanks, man."

I whistle for my temporary pet, who is clearly annoyed I interrupted his nap. Eventually, he rolls off the couch and comes to my side.

"I have a feeling this isn't going to end well." Carter bends down and gives Gus a scratch behind the ears.

"It will be fine." I open the door. "It's just Gabby and me having dinner. What could go wrong?"

12

Gabby

Fumbling around the kitchen, I make sure everything is in place. I'm usually so confident with my cooking, but tonight is a little different. Michelle had a late-night study group, and I invited Alex to come over...alone. It's not like we haven't been alone before, but this time will be different. I decided I need to sit down with him and have a heart-to-heart conversation. I'll tell him that I found his list and that a relationship with me is not going to work. I'm willing to still be his friend, and I'll go with him as his plus-one to his parents' anniversary dinner (after all, I agreed before I saw the list), but nothing can go further.

I also changed up a few things for our dinner tonight. If I'm going to let him down, I might as well make myself as unappealing as possible.

My nerves are at their wits' end when a knock at the door makes me jump. "Come in!" I yell.

"Hello!" Alex appears in the doorway.

"Why did you knock? You know we have an open-door policy." The only time we keep our doors locked is at night or when everyone is out. Carter and Alex do the same. Jax and Aly are a little more private, which is probably a good thing because no one wants to accidently walk in on them and see something they shouldn't.

"I know, but things felt more formal for some reason. I felt like I should knock." He strolls in holding a purple gift bag. Instead of his usual SBFD T-shirt, he's wearing a baby blue polo that accentuates his eyes. It was the first thing I noticed about him when we met in the parking lot. His light blue eyes shone like a beacon through the darkness and rain surrounding us. I was so taken aback by his presence and the immediate sense of tranquility I felt standing next to a complete stranger, I could barely get any words out to speak. Thankfully, Alex never seems to be at a loss for words and did most of the talking that day. It was heartbreaking to learn that he was a firefighter. Even though I had just met him, I was already afraid to lose him.

As Alex walks farther into the condo, I notice a three-legged dog beside him.

"Is that…Gus?" I don't know Travis too well, but I know he doesn't leave home much without his dog.

"Yup!" Alex smiles. "Travis…uh…had something to do and asked me to watch him so he wouldn't get lonely. Are you okay that I brought him along?"

"Of course! Gus is no trouble at all. I'm just surprised Travis left him with anyone." I walk over to give the furry hound mix a scratch behind the ears. I've always had a soft spot for animals but never had a pet of my own.

"Yeah, well, you know…" Alex saunters farther into the condo. "Travis knows how responsible I am."

"Okay…" That's kind of a weird thing to say, but I brush it off and look down at the bag he's holding.

"Oh, I almost forgot. Happy first day of Peds!" He hands me the gift bag. I started my new position a few days ago, but Alex and I have been two ships passing in the night since then.

"You didn't have to get me anything. It's not like I got a promotion. I just moved to a different floor." I poke through the white tissue paper and pull out some sort of light beige stuffed animal wrapped in a…banana peel?

"It's a bananasaurus rex!" Alex beams and puffs out his chest. He's clearly proud of his gift-giving skills.

"It's so odd but so adorable." I laugh, hugging the hybrid dinosaur banana to my chest.

"I know you don't like flowers, but I wanted to get you something."

"That's very sweet of you." I give him a hug. Crap, how am I going to let him down after he just gave me a gift?

"Huh." I hear him sniff as he lets go from our embrace. "Are you wearing bug spray or something?"

"Oh, umm, no." I brush a curl behind my ear. "I'm trying out a new shampoo. It has rosemary in it. It's supposed to be good for hair."

"It smells a little weird." He scrunches up his nose. "But whatever you're cooking smells great!" He walks toward the kitchen while Gus hops on our love seat and promptly falls asleep.

"I hope you don't mind. I tried something new." I grab the salad bowl and place it on the table. Besides our drinks, it's the only thing I haven't altered. "The girls in Peds were talking about going on a diet," I lie. "They mentioned how much healthier they felt, so I decided to try one of their recipes."

"Diet?" He makes a face. "You do not need to go on a diet. You're perfect just the way you are."

"Thank you." Heat creeps up my cheeks. "But it's not about losing weight, just a healthier lifestyle." I've never been super skinny, but over the years, I've learned to embrace my curves. My confidence has grown even stronger this past year since Alex tells me on a frequent basis how attractive I am to him.

"I guess I can't argue with wanting to be healthy." He shrugs.

We sit down for dinner while Gus snores away in our living room. We talk mainly about my first few days at Peds while we eat our salad. There's nothing unusual about that, but next comes the main course, which, surprisingly, smells pretty good. I wonder if my plan will backfire.

"I know these look like regular cheeseburgers, but I swapped some of the ingredients for healthier ones."

I hold my breath as Alex takes a huge bite. He chews and chews...and chews.

"Umm...what did you say were in these?" he says with his mouth still full. I'm a little worried he hasn't swallowed yet.

"I used some plant-based meat in place of ground beef," I answer.

"You used imposter meat?" He finally swallows.

"It's not imposter. It's plant-based."

"Plants and meat are two totally separate things." He lifts up the top of the bun. "Is the cheese fake too?"

"Umm...yeah." I chew on my lower lip. "And the bun is gluten free. I got it from the health food section of the grocery store."

Alex stands up, abandons his plate, and begins rummaging in the kitchen. He picks the empty cheese package from the top of the garbage can and studies it. "Dairy free, nut free, wheat free, gluten free, soy free, salt free, BPA free—what the hell?! Why would they even put that on the label?"

"Stop!" I burst into a fit of giggles, watching Alex's facial expressions morph into various shades of repulsion as he continues to study the label. The nerves I felt earlier diminish the more I laugh. I love his sense of humor. "You've got to be making this up."

"Am not!" He walks over and holds the packaging out for me to see. Sure enough, he wasn't making anything up. I was so nervous about tonight that I didn't pay attention to all the ingredients. I just kind of threw everything in my cart.

"It can't be that bad." I take a bite to prove him wrong and promptly spit it out into a napkin. "Oh God! *Sabe a zapato de cuero mojado en huevos podridos y colgado a secar en una granja de cerdos.* That tastes like a leather shoe dipped in melted rotten eggs and hung out to dry on a pig farm."

"That is a horrifyingly accurate description."

"How did you manage to swallow that bite?" I grab my iced tea and begin chugging.

"I didn't want to insult you. You always make such delicious meals." He looks down at the floor. "I may need my stomach pumped."

"I would agree if you ate the entire thing, but I think you'll be okay." I figured dinner would be subpar, but I wasn't expecting it to be inedible. "How about we order a pizza and watch a movie?"

"That sounds like a much better plan," Alex agrees.

While I place an order for a pizza, Alex cleans up our disaster dinner. We argue over what type of movie to watch. He wants a thriller while I prefer a fluffy rom-com.

"You win." Alex plops himself on the couch. "I think we had enough horror with that meal you made."

"You're not going to let me live this down, are you?" I groan, taking a seat next to him.

"Nope." He grins and presses play on the remote.

Our food arrives about twenty minutes later, and we decide to eat our meal in the living room while continuing to watch the movie. Since things have calmed down, I decide there's no time like the present to have the hard conversation I've been putting off.

"Alex." I turn to him. "There's something I need to talk to you about."

He cocks his head to the side, watching me curiously. God, I love his face, his defined features, and his enormous smile. Those dimples. Those freaking dimples of his always send my stomach into a flutter, making me feel like I'm a teenager with a huge crush.

"Are you okay?"

"Yeah, umm...just got distracted there. As I was saying, I wanted to talk to you about..." I stop and sniff the air. "Do you smell something?"

"Yeah, where's it coming from?" He looks around the couch. "It almost smells like how those fraudulent cheeseburgers tasted."

As if we can read each other's minds, we both turn to look at the love seat, which has been abandoned.

"Where's Gus?" I pray he went into another room to nap and the smell is just some random phenomenon.

We spring off the couch and run toward the kitchen island.

"Oh no!" I cover my mouth with my hands as I take in the overturned garbage can and Gus happily devouring what's left of our grotesque dinner. His floppy ears are covered in ketchup and melted fake cheese. A squeaking sound comes from Gus's rear and his wagging tail helps spread the smell throughout the room.

"Oh God, that's so bad!" I wave my hand over my nose, hoping to fan the stench away. "He's the slowest dog in the world. How can that food process through him so quickly?!"

"Maybe because it's not real food," Alex deadpans.

"You really want to debate that right now?" I put my hands on my hips.

"Later? Yes. But right now, I have to get him away from that plastic food."

"It's not plastic!" I smirk. "Remember the label said it was BPA free."

"Woman!" he huffs. "I'm not in the mood to argue about this!"

The muscles in my face begin to ache as I try to hold back a laugh. He usually refers to me as "baby girl" when he's flirting and "woman" when I get under his skin. Honestly, I adore both.

Alex walks over to Gus, bends down, and gently tugs on the smelly hound's collar. "Come on, buddy, you shouldn't be eating that." Gus responds with a warning growl and Alex immediately straightens. "Oh, boy. I wasn't expecting that."

"He's just hyper focused on the food right now. He's not even registering who's behind him," I reason and try to think of an alternative plan. The garbage can is wedged in the corner between the counter and fridge. With Gus blocking the way, the only other way to access the trash is from above.

I hop up on the counter. "I can lift the garbage can up and away if you can just pull him back an inch or two."

"Okay, but we need to be fast." Alex gets into position by squatting down and hovering his arms over Gus's torso.

"On the count of three. One. Two—" PRFFTT!

I stand upright on the counter with the garbage can in my hands feeling super proud that my plan was successful. But...

"I've been skunked! I've been skunked!" Alex starts jumping around the kitchen.

A second later, I notice a rancid smell wafting upward.

"How can it be even worse than before?!" I cover my nose, still watching Alex wiggle all over the place. I imagine that's how I look when I accidently walk through a spiderweb.

"I think I pulled a little too hard on his stomach and released something from the depths of his bowels. Oh my God, I've been skunked!"

"You can't get skunked by a dog." I place the garbage can on top of the counter and jump down. I try my hardest not to laugh, but I can't take it anymore. Between the stress I put on myself today and the craziness of our night, I lose all control and burst out into hysterical laughter.

"This isn't funny! If the smell is permanent, you're going to have to marry me now because no one will be able to tolerate being in the same room as me. Oh. My. God. Is this what happened to Stinky?" He begins rummaging through our refrigerator.

"What—what are you doing?" I wipe the tears springing from my eyes. I haven't had a full-on belly laugh like this since the time Aly told me the story of how Jax was doped up on pain meds and thought he lost his penis.

"Tomato juice!" Alex waves his arms frantically. "I'm looking for tomato juice. Isn't that how you get the skunk smell out? I think the scent seeped into my pores. Maybe if I drink it, it will counteract everything and I won't smell like this for the rest of my life!"

"You. Are. Nuts." I grab onto the countertop, trying to gain what little composure I have left. "One, the tomato juice thing is a myth. Two, we don't have any. And three, Gus is a dog, not a skunk. We probably need some fresh air." I walk over to the window in the living room and open it, welcoming the cool breeze that drifts through.

"Fresh air," Alex says to himself. "Yes, that's what we need. Come on, Gus!" he yells to the hound, who obediently follows. As he gets to the door, he turns around, giving me a sheepish look. "Umm...sorry about tonight. Rain check?"

"Yeah." I laugh and wave toward the door. "Go take care of Gus. Hopefully, he can get everything out of his system before you bring him back to Travis."

"God, I hope so," Alex says and closes the door.

I walk back to the kitchen and place the garbage can on the floor. Turning, I notice the purple gift bag on the table. I grab it, pull out my wacky present, and give it a squeeze. It's so uniquely Alex and I love it.

Once things have calmed down, I decide to finish the movie that's only halfway through. It's a rom-com about a boy who's in love with his best friend, but the girl is scared to get into a relationship and keeps pushing him away. *Oh, how relatable.* I settle on the couch with my bananasaurus rex and realize we never had the chance to talk about his list.

I can't help but wonder if maybe that's for the best.

13

Alex

The walk of shame.

Never in a million years did I expect to do one...especially with a dog.

The ride back to Travis's was fragrantly painful despite keeping all the windows down and the air conditioner on full blast. It's a pretty chilly night and I can't feel my fingers. Still, I have bigger things to worry about at the moment.

Gus appears no worse for wear despite the never-ending flatulence. I took him for a long walk around the condo, hoping he would clear out his system, but we had no such luck. I even called a twenty-four-hour emergency vet hotline to see if there was something I should do or if I needed to bring him in to get checked out. Since the furry guy is showing zero signs of distress, it looks like we're in the clear.

"Might as well get this over with," I say to Gus as I open the passenger side door to let him out. He happily hops down and looks up at me, anticipating my next move.

"Let's go, Sir Smelly Butt." I begin walking down the gravel path toward Travis's house.

"Hey!" Travis opens the door as we make our way up the walkway. "You're back earlier than I thought. Everything okay?"

"Umm...yeah." I look down at Gus, who seems completely normal. Maybe I can get out of this without Travis knowing. After all, the vet said he's fine. No harm, no foul. "The dinner Gabby made was...unexpected, and things ended early."

"Really?" Travis crosses his arms and leans into the door-frame. "What happened?"

"Gabby decided to try out some new ingredients that didn't go over very well. We ended up ordering pizza and had an early night." I take a step backward, hoping Travis isn't in a chatty mood. Gus happily hops up the two front steps and leans into his owner's side.

"Did she say why she wanted to see you alone?"

Ugh. Why can't this guy be like his best friend? Jax would've already ended the conversation and closed the door...probably right in my face. Still, he brings up a good point.

"You know, she didn't." I scratch my head. "I mean, it's not unusual for us to do something without the rest of the group, but it did seem like she wanted me there for a particular reason."

"Maybe your plan is working and she wanted some quality time with you." Travis mindlessly pats the top of Gus's head.

"Maybe..." My voice trails off. Something about Gabby was off tonight and I don't think it had anything to do with what happened with Gus. She seemed nervous for some reason. Speaking of nervous, I look down at Gus, who's happily wagging his tail next to Travis. I really should tell him about what happened, but the person who answered at the vet hotline said he'd be okay. "I better go." I take another step backward.

"You sure you don't want to come in for a beer or some-thing?"

"Umm...no. I have to be at the station early tomorrow, so it's probably for the best I turn in early." Just a few more steps to freedom.

"All right then." Travis shrugs. "If you ever need to borrow Gus again, let me know."

"Thanks." I pull my keys out of my pocket. "He didn't quite pull off the part of wingman like I was hoping, but maybe we can give it another try."

We say our goodbyes and I hustle back to my SUV, praying that Gus got everything out of his system while still with me. But then I hear Travis's voice through the closed door.

"Come on, Gus, let's go... What was that? What? Oh my God! The smell! What did you eat?!" The door swings back open. "Jones! What the hell did you do to my dog?"

14

Gabby

"How'd it go?" Michelle puts out a plate of freshly baked cranberry orange muffins on our farmhouse-style table. The citrusy sweet smell makes it feel like an autumn day, even though we're still several months off.

"Great. Just fan-freaking-tastic." I grab my coffee mug and take a seat across from Aly. Thanks to my work schedule, I haven't had the chance to update the girls on the disaster dinner. This wasn't something I could explain over a group text and I wanted to make sure they were both present when I told them. Telling the story twice would have been torturous, although with Travis being Jax's best friend, I'm sure Aly is aware of some of it.

"Uh-oh. Did he get mad when you told him you found out about his plan?" Michelle asks while placing a muffin on her plate. Her freshly manicured nails match the pink hearts on her coffee cup. Even in jeans and a T-shirt, she always looks so put together—a trait, she says, of being a member of her prestigious family.

"I didn't have a chance." I add way too much sugar to my extra-large coffee. I'm going to need all the caffeine I can get today. "First, he gave me a gift for starting my new job, so I waited a bit because that just seemed like awful timing. Then the dinner, which I expected to be subpar, turned out to be a repulsive mess. So, we ordered pizza and watched a movie. I figured once things settled down, I'd tell him. But then Gus got into the garbage—"

"Oh no!" Michelle gasps.

"Yeah." Aly winces. "Jax told me about that part. He said that Travis was pretty pissed that he had to sleep with all his windows open and fans on," Aly explains to Michelle. "Gus had a major case of flatulence that stunk up the entire house."

"Oh my gosh! I'm sorry, but that's so funny." Michelle cracks up.

"You should've seen Alex when he tried to pull Gus away from the garbage and tugged on his stomach too hard." The memory stirs up some giggles. I don't think it would've been as funny had it happened to someone else in our group of friends. There's just something special about Alex. It's impossible to say his name without smiling.

"But in all seriousness." I look at Aly. "Do you know if Gus is okay?" I wouldn't be able to live with myself if I caused any pain or suffering to the furry guy. Granted, it was accidental, but we still should've paid more attention to where he was.

"He's completely fine. I saw him the other day when I went to the house to drop off paint samples for the baby's nursery." Aly places her hand over her stomach. She's finally starting to show.

"Why would Alex bring Gus over?" Michelle asks. "I thought he and Travis were attached at the hip."

"It was part of Alex's plan to prove to Gabby that he's responsible." Aly picks at her muffin. "I also thought it was weird Travis would let Alex take Gus, so I pressed Jax for more information."

"I'm surprised Jax gave that knowledge up so willingly." Michelle looks at Aly.

"Oh, he didn't...at first." A mischievous grin spreads across Aly's face. "But I've found ways to persuade him."

"Aly! That's so underhanded." I reach across the table to high-five her. "I love it!"

"I'm not going to lie, I had fun. Next time, I'm going to try to figure out what he got me for my birthday." She tilts her head to the side as if in deep thought. "I think he's hiding it at his sister's house. But anyway, if there's anything else you want to find out, just let me know."

"Not right now. It makes sense that he was trying to check things off his list." I look at Aly. "I'm glad to know I have a secret weapon in case I have more questions."

"Happy to help." She gives a fake salute.

"What are you going to do now?" Michelle stirs her coffee.

"I have no idea." I shake my head, defeated. "Did I tell you that I agreed to be his plus-one at his parents' anniversary party? It was before I found the list."

"Are you going to cancel on him?" Aly gives me a melancholy look. I'm sure she thinks I'm being ridiculous about this whole thing. I mean, who in their right mind would give up an opportunity to be with a man like Alex?

"No. If I had found his list beforehand, I would've made up an excuse that I couldn't get out of work. He was so excited when I told him I'd go. I can't do that to him."

"Maybe that's when you can have a talk with him," Michelle suggests. "Isn't it a long car ride?"

"About three hours each way. But I can't do it then. I don't want to make the trip awkward." I rest my chin on my hand and let out a sigh. "It just seems like it's never the right time."

"Have you considered there's a reason why it's never the right time?" Aly asks.

"What do you mean?"

"Maybe it's never a good time to have a talk with him because you're supposed to be together."

I'd be lying if I said that hasn't crossed my mind.

***

I shuffle my feet while waiting in line at the hospital cafeteria. Starboard Beach Community Hospital isn't known for their stellar selection of food, but they do make a decent buffalo chicken salad. I planned on having leftover chili, but someone must've beat me to it. I smile to myself thinking of Alex—it had to be him—although Carter would eat us out of the condo if we let him. I really don't mind it. It's in my nature to take care of people and cooking is sort of my love language. I might not be able to give my heart to anyone, but I can show I care with a home-cooked meal.

"What do you recommend?" a voice says, startling me.

"Excuse me?" I turn to see a slender, fair-haired man standing next to me in dark dress pants and a crisp gray button-down shirt. His name tag reads Dr. Joshua Payne, Proctology.

"I'm sorry, I didn't mean to scare you. I never eat here, but I forgot my lunch. I was wondering if you have any recommendations." He smiles. It's a nice smile, but nothing compared to Alex's megawatt smile. I'm a sucker for those dimples of his.

Dammit, I have to stop thinking about him.

"Oh, well, I'm getting the buffalo chicken salad. The turkey club is okay too. But stay away from the meatloaf and roast beef." I scrunch up my nose and shake my head.

"Got it. Stick with the food that clucks."

"Pretty much." I laugh and size him up again. "I haven't seen you around. Are you new here?" Our hospital is small compared to others, but it's still big enough that you can work in the same building for years and not know everyone.

"Sorta." He grabs a turkey club sandwich and places it on his tray as we make our way through the cafeteria line. "I was a resident here a few years ago, then I worked as a traveling doctor for a bit. That contract ended, so I decided to come back to where I started. I'm Josh, by the way." He extends his hand to shake mine.

"I'm Gabriella, but most of my friends call me Gabby." I return his handshake.

"Can I call you Gabriella or Gabby?" He gives a little wink.

"You seem friendly enough. I guess you can call me Gabby."

"Well, it's nice to meet you, Gabby. Can I join you for lunch?" he asks as we scan our ID cards to pay for our meals.

"Sure," I reply. I usually sit alone on my lunch break and read, but I guess I can make an exception today. Especially if he's new...or sort of new. I know what it feels like to be in a place where you don't know anyone. Although, lucky for me, it didn't take as long as I thought it would to adjust. I glance around the cafeteria and spot an empty table that overlooks the courtyard. "How about we grab that spot over there?" I point.

"Looks great," Josh replies and makes a sweeping movement with his hands. "Ladies first."

As soon as I settle in at the table, I realize I've made a terrible mistake. On sunny days, the crew from the firehouse and first aid squad like to relax in the courtyard for some fresh air in between calls. Looking out the window, I see a couple of guys wearing matching Starboard Beach Fire Department shirts gathered round a table. My eyes fixate on a tall, dark, and handsome man holding what looks to be an energy drink in one hand while his other hand waves frantically in the air. No doubt, he's telling some elaborate story to his buddies.

The sound of Josh's tray hitting the table snaps me back to reality. He sits down across from me, completely oblivious to the crowd in the courtyard.

"I don't remember you from last time I was here. Although you might not have been old enough to work here a few years ago. Are you new?" Josh asks while unwrapping his sandwich.

"I'm twenty-seven." I pop open my can of Diet Coke. I know I look younger. I've had patients ask me if I was even old enough to be a nurse. My short stature doesn't help either. "I moved here from Arizona a little over a year ago."

"Oh yeah, what part?"

"Phoenix."

"Ah, that's a great area." Josh sits back in his chair. "I went to a conference in Sedona a few years back and stayed a week longer to explore. Red Rock State Park was captivating and the weather was fantastic. I'm surprised you'd want to leave."

"It's a gorgeous place," I agree. My parents couldn't afford to take us on big vacations like some of my classmates. While my peers recounted stories of summers spent at Disney or on a cruise, we stayed within driving distance of our apartment. I never minded or felt like I was missing out. Arizona has plenty to explore, and my family always had a blast on our road trips. It's probably why I was so quick to accept Alex's offer when he asked me to take the ride with him.

"What brought you here? A significant other, perhaps?" His eyes home in on my left hand, presumably looking for a ring.

"Oh no. Nothing like that. I just…needed a change." I grab my fork and start picking at my salad, then subtly change the subject. "You mentioned you traveled. Tell me about where else you've gone."

Josh takes the bait and excitedly tells me about the places he's seen, people he's met, and food he's tried. I half listen, trying to keep my focus on my company in front of me and not out the window. From the angle I'm sitting, I can see Alex perfectly, but he can't see me. I kind of like this advantage.

The guys from the station gather up their lunch, and I'm disappointed that they're leaving so soon. Alex stands and tosses his drink into a trash can like he's sinking a basketball into a net. He does a small celebration dance when the can hits its intended target. I try to pull my eyes away, but then he lifts the hem of his shirt and uses it to wipe some sweat above his brow. I see him with less clothes on all the time, but it's a view I don't think I'll ever tire of. His defined abs make a perfect "V" that leads straight to his—

"Are you free Saturday night?" Josh asks.

I snap my gaze from the window so fast, I feel like I've given myself a minor case of whiplash.

"I'm sorry. I didn't hear you." I flush, thinking I've been caught ogling my neighbor, but Josh seems completely oblivious.

"I asked if you were free Saturday night." He gives a pleasant smile. "I'd love to take you out to dinner."

"Oh, umm." I chew on my lower lip.

"I'm sorry." Josh's face falters. "Is there someone else?"

"Oh no," I stammer and wave my hand around nonchalantly. "Nothing like that." My immediate reaction is to turn him down. I've never had trouble turning down other offers in the past. But an idea pops in my head. If I go on a date with Josh, maybe Alex will move on from me and find someone else.

Someone he deserves. Someone who's not broken and who's capable of loving him with their whole heart. My stomach sinks thinking of what I'm about to do, but I'm doing this for him.

Josh watches me with bated breath.

"I'm actually working Saturday night." I fidget with my napkin. "But I'm free on Friday."

Josh's hazel eyes light up at my response. He pulls out his phone and taps it a few times. "I have a late meeting on Friday, but if you don't mind, I can leave from there and meet you somewhere. Have you ever eaten at The Lighthouse?"

"No, but I've heard good things about it." I know it's slightly more upscale than The Local, which is my friends' usual go-to. And though I love the food there, it might be nice to try something different. Maybe this will turn out okay after all.

"Perfect!" Josh says gleefully. "Want to meet there at seven?"

"Sure. That will work." I force a smile, convincing myself this is for the best.

"Then it's a date!" Josh winks.

We say our goodbyes. I throw out my barely touched lunch and head back to my department. My stomach feels like I'm on the downside of a roller coaster and there's no end in sight. I try to convince myself that I'm doing the best thing for my heart. The best thing for me, so I don't have to go through that pain of losing someone again. But the pain I'm feeling now, with the potential of hurting Alex all for the purpose of getting him to move on and find someone else, completely destroys me.

If I'm being truthful with myself, I'm not sure whether I hope this will work or not.

<h1 style="text-align:center">15</h1>

<h1 style="text-align:center">Alex</h1>

"Looking a little formal for some lasagna, baby girl, not that I mind, of course." I give Gabby an appreciative once-over as she steps out of her bedroom wearing a little black dress. It's certainly a different sight from her regular attire of scrubs or the leggings and oversized sweatshirts she wears on her days off.

"I'm not having dinner here tonight. I'm going out," she says, looking a little distracted.

"I found the necklace!" Aly barrels through the door. "This will look perfect with that dress!"

"Wait! Where are you going?" I stand from the couch, irritated. It was my understanding that everyone was off tonight and we'd all have dinner together. Michelle sent a group text a few days ago to make sure she had enough food for all of us.

"I told you. I'm going out." She turns her attention toward Aly and takes the necklace. "Thank you. It's beautiful. Are you sure you don't mind?"

"Not at all!" Aly smiles. "I'm not going anywhere fancy, and it's the perfect length to go with that neckline."

"What's this about going somewhere fancy?" And why am I just hearing about this now?

"She's got a hot date with a doctor." Michelle's head pops up from beneath the counter where she must've been grabbing some utensils. We have a rule that if the girls cook, the guys stay out of the way until it's time to clean up. Then that's on us.

"You have a date?" I ask with bitterness laced in my voice. It's impossible to hide my anger.

"It's not a big deal, but if you must know, I met a guy—"

"You mean a doctor!" Michelle interrupts.

"Fine. Doctor," she huffs. "Anyway, we were in line next to each other at the cafeteria. One thing led to another and he asked me out for dinner."

"A doctor from the hospital?" I rub my chin. "Who?" It can't be any of the doctors from the Emergency Department. They're either married or nearing retirement.

"His name is Josh Payne. He's new...sort of. He said he was a resident but left and came back."

"I haven't heard that name." I try scanning my memory for any recognition. "What does he practice?"

"Alex. I need to go."

"Just tell me what he does, and why isn't he picking you up here?" It pisses me off that she's being so vague.

"Because he had a meeting. We agreed to meet at The Lighthouse for dinner."

"Ohh. The Lighthouse. That's more than just a casual dinner. He still should've offered to pick you up so I can vet him."

"You do not need to vet him. He seems perfectly fine."

"Perfectly fine..." I make a clicking sound with my tongue. "He sounds like an exciting guy. Just tell me what he does."

"Fine!" She taps her foot in frustration. "If you must know, he's a proctologist."

"Eww." Aly scrunches up her nose, then catches her faux pas. "I was so surprised about you going on a date that I didn't think to ask what he specialized in."

"Neither did I," Michelle says as she continues to flutter about the kitchen.

"Oh, come on. It might not be as glamorous as say, a cardiologist or brain surgeon, but someone's gotta do it," she tries to rationalize.

"Someone's gotta do what?" Jax walks through the door and makes a beeline for his wife. He places his arm around Aly's waist and she leans into him with a sigh of contentment. A pang of jealousy hits me. I want that. I want what they have and I want it with Gabby. And now she's going out with someone else? This is bullshit.

"Gabby is going out to dinner with a proctologist," Michelle answers.

"Eww." Jax recoils a bit and Aly shoots him a look. "I mean, wow! That's a very important job. You never know when you need an expert to examine your ass."

Aly elbows Jax in the stomach.

"I mean butt."

Aly takes her heel and presses it against the top of Jax's foot.

"I mean tush."

"Really?" Aly says exasperatedly.

"What? That's what my mom calls it."

"Hey, guys!" Carter saunters in. "Wow, Gabby, you look great!"

"Thank you." She grabs her purse and tries to make a quick exit.

"She's going on a date with a proctologist," Jax blurts out, earning him another dirty look from his wife.

"Eww." Carter winces. "I hope I never have to see one of those."

"Oh my God, will you all just grow up?" Gabby yells at everyone and stomps out of the condo.

I run down the hall after her. "Gabby, wait!"

"What?" She turns around and folds her arms across her chest.

"I'm sorry we were making fun of your date. I'm just surprised you're even going on one. How many times have you turned me down? You have been adamant that you don't date and now suddenly you've changed your mind?"

"I can't date you, Alex." She looks down, avoiding any eye contact, and pushes the button for the elevator.

"Yes. You've told me many times. In the past, you've told me that you weren't looking to get into a relationship with anyone. Now all of a sudden you're going out with some guy who shows up out of nowhere?" I'm trying to stay calm but am failing miserably. Every nerve in my body vibrates with anger and a bit of betrayal.

"He didn't just show up out of nowhere. We work in the same building. He seemed nice."

The doors to the elevator open and Gabby steps on. I put my hand against the frame, preventing it from closing.

"Nice or safe?" Is that what this is all about? Maybe Jax was right when he mentioned my history with women worries her. I really haven't been with anyone since I set my sights on Gabby, but I know my reputation precedes me. Still, Jax was just as bad (if not worse) and Aly was able to overlook his past.

"What?" She looks up, finally making full eye contact with me. There's a sadness to her. She doesn't want to go on this date. I can feel it.

"Are you choosing him because he's the safe choice?"

"Alex...I...I can't be late," she pleads.

My heart plummets to the floor at the thought of her spending time with another man. But I can't force her to do anything.

"Fine." I remove my hand from the door. "Just promise me you'll call if you need anything."

She somberly nods as the doors close. I stay frozen in place, trying to think of what I could have done or said differently to change her mind.

The door to 312 opens. Carter sticks his head into the hallway and yells, "You coming to dinner or what?"

"No." I don't even bother looking at him. "You guys go ahead and eat without me. I've lost my appetite."

16

Gabby

The sun is still high in the sky and the breeze flowing through my open car windows feels like a warm blanket as I pull into the restaurant's parking lot. Summer is in full swing and it's by far my favorite time of year. I hope this is a sign of good things to come. Seeing Alex's reaction tonight nearly gutted me, and I almost called the whole thing off. But Alex deserves someone who can love him unconditionally, and while I want to, I just can't.

It's not like I haven't tried to work past my grief. I went to counseling and even joined a support group for a short time. Maybe it was due to my young age, but I never found anyone I connected with or felt safe enough around to fully open up about my feelings. Eventually, I gave up and decided to figure out how to get through life on my own. Which brings me back to my current situation.

Parking Stinky, I scan the lot, looking for Josh's car, and kick myself when it dawns on me that I don't know what he drives. Thankfully, we exchanged numbers earlier, so I send him a quick text to let him know I'm here. He replies instantly, saying he'll meet me outside. I walk toward the front of the restaurant. Its dark awning is covered with tiny fairy lights, and for a moment, it reminds me of a few weeks ago when Alex took me to count the stars. God, that felt like such a magical evening. Some nights I lie in bed and pretend I'm back there with him all snuggled up under the blankets. Once, I even typed out a text to see if we could count stars again, but then I realized I'd be leading him on and deleted it before I hit send. I'm sure I'm giving him mixed signals and that's not fair to Alex.

"Gabby, you look stunning." Josh interrupts my thoughts as he walks up to me and hands me a small bouquet of flowers.

"Thank you." I politely accept the gift. Flowers—ugh. But it's not his fault. It's not like I announce my aversion to everyone. Aly is petrified of seafood and all things related to what goes on beneath the ocean's surface. She uses the excuse of allergies to get by. It sounds kind of crazy, but now I wonder if I should borrow that idea. "I'm surprised you had time to get flowers. How was your meeting?"

"It ended earlier than expected." He opens the door to the restaurant. "So I stopped by the florist and had a few drinks at the bar while waiting for you."

I look down and fidget with the bouquet. If he got out of his meeting early, why didn't he let me know or at least offer to pick me up? I'm sure it's for the best this way. Alex would've grilled him with questions.

Josh reads the confusion written all over my face. "I hope you don't mind. The meeting didn't go as planned and I figured a few drinks would help me unwind before seeing you."

"Oh." I chew on my bottom lip. "I guess that makes sense. I'm sorry your meeting didn't go well."

"At least I had something to look forward to tonight." He takes a lock of my hair and twirls it. I brush his hand away and take a step back. Unfazed by my response, Josh just gives a grin that doesn't sit well with me. I shake off the alarm bells in my head. I've never dated as an adult. Maybe this is normal behavior and I'm unfamiliar with it. Or maybe I'm just worried about Alex and it's clouding my judgment.

The hostess shows us to our table. It's right in the center of the dining room and covered with a crisp white tablecloth. A candle in a hurricane lamp flickers off to the side. I've passed this place many times but have never eaten here. It's not super upscale, but it's definitely classier than The Local. Josh, acting like a gentleman, pulls out my chair. As I sit down, I notice a faint smell of alcohol. I wonder how much he had to drink before I arrived.

"How early did your meeting end?" I ask as he takes a seat across from me. A waiter comes over, hands us our menus, and fills our glasses with water.

"Oh, I don't know." Josh's head bobs a bit. "Two maybe three hours ago."

"Two or three hours?!" My mouth gapes open at his answer.

"I'll have another one of those Long Island iced teas," he says to the waiter, then points to me. "She'll have one too."

"Oh! Umm...I'm fine with water." I smile politely at the waiter. I'm not much of a drinker, but on the occasion when I do indulge, it's usually something decadent and chocolaty.

"No, no, I insist. The bartender here makes them just right." Josh brushes me off and I realize the waiter has already left.

"Okay," I concede. I suppose I can take a sip or two. "Do you come here often?"

"This is my first time back since I left a few years ago." Josh pokes at the candle in the hurricane lamp and I'm grateful that there's a glass barrier between the flame and his finger. "In all those years, everything has stayed the same. Starboard Beach is stuck in a time warp."

"You really feel that way?" I ask, feeling defensive of the town I've grown to love. Growing up in a more urban area, I was used to constant changes. Businesses were always changing and moving, trying to keep up with the latest trends. It felt like every year, I had to find a new coffee shop to frequent because the ones I loved would inevitably go under due to all the competition. Starboard Beach might not be the most modern place in the world, but it's consistent and I appreciate that.

"I do. I've always felt like this town has suffocated me. I'm bigger and better than this." He puffs out his skinny chest. "There's more to life for me than just this place."

The waiter comes back with our drinks, and we place our orders. I stay conservative with a small pasta dish while Josh chooses a prime rib dinner with a ton of sides. I hope the large meal will help absorb some of the alcohol he's consumed. I don't think he's as sober as he's pretending to be.

"If you don't like this place, why did you come back?" Annoyance stirs within me. Who the hell is this guy to think he's better than, well, anyone?

"It was the only place that would take me back."

"It was what?" I ask incredulously. A million questions enter my mind, but I'm left dumbstruck as Josh takes his drink and begins to chug it. "I...umm...I don't think you're supposed to do that."

"It's fine." He slams his empty glass on the table, making everything shake. I feel all eyes on me as diners from surrounding tables turn toward the source of the noise.

"You know what? Maybe we should call this a night. Something must've really stressed you out today." I try to make my voice sound as gentle as possible. I don't want to draw any more of a crowd.

"My life is over," Josh slurs, ignoring my request. "I can't keep running like this."

"Um...running?" I nervously scan the restaurant, wondering if anyone can hear my dining companion.

"You perform one wrong surgery on a patient and suddenly you're slapped with a malpractice suit." He reaches across the table, grabs my drink, and proceeds to chug it like the last one.

I open my mouth to say something but quickly snap it shut. How do you even respond to that? *¿Cómo me metí en este lío?* How did I get myself into this mess? I would give anything to be back home surrounded by my friends.

"Did it ever occur to anyone that I'm under stress? It's not easy being a proctologist," Josh says rhetorically. "And the jokes. I'm always the butt of everyone's jokes." He waves his hand, knocking his water glass to the floor. Thankfully, it doesn't shatter, but my dress is now soaked.

"Is everything okay here?" the waiter asks while placing our meals before us.

"I-I'm not sure." A clunking noise makes everyone in the room jump. I turn my focus away from the waiter to see Josh has face-planted right into his plate.

"Is he dead?!" The waiter jumps back and yells. If we didn't have everyone's attention a few minutes ago, we sure do now.

I jump out of my seat, remove his head from the mashed potatoes, and check his pulse. "No, he's just passed out," I assure the petrified waiter. "I need to go make a phone call." I grab my purse and scramble out the door. Part of me wants to jump in my car and hightail it out of there, but morally and ethically, I can't do that. Instead, I pull out my phone and call the one person who I know will always come to my rescue.

17

Alex

"Where's the son of a bitch?" I growl as I walk up to Gabby, who's nervously pacing outside the restaurant. I take a moment to reel in my anger. I'm not mad at her. I'm mad at Dr. Hemorrhoid Helper for putting her in an uncomfortable situation. The moment I saw her picture flash on my phone's screen, I knew something was wrong. I'm glad she called me, though. Even though she gutted me tonight, I'll always come to her rescue.

"He's still passed out at the table. One of the waiters offered to help get him to the car, but what would I do with him after that?"

"Why don't you just leave him at the table? Let the restaurant call the cops on him or something."

"I thought about that, but we work in the same building. I don't want to be the girl who left Dr. Payne unconscious at a restaurant. Although from what he was saying, he might not be a doctor much longer," she mumbles.

"He deserves whatever he has coming."

"Maybe he does, but who knows? I really don't know him well and it's possible I misunderstood him since he was slurring. He might've had a hard day and needed to blow off some steam and went a little too far."

I can't believe she's willing to give this guy the benefit of the doubt. I, for one, have already judged him for the asshole that he is.

"Do you know where he lives?"

She shakes her head.

"Great." I blow out a breath, trying to come up with a plan. "Well, we're going to need his wallet and keys. We'll find his address and take him home. I'll stick Dr. Payne in the Ass in my car. I don't want him trying anything with you if he wakes up. Do you think you can drive his car? We'll drop him off at his house and then swing back around here for Stinky. Does that sound like a plan?"

"I guess so. But how are we going to get him out here and to your car?"

"We have that covered," a male voice says from behind me. I turn around to see a stout man in a three-piece-suit standing next to a humongous teenage boy who has a lanky man wrapped around the back of his neck like he's wearing a human boa.

"Hi, I'm Jared," the guy in the suit says. "I'm the general manager and this here is Nickolas, one of our busboys. Your date started to disrupt other customers with his snoring, so we figured we'd save everyone a headache and bring him out here. Thankfully, Nick is a star athlete. We call him Nick the Brick."

"Thank you," Gabby says sheepishly and digs in her purse.

"No need, ma'am." Jared holds his palm up and shakes his head. "Your date already settled his tab at the bar, and dinner is on us."

"No." Gabby gasps. "I can't let you do that."

"I insist. You've already had a horrendous date. You don't need to get stuck with a bill on top of it."

"I-I don't know what else to say." Gabby shakes Jared's hand. "Thank you for your compassion."

"As much as I appreciate this moment," I interrupt, "we need to get this guy out of here." I look over at Nick the Brick, who still has Dr. Ass Analyzer in a firm grip. "Can you hold on to him while I bring my car around?"

"No problem at all, sir." The Brick puffs out his chest. "I can bench up to 225 pounds and I would say this guy is about"—he jiggles the drunk doctor a bit—"one hundred seventyish."

"Good to know." I roll my eyes, although I'm impressed with Nick's stats.

I jog to my car while Gabby thanks Jared and Nick over and over again. In less than a minute, I pull up to the curb. Jared opens the passenger side door and Nick dumps Dr. Colon Cleaner into the seat. Once their work is done, they head back into the restaurant.

"What do we do now?" Gabby asks as I click her deadbeat date's seat belt into place. I might hate the guy, but I don't need him getting hurt on my watch.

"We need his keys and wallet to find his address." I turn my attention back toward her.

"Okay, umm...I guess they're in the pocket of his pants." She bends down next to where Josh is seated.

"Hold it!" I place my hand on her upper arm and gently pull her back. "The last thing I need tonight is to watch you digging around in some other man's pants."

I reach around Dr. Posterior Prober's waist, wishing I had thought to get his belongings while Nick the Brick was still holding on to him. It's a lot harder to access his pockets now that he's sitting down.

I successfully pull out his belongings and read the address on his license. "Okay, Dr. Douchebag lives on Riverside Drive and..." I hit a button on the key fob. A black Mercedes lights up. "His car is right over there."

I give Gabby strict instructions to follow directly behind. About ten minutes later, we pull up to a small bungalow-looking house that's seen better days. The dilapidated porch is covered with chipped paint, and the screen door is barely hanging on to one hinge.

"Huh." I step out of my SUV. "I guess he put all his money into his car rather than his home," I say to myself.

"How was he on the drive?" Gabby asks while walking up to me.

"Inebriated," I deadpan, though I'm happy he did nothing but sleep. "Give me his keys. I'll open the door and drag his ass inside. Did he mention if he had any pets, like a guard dog or anything?"

"No, he never mentioned any pets." She chews on her bottom lip. She always does that when she's nervous. "I really don't know much about him."

"No kidding."

I walk up the two steps to Dr. Cheek Checker's front door and listen for any clue that something or someone might be inside. Everything seems quiet, so I unlock it and feel the wall for a light switch. Finding what I'm looking for, I flip on a light to the sight of one shithole of a house. The place looks like a 1970s bachelor pad complete with dirty shag carpet, wood paneling on the walls, and a dark green sofa and recliner set. Perfect. I'll drag Dr. Tush Tester to the recliner, where he can sleep his drunk ass off.

"You so dodged a bullet on this one." I smirk and walk past Gabby to get the drunkard.

"What do you mean?"

"Go inside and have a look for yourself." I nod my chin toward the front of the house. She gives me a hesitant look but walks toward the house.

I open my passenger side door, unclick the drunk doctor's seat belt, and lift him over my shoulder. The dude is dead-weight, but Nick the Brick was right on the money. I'd say he weighs just about one hundred seventy pounds if not slightly lighter.

"I'm getting too old for this shit," I mumble, schlepping Dr. Deadweight from the side of the road and into his shack of a house. He's not the first passed-out guy I've carried before, although it's usually out of a building and not into it. I dump his butt in the recliner, then turn to Gabby, who's still taking in the scenery with a horrified look on her face.

"Is it okay to just leave him here like this?" She fidgets with her hands, still trying to take in the retro scene surrounding us.

"He should be fine." I shrug and start to explore the rest of the place out of sheer curiosity.

"I'm just going to leave him a note so he doesn't wonder how he got back here." Gabby starts looking around for something to write on.

"Maybe he has something in here." I open a door and... "No...freaking...way!"

I figured the rest of the house would look similar to the living room, but this is more than I ever could've imagined.

"What's going on?" Gabby walks up beside me and peers into the funhouse-looking room. I'm all too familiar with the sight. It looks just like the mirrored room I helped demolish in Jax and Aly's future home. Jax and Travis had dubbed it the "Hotel California Room" because it was hard to find your way out once the door was shut. We had endless ideas about who the previous tenant was. Now I think I have the answer.

She gasps as I take out my phone and snap a few pictures.

"You said this guy used to live here, moved away, and came back, right?"

"That's what he told me," she confirms. "Why do you ask?"

"I think I just found out who used to live at Jax and Aly's new place." I snap a few more photos. The only difference between this room and the previous one is that this one has a bed smack dab in the middle.

"I can't believe this." She shakes her head.

"I can. He's probably a narcissist who gets off on looking at himself from all angles. I can't imagine that with this house and his stellar personality, he brings many women back here. Like I said before, you dodged a bullet."

"I never planned to go home with him," she replies defensively.

"What were your plans exactly?" A muscle in my jaw twitches.

"I don't know!" She takes a step back. "I told you. He seemed nice enough and I didn't think going out to dinner would do any harm."

"Well, it might've done a lot of harm. Who knows what this guy had planned for you." I stare her down, so agitated by her recent actions. She's better than this.

"Let's just get out of here." She crosses her arms over her chest and pivots towards the living room.

With one last check that Josh is fine and propped in an upright position, I place his keys on the side table, turn the bottom lock, and close the door. He's in for a hell of a hangover, but that's not my problem.

Walking back to my SUV, I notice that Gabby has already settled into the passenger side, undoubtedly waiting for me to drive her back to the restaurant to retrieve her car. Too bad I have other plans. This whole cat-and-mouse chase she's put me through needs to stop and I'm declaring it ends tonight.

18

Gabby

I slouch in the passenger seat of Alex's car, upset with myself. What was I thinking accepting some random guy's offer for a date? Okay, he wasn't totally random, but clearly, I should've gotten to know him better before agreeing to dinner. Still, I was just trying to keep Alex at arm's length. I can't believe how much my plan backfired. I chew on the inside of my cheek, not knowing whether to laugh or cry at this ridiculous situation.

Alex gets behind the wheel of his SUV and starts up the engine.

"If I didn't say it before, thank you for coming to my rescue."

His only response is a curt nod, making me feel even worse. The atmosphere inside the vehicle is heavy and the ride remains silent until I notice he makes a left turn instead of a right, leading us away from our intended destination.

"Umm..." I pipe up. "Did you forget I left my car at the restaurant?"

"Nope." The one-word answer has such acidity to it.

"Are you okay? Where are we going?" If this were anyone else, I'd be worried, but just like the night he took me to count the stars, I trust him with all my heart.

"Need to blow off some steam and you're coming with me." He keeps his eyes focused on the road and a death grip on the steering wheel.

I rest back in my seat and look out the window. If we stay on this street, we'll eventually merge with the main road that leads to the beach. A few minutes later, we arrive at the lookout spot we sat at several weeks ago. The SUV is barely in park before Alex jumps out and starts pacing the gravelly terrain.

"Alex, are you okay?" I call out as I climb out of my seat. I cautiously approach him, careful not to misstep in these ridiculous heels Michelle loaned me.

"No!" he snaps. "I am not okay. I'm confused. From the moment I met you, I have felt like there has been something between us."

"I—"

"Let me finish," he cuts me off. "The least you can do is give me a chance to finish my thoughts."

I snap my mouth shut and nod for him to continue. Fresh tears prickle behind my eyes. I've never seen Alex look so lost, so disheveled. It kills me to think that I'm the cause of it and why.

"I've come to your rescue countless times in the pouring rain and snow when you've locked your keys in your car. When your condo flooded, I gladly gave up my bed for you. Hell! I've even sung to your bashful bladder. I have been very open about my feelings for you, Gabby, and call me crazy, but I've always felt like you have feelings for me too."

Heat creeps up my face. It's been so hard to deny my pull toward him and I can't... I can't lie. Not to the man who's become my best friend. To the man I've denied loving.

"I know you claim you don't want to be with me because of the amount of women you heard I've been with, but how many times have you seen me with someone else?"

"Umm...never," I say sheepishly. I've always relied on the rumor mill to be my excuse and I'm not proud of that. But let's face it, it suited my needs—my reason not to date Alex.

"I swear, you're trying to sabotage whatever we can have." Alex stops pacing. "I'm done skirting around this question. I want answers and I think after what happened tonight, I deserve the truth. Why are you doing this? Why are you not allowing us the chance to find out what it is we have between us?"

An internal war ignites within me. Alex has been so sincere and he's right; there is something between us. I tried my best to ignore him when I first moved in, but the pure joy I get from spending time with him has such a magnetic pull. He brings me peace, a sense of belonging, and comfort. It's so hard to do this, but he deserves to know the truth. I owe him that much.

"I lost them." My voice comes out in a whisper and is drowned out by the waves crashing against the shore. I don't know if I have the strength to repeat my words, but I can tell Alex didn't hear me.

"What?" He takes a step closer to me.

"I-I lost them," I say again a little louder. *God, this hurts so much.*

"Lost who?" Another step closer and we're standing toe to toe.

"I can't do this." I can't talk about them. If I do, I'll have to relive that night and I'm not strong enough for that. I look down at my feet, but Alex places his hand under my chin and lifts it up so I'm looking straight at him.

"You need to," he says with a mixture of gentleness and sternness in his voice. "I think I've proven to you that I'll stick by your side no matter the issue. Whatever it is, you can tell me. No more secrets."

Secrets. I never thought of my omissions as secrets before, but I suppose that's just what they are. A pang of guilt hits me. If anyone deserves to hear the truth, the reason why I try not to get too close to anyone, it's him. Not even Michelle or Aly know what I'm about to tell Alex.

"I'm going to ask you again." He grabs my hand and splays it against his chest. The forceful beating of his heart begins to subside as his anger is replaced with compassion. "Who did you lose?"

"Everyone I ever loved." I barely get the words out before I burrow my face into his chest and begin sobbing. He holds me and lets me cry all while lovingly rubbing my back. My initial tears turn to complete wails. My body quivers and my knees feel weak. I know I'd be a heap on the ground if it weren't for Alex supporting me. I've been bottling these emotions up for far too long and now I can no longer control them.

I have no idea how much time has passed, but when I calm down enough to peel myself away from Alex's tear-stained shirt, I realize the sun has already set.

"I soaked your shirt." I place my hand on his chest. It feels like he just pulled his clothes out of the washing machine and put them on. "I didn't mean to do that."

"It's fine." He motions to a nearby bench, and we sit down next to each other. I shift as close to him as possible. Feeling him near brings me a sense of calm even though I'm nowhere near done with my turmoil for tonight.

"I-I was sixteen. I had just gotten my driver's license and was loving the freedom, you know?" I look at him for confirmation.

"I get that. When I was sixteen, I thought I was a full-fledged adult and no one could stop me from making dumbass decisions."

"Exactly." I give a sad smile. "Anyway, there was this group of girls that were really popular and for some reason, I always wanted to be like them. You know, the whole grass is greener thing?"

Alex gives a nod, then grabs my hand and squeezes it.

"My life wasn't bad or anything. As a matter of fact, it was pretty amazing. I had my parents and my sister, Mari—she was fourteen. We were so close. She was my best friend, but things changed when I went to high school and she was still in middle school. I felt like I was too cool to be around her and we began to fight a lot." I pause, realizing that my thoughts are all over the place. "Anyway, some of the popular girls from school were throwing a party and, to my surprise, they invited me. I was so excited, I felt like this was my moment, my chance to get in with the popular kids, you know?"

"Sounds like a typical teenager," Alex agrees.

"Yeah, I guess so." I fidget with Alex's hand for a moment. "It was a school night and I knew my parents wouldn't allow me to go. So I made the decision to sneak out of our apartment. Mari and I shared a bedroom and she begged me not to go, but I waited until she fell asleep and snuck out anyway."

I push down the lump forming in my throat because that night, I betrayed my sister, my best friend.

"I went to the party," I continue. "It was lame and I realized that these so-called popular girls were just regular people that I idolized for some ridiculous reason. Suddenly, I had a strong urge to be back home with my family. I decided to leave, but when I got to my car, I realized I had locked my keys inside."

I look up and out toward the ocean. God, I hope they are okay. I feel Alex give my hand another squeeze and realize I stopped talking.

"Some neighbor of one of the girls came out and managed to break into my car. By then, I had been gone for several hours. I started heading back home, but when I turned the corner to our apartment complex, I noticed a ton of smoke and emergency vehicles everywhere."

Alex audibly sucks in a breath. I have no doubt that he of all people knows what's coming next.

"My family—we...we weren't poor, but we didn't have a lot either. The building we lived in wasn't the greatest. The landlords cared more about making money than the safety of their tenants. It's believed that the fire started on the floor below my family's. Someone left a candle burning too close to their curtains. The building wasn't up to code and the smoke alarms didn't work. The-they—"

Queasiness washes over me as I fight to finish my story.

"E-eleven people passed away that night. My mom, dad, and s-sister. I lost them all." For the first time since starting my story, I look up at Alex. The sun has fully set, but the moonlight reflecting off the ocean provides enough light to see his face. His eyes are filled with sadness, compassion, and love.

"Gabby, I'm so sorry." He brushes a piece of my hair away from my face.

"I should've been with them," I say. "If I hadn't locked my keys in my car, I could've warned them, gotten them out—and the others too. It's my fault."

"No!" The tone in Alex's voice makes me jump. "No. It's not your fault. You did not start the fire and if you had been home, you probably would've died too."

"But maybe I would've survived and been able to wake everyone," I argue.

"How? You said it yourself: the smoke detectors weren't functional."

"But—"

"No buts." Alex shakes his head. "I'm so deeply sorry that you had to go through something like that and especially at a young age, but did it ever occur to you that you locked your keys in your car for a reason? You weren't supposed to be there that night, Gabby. You were meant to live."

"Meant to live?!" I jump up from the bench. "Why? So I could be spared and tortured for the rest of my life? The apartment complex was torn down and the city replaced it with a flower garden. A fucking flower garden with a cheap plaque remembering the victims. I purposely drove fifteen minutes out of the way to work just so I could avoid passing the area. I stopped going downtown because I couldn't bear to be near the restaurant where my dad was a sous chef. I accepted a job at the worst hospital in the city because I couldn't bring myself to step foot in the nicer one where my mom worked. I wanted to be a nurse and follow in her footsteps, but I wasn't prepared for the burn victims. I had a panic attack the first time one was brought in. I—"

Two large hands grab hold of my shoulders. "Gabby, you're spiraling!"

"Spiraling?" I laugh maniacally. Anger replaces my sadness. "That's not even all of it. I finally decided that maybe a fresh start would be just what I needed. So I packed up everything to start a new life. Wouldn't you know that my first full day here, I meet the most amazing man I could ever dream up?" Because I locked my keys in my car...how ironic.

I pause for a moment and flex my hands into fists. My frustration only grows at the thought of my cruel twist of fate. Alex keeps his focus on me, but I know he's not sure how to react to my outburst. I can't stop now. Once the floodgates have opened, there's no going back.

"The one person who brings me so much joy...who makes me feel like I'm finally whole again...is also a man who runs into burning buildings for a living. That is why I fight so hard not to love you!"

19

Alex

I stand before Gabby, completely dumbfounded by her confession. I cringe thinking of all the times I recanted my craziest stories and my close calls on the job. All this time, I thought I was earning extra points by showing her how heroic I could be, but instead, I was pushing her farther away.

Gabby starts crying again, so I pull her in close to me and hold her tight. I'm already emotionally spent from this night. I can't imagine how she's still upright. Resting my chin on the top of her head, I tell her how sorry I am over and over again. I wish I had better words to say, and for a moment, I wonder what Carter would do in this situation. He's the one who's never at a loss for words in these circumstances.

"Stop saying you're sorry," she mumbles into my extra-tear-soaked shirt. "It's not your fault."

"It's not your fault either," I counter as revelations and more questions invade my mind. "What happened to you? You know, after everything happened?"

"I was sent to a group home with the clothes on my back." She pulls away from our embrace and uses her hand to wipe away her tears. "My family's car was impounded. It's not like I had the money to afford the payments. I don't have any other relatives and people don't chomp at the bit to foster a teenager who just lost her entire family. I was a mess and so angry."

I rub my hand up and down her arm, hoping to calm her but also trying to satisfy my need to touch her...to be close to her. As horrible a situation she's been through, I can't help but think of the strength it took for this young, beautiful, smart teenager to muster through it all. My admiration for Gabby hit a new level.

"The first group home didn't work out," she continues. "So I was sent to another...then another. Eventually, I aged out of the system. My parents had a small life insurance policy that I received when I turned eighteen. I used that to get myself a little apartment and enroll in nursing school."

"That was so brave of you. To do that at such a young age," I say with true adoration. I floundered after high school. My parents pushed college on me. They wanted me to follow in the footsteps of my siblings, which included multiple degrees and cushy jobs. I wanted to appease them but always felt like a fish out of water. I changed my major three times with the hope that I would find something that would make me happy, but nothing ever did.

Then one day changed everything. I was driving home from a class and witnessed a car wrapped around a tree. I ran to help the driver but had no clue what I was doing. An off-duty fireman came upon the scene and started barking orders at me. Everything he told me to do made perfect sense. We worked seamlessly together to safely extract the victim and tend to his injuries. I later learned that he lived because of our quick response. I had never felt such a sense of purpose until that night.

The very next day, I dropped out of school and signed up for the Fire Academy. While waiting for the semester to start, I took classes to become an Emergency Medical Technician and later became a paramedic. I love being a first responder. My family, on the other hand, is still livid that I choose to live my life so recklessly. Their words, not mine.

There are times I feel like I've never been so sure of my decision to leave. Then there are times that I become overrun with guilt because I abandoned the rest of my family. I've overheard the snarky remarks and seen comments on social media. I may not live a glamorous life like the rest of them, but I finally feel like I found my calling.

A breeze from the ocean comes rolling in and I watch as Gabby shivers. It's then that it dawns on me that she's only in her dress from her horrible date earlier. God, that feels like a lifetime ago.

"You must be freezing." I want to hold her again but realize that my wet shirt will do nothing to provide warmth.

"I think I'm more numb than anything." She wraps her arms around herself.

"Come on, we don't have to go home yet, but we can at least sit in my car, and I can put the heat on."

She agrees and I run over to the passenger side to open the door for her. The scent of her lemony shampoo hits my nose and something dawns on me.

"You're using your normal shampoo again," I say when I slip into the driver's seat. I'm very familiar with the scent. When the girls' condo flooded, Gabby not only moved into my bedroom but my bathroom as well. I loved the fresh clean scent that was always left behind from her showers...and also on my pillows.

"Oh yeah. I wasn't fond of the new stuff I tried either." She bites down on her lip.

"You did that on purpose, didn't you?"

Her big, beautiful brown eyes look up at me as she shamefully nods.

"And the imposter burgers?" I rub my chin. Things are starting to make a bit more sense.

"I found your list and got worried that you were planning to try harder. To, ahh—" Her cheeks flush. "I'm so sorry, Alex. I didn't want to push you away. I was just so scared. I still am. I can't lose you too."

"I'm not going anywhere," I assure her.

"But you don't know that!"

"Do you want me to quit?" I challenge, knowing she'd never ask that of me.

"No!" she says emphatically. "You love your job and you're damn good at it too. I would never ask you to change yourself for me. The world is a better place because of people like you."

"The world is a better place with you in it too." I start up my engine and blast the heat. "I understand that you worry for me, but crazy things happen all the time. You can't avoid everything in your life, hoping you'll get by unscathed. One of us could become terminally ill, or the world could end tomorrow and you never got a chance to live while you had the time."

"You sound like Miss Ruby."

"You talked with Miss Ruby?" I don't know why that surprises me. Miss Ruby tends to be privy to lots of people's innermost thoughts. She has that effect on people. Still, I wish Gabby had opened up to me sooner. She's been grieving all alone.

"Not exactly about this, but we did talk the last time she was in." Gabby nods. "She figured out that I was scared to be with you because I'm petrified to lose you."

"She's a wise woman. What else did she say?"

"Well, I'm paraphrasing, but she thinks I should give you a chance." Her lips turn up ever so slightly. "She's also quite fond of your muscles."

"Like I said, she's a wise woman." I let out a chuckle while flexing my arms. It feels good to release some of this tension. The atmosphere in the car begins to lighten, and Gabby starts to relax.

"What happens now?" Her voice is a little more than a whisper.

"I really don't know. My feelings for you haven't changed, but I know now that I have been way too forceful with how I've dealt with them. I'm sorry for coming on so strong." I shake my head, upset with how I've handled things. "All those times I proposed to you..." I slap myself in the forehead.

"I'm pretty sure I hold the record for most rejected proposals." She lets out a small sigh. "I guess we both went about this the wrong way."

"Are you upset with me?"

"Absolutely not." She reaches over the center console and wraps her arms around my neck. I begin rubbing slow circles on her back, and her body presses further against me.

"You're exhausted."

"I feel like I just ran a marathon."

"In a way, you have. It was just an emotional marathon instead of a physical one." I pull away from our embrace. "Come on, let's go home. You need some rest."

"Umm..." She sits back in her seat. "I don't think I'm ready to go home. Do you think we can count stars instead?"

My heart is so happy to hear those words. That was one of the most memorable nights ever and I love that it obviously meant something to her as well. There's hope for us yet. I know it.

I crawl over my seat to see if I still have the blankets and pillows. Sure enough, I do. I hold up the bag. "Looks like we're in luck."

"So we can?" she asks hopefully.

"Sure." We pull away from the lookout spot and head to our little slice of heaven.

"Oh no!" Gabby gasps. "We forgot about Stinky."

"We can wait until tomorrow. I don't think Stinky is going anywhere." I shoot her a look and for the first time tonight, she gives me a smile, and it's then I know everything will be all right.

20

Gabby

"Ugh." I lift my head off Alex's chest. It feels like it's made of lead. I try to blink away the sunlight that's invading my eyes. Our attempt to count stars was futile. We fell asleep as soon as we got comfy in the back of the SUV. I think Alex and I both knew the real reason why I wanted to come back out here. I couldn't bring myself to go home after such an emotionally charged night, and I didn't want to fall asleep alone. I needed to be close to him, to feel his comfort and support.

"What time is it?" My voice sounds hoarse, undoubtedly from all the crying I've done. I'm sure my eyes are a swollen mess as well.

"Dunno," Alex mumbles. I love that our bodies are right up against each other. I can feel the vibration of his baritone voice right down to my toes.

I search around the vehicle for my phone or Alex's. It doesn't really matter. I just need to figure out the time. Digging through the blankets, I hear a thud and discover Alex's phone first. I hit a button and the time flashes on the screen. Nine twenty in the morning. It's later than I expected but not too bad. Unless...

"Do you work today?" I hope Alex didn't miss a shift.

"Uh-uh." He shakes his head. "I had to switch with Mickelson a few days ago 'cause his kid got sick. I have off today and tomorrow."

"Okay." I blow out a sigh of relief. "I don't go in until tonight, so we're in good shape."

"Perfect." Alex reaches up and pulls me back to him. The idea of going back to sleep is tempting, but I have too much running through my mind to fully relax.

"Oh no!" I pull away from him. "I forgot to text Michelle. She's probably worried that I didn't come home last night."

"I messaged Carter last night. Everything's good."

"Okay." I rest my head back on him, relieved no one is sending out a search party for us. "What do we do now?"

"We go back to sleep," he replies like the answer is obvious.

"No, I mean after this. I don't think I can go back home and just go about my life as normal."

"That's 'cause you can't." He shifts to sit upright and rubs his eyes. "You experienced a traumatic event and for over a decade, you kept that to yourself. Now it's out."

"I was trying to protect myself," I say meekly.

"I get it. I'm not mad at you, but after revealing something like that, I can imagine you probably feel a little different."

"I feel like my whole world has shifted," I agree. "It probably sounds ridiculous, but I felt like if I talked about them, I was acknowledging their deaths. If I kept everything bottled up, they were all still alive somehow."

"I see where you're coming from." Alex scratches his chin pensively. "But did it ever occur to you that talking about them keeps their memory alive?"

My mouth opens and closes like a fish out of water. "I-I never thought about it that way."

"Hey." He cups his hand to the side of my face so we're looking directly at each other. "You experienced more tragedy at sixteen than some people go through in a lifetime. You did what you had to do to survive. From that fire, you rose from the ashes. You took care of yourself the best way you knew how and you did a damn good job. I'm sure your parents and sister are so freaking proud of you. For what it's worth, I'm proud of you too."

"How do you know just what to say?" My heart feels so full.

"I actually had trouble sleeping last night, so I texted with my sister Lilli. She's a psychologist. I was worried that I'd say something dumb and screw things up. I didn't want to risk that."

"You sought professional help?" I cock my head to the side in amazement.

"Are you mad I told someone?" He winces, waiting for some type of backlash.

"No. Actually, I'm impressed that you wanted to make sure you said the right things. It sounds like you're starting to take life seriously. I believe that was step three on the list." I nudge him with my elbow.

"Where did you even find that thing?" He groans.

"On the laundry room floor. I almost mistook it for garbage, but then I saw my name on it."

"Wait. I just thought of something." He perks up. "The last item on the list was to find out why you don't like flowers. Is that because the city changed the site to a garden?"

"Partially." I nod. "The first few days and weeks after every-thing happened was a blur, but the one thing that has always stood out in my mind was the amount of flowers everywhere. There must've been thousands of them stacked high on the road near the complex. You could barely see the caution tape the police used to close off the area. There were even more at the vigils and memorials. People thought it was a nice way to send their condolences, but I hated it. I didn't need flowers. I needed my family." My eyes fill again with tears. But I push them back.

No more. Only happy memories now.

"I can see that."

"Most people don't, and flowers can be a sweet gesture, just not for me." I rest my head on Alex's shoulder. "I'm more of a bananasaurus rex girl."

"I'm glad you liked the gift."

"It's so cute. I put it in the corner of my bed."

"It gets to sleep with you every night? Well, now I'm jealous of the thing."

This sets me into a fit of giggles, and the tension in my shoulders starts to ease. I need this release. I don't want this moment to end, but I know I have to go back and face reality.

"What do we do now?" I ask after a moment of peaceful silence. A warm breeze blows past, carrying the scent of the pine trees surrounding us. Coming from a landlocked state, I was pleasantly surprised to discover Starboard Beach has a variety of beaches, mountains, and forests. The place has always had such a magical feel to it, and I begin to wonder if maybe there is some hope for me.

"The first thing I'd like to do"—Alex stands and stretches—"is go home and shower. I need to change out of these clothes." He pulls at this shirt. "The thing has seen better days between all of your tears and drool."

"What?!" I shriek. "I do not drool!"

"Yes, you do. But I'll give you a pass this time."

"Hmph." I place my arms across my chest.

"I'm just playing with ya, baby girl." Alex lets out a deep chuckle and leans in to place a chaste kiss on my forehead.

"Seriously, though." I try to push down the mixture of butterflies and all the other emotions I've been feeling in my stomach. "What do I do now?"

"Whatever happens is up to you, but if you're asking me for suggestions, I think you need to come clean to the rest of the group about your past."

"Do you think Michelle and Aly will be upset that I was hiding this from them?" I look down at my feet.

"Nah, they're good friends. I think they'll understand." He begins to gather the blankets. My heart sinks, knowing this morning is coming to an end, but we really do need to head back home.

"What about the guys?" I ask, jumping down from the back of the SUV.

"You can rip off the Band-Aid and talk to everyone together," he suggests.

"I think I'd like to talk to the girls first," I decide. I adore Carter and Jax, but I feel more comfortable around Aly and Michelle.

"Okay, sounds like you've got a plan going. That's good progress." He nods for me to get into the car.

"Umm...what about us?" I sit down and strap my seat belt into place.

"What about us?" He mirrors my actions.

"You know...about everything."

"Like I said last night, my feelings for you haven't changed. If anything, they're stronger because I have so much admiration for what you've overcome."

"I can't get past the fear of losing you, Alex. Nothing's changed that way." Is it possible to overcome this phobia over time? If you had asked me yesterday, I would have immediately responded no. But now? Just talking about my past has made me feel...lighter. I kept everything bottled up for so long, I didn't realize how badly I needed to release my emotions. I really needed that cry last night.

"I understand, but no one knows what life will bring them. There are no guarantees for any of us. So you have a choice. You can go through the rest of your life keeping everyone at arm's length, expecting the worst, or you can jump right in with both feet and hope for the best. I know it sounds scary, but I promise to be with you every step of the way. Whatever you need from me, I'll be there." He pauses to wag his eyebrows. "And I do mean whatever you need from me."

"Alex." My voice carries no hint of annoyance.

"Sorry, baby girl, but old habits die hard." He grins at me with those damn dimples. Gah, the feelings I have for him.

"Honestly, I think I'd be more worried if you didn't try to turn a situation into something sexual."

"Yeah, but I really should tone it down. Like the list said, I need to show you that I can take life seriously."

"I know you can take life seriously." I throw my hands up. "And I adore your sense of humor. It makes things more fun."

"Well..." He scratches his chin. "If you say so."

"I do say so."

"Does that mean I can have the list back?"

"Oh no, I'm totally keeping it as a souvenir."

"Ugh." He hangs his head and starts the ignition.

I giggle at his reaction, but a wave of reality sweeps over me. I can't just transform my way of thinking overnight...or possibly ever. Although a certain patient of mine was able to change. If she could, maybe I can too.

"Miss Ruby said she didn't start living until she turned eighty-three."

"Do you plan to wait that long too?" Alex puts the car in drive and we make our way down the dirt road. He makes a left instead of a right and I realize he's driving me back to The Lighthouse to pick up Stinky. "Because like I said, I'll wait with ya, but a lot of stuff won't be working as good as they do in my prime."

"No. Like you said, there are no guarantees. I mean, what if I don't even make it to eighty-three?"

"Now you're starting to get it." He winks. "Miss Ruby is a smart woman, and I'll have to thank her next time I see her."

"That probably won't be too long." I smile. I know Miss Ruby will be proud of me for opening up to Alex. Yet I have to admit... "I'm still scared."

"I know, but think about it this way: Yes, Miss Ruby waited a long time to start her life, but she also didn't have something that you have."

"What's that?"

"An amazing group of friends to get you through."

My heart warms at the thought. I tried not to get attached to the 3rd East crew, but I did anyway. They're some of the most loving and compassionate people I've ever met.

We turn onto the main road, headed back to grab my trusty car.

"Alex?"

"Hmm?"

"Tell me everything is going to be okay."

He reaches down and threads his hand through mine. "Everything is going to be okay."

21

Gabby

"So that's my story." I shrug my shoulders, watching for Aly's and Michelle's reactions. I predicted Aly would cry and Michelle would be stunned silent, but somehow it worked out just the opposite. I'm grateful that both of my friends were home this morning so I didn't have time to dwell over talking to them. The fact that we're in the comfy surroundings of our living room also helped ease some nerves. Telling them about losing my family wasn't easy, but it didn't have the emotional drain that it did when I told Alex.

"Oh, Gabby." Michelle throws her arms around my neck. "I'm so, so sorry. I wish you had told me sooner. Not that it would've changed the outcome, but maybe I could've helped in a way to make life more bearable. Please let me know if you need anything."

"Thanks, Michelle." I hug her back. "Honestly, just telling you both feels like a weight lifted off my shoulders."

"It all makes sense now," Aly says almost to herself, then turns to me. "I mean, with you and Alex. I never understood

why you insisted that you two weren't right for each other."
She gets up, walks over to me, and gives me a hug. "I'm so sorry
for your losses."

"Thank you." I give her a squeeze back, then place my hand
on her growing belly.

"Nonna Grace always said that babies are a sign that the
world will keep going." She looks down at her stomach and
smiles.

"Is that a hint?" I smirk.

"All I'm saying is that you're here and Alex is here and you
two would make adorable babies and then our children could
become friends or—" Aly gasps. "My babies can marry your
babies and we'll be family."

"You are getting way ahead of yourself." I laugh at Aly's
enthusiasm as she happily plops herself in the space between
Michelle and me on the couch. "Alex and I are not even together."

"Yet," Aly adds. "You're not together yet, but come on,
anyone with eyes can see it's coming."

"I guess." Heat creeps up my neck. "Alex is letting me take
the reins with everything. We talked and he realized he was
coming on too strong. For now, I need to take things slow. I
mean, I never even planned on getting into a relationship."

"Neither did I and look where it got me." Aly winks.

"Speaking of relationships," Michelle pipes up. "What happened during that date with Josh? Carter got a text from Alex
saying that you were safe with him and not to expect either of
you home until the morning. We didn't even know Alex left."

"He wasn't having dinner with you all when I called him?"
I cock my head to the side.

"No." Aly frowns. "He went back to his place right after you
went on your date. He said he wasn't hungry."

"Ugh," I groan. "That just makes everything even worse. The date with Josh was a total nightmare. He started drinking before I even got there and was mumbling something about a malpractice suit. He made a complete spectacle of himself before he passed out in his potatoes. It was so embarrassing."

"He—passed out in potatoes?" Aly fights back a case of giggles.

"Yeah. I had to pull his face out and make sure his airway was clear."

"Oh my God." Aly loses her fight with the giggles. "I'm sorry. It's rude to laugh, but it's funny."

"Go ahead." I sigh. "I'm sure I'll find this funny one day...maybe in like twenty years."

"So that's when you called Alex?" Michelle asks while Aly tries to compose herself.

"Of course. I knew he'd come to my rescue. He's basically my knight in shining armor." I fill the girls in on the rest of the details. I tell them about the helpful employees, how Alex swooped in to save the day, and how we got Josh safely back to his house. "That reminds me." I look at Aly. "The next time you see Alex, ask him to see the pictures he took of Josh's place."

"What?" My former roommate scrunches up her nose. "Why?"

"Trust me. I'd describe it to you, but I think Alex would enjoy telling you more, and honestly, he deserves that."

"I think this is a perfect time for cupcakes." Michelle changes the subject.

I'm happy for the reprieve. I've bared my soul and my embarrassment all in a matter of minutes. I'm spent. I don't think I have it in me to talk more about my horrible date or discuss the potential future of Alex and me. Part of me feels like jumping into a relationship with him would be the most natural thing in the world. The butterflies in my stomach haven't stopped fluttering since that little forehead kiss back at his car. But I'm still petrified to lose him, and I'm not sure how to deal with that.

And if I'm honest with myself, it's not just about him dying in a fire, although that would be the worst of the worst. It's also about us not working out, us breaking up, me losing him to someone else. You name the scenario of loss and I'm worried about it. I realize how irrational all of this is, but I can't stop myself. And I'm not sure if I'm ready to talk about that with anyone either.

All the what-ifs that go through my head are enough to scare me into my own little cocoon. But then I think back to my conversation with Miss Ruby. All that worrying is going to make me miss out on all the things I could have with Alex.

Yes, I definitely need a cupcake.

"That is one of the best things I've heard all morning." I take a seat at our table while Michelle puts down a huge plate of pastries.

"Whoa!" Aly says, looking at the number of treats. "This is way more than cupcakes."

"Yeah." Michelle sighs. "I failed another test this week and couldn't sleep last night. I made peanut butter cupcakes with vanilla frosting, lemon bars, white chocolate raspberry scones, and pistachio macarons."

"Oh, man, I'm sorry about the test, but I'm excited to try these." Aly grabs a lemon bar and puts in on her plate. "There's no way we can eat all this. Even if the guys come over and help."

"That's okay," Michelle states. "I can send Alex over to the firehouse with whatever we don't finish."

"That's a great idea," Aly gushes.

"I've sent him with extras before. It's the best of both worlds," Michelle agrees. "I get to test out new recipes and the guys down at the station get some treats."

"Alex is off today and tomorrow," I inform Michelle. "But I'm working tonight. I can run some stuff over to the station." It wouldn't be the first time I've brought over food for the firefighters.

"Perfect!" Michelle claps her hands. "I do have a question, if you don't mind me asking."

"Go for it." I bite into a pistachio macaron. Heavens above, this girl needs to drop out of law school and open up her own bakery. I have no doubt I'd be her best customer.

"You said that after the fire, you went to live in a group home because you didn't have any relatives to take you in?" Michelle asks, pulling me out of my sugary bliss. "I can't imagine anyone refusing to do so."

"It's not that anyone refused." I shake my head. "The only family I had were my parents and sister."

"Wait." Aly puts down her pastry. "You mean to tell us that you don't know any of your relatives?"

"Nope." I grab another macaron, choosing to focus on something sweet.

"No grandparents, aunts, or uncles?" Michelle asks.

"Not even a third cousin twice removed or whatever."

"How is that possible?"

"All I know is that my parents ran away from home shortly after they graduated high school. I never met any blood relatives. I have no idea who my grandparents are or if they are even still alive. I could have cousins or extended family living right around me and I wouldn't know."

Aly and Michelle watch me wide-eyed as if expecting me to reveal some dark, life-altering secret.

"Umm...that's basically it."

"Wow." Aly finally breaks the odd silence. "I mean, I thought I didn't know much about my family, but this is...wow."

"Did you ever ask about other family members?" Michelle cocks her head to the side, still trying to make sense of what I just told her.

"It's funny, you know? I don't remember ever asking or really wondering. I would see my classmates with grandparents and cousins or whomever, but I was just kind of happy in my own little world. We had each other and that was enough. There is one thing, though."

Both girls lean in close.

"A few years before everything happened, my sister and I went rummaging through our parents' closet. We were trying to get a sneak peek of our Christmas presents and discovered a high school diploma from my mom. The school was located in Manhattan."

"Manhattan," Aly repeats. "As in New York?"

"Yup. We showed the diploma to my mom. She just mumbled about it being a lifetime ago and told us to never speak of it again."

"Have you ever traveled to New York?" Michelle asks.

"No. If we went anywhere, it was always within driving distance of where we lived at the time. We never brought up the subject again, but my sister and I always wondered whether our parents originated from New York. If so, that means they traveled thousands of miles to begin their new lives. Why? What motivated them to go?"

"There are a lot of reasons to move thousands of miles away and start over. I did it to get away from my ex, and you did it because you needed a change," Aly answers. "New York is super expensive. Maybe they moved to somewhere more affordable, or for a job, or simply because they wanted nicer weather."

"Maybe," Michelle ponders. "But if they left for new career opportunities or better weather, wouldn't they keep in touch with their family or friends back home? What if something bad happened and they had to flee a dangerous situation?"

"I don't know." I contemplate Michelle's idea. "Mari and I never felt unsafe, but you do make a good point about not keeping in touch with people from back home."

"Exactly." Michelle points a fork at me. "It's not like phones or computers didn't exist back then and—" She slams her palm on the table. "Maybe your parents were in the Witness Protection Program!"

Aly chokes on her coffee. "What on earth would give you that idea?"

"New York has some sketchy areas. Maybe they saw something they shouldn't have or were in the wrong place at the wrong time. It happens more than you think." Michelle goes on the defense, but she's not wrong. I know she's been studying criminal cases for one of her classes.

"Have you ever considered trying to find other relatives?" Aly asks.

"I'd be lying if I said I haven't considered researching or doing one of those DNA tests, but the unknown is kind of scary...especially if Michelle is actually right."

"Sorry about that." Michelle shrinks back in her seat.

"It's okay. I know you're just considering the possibilities and looking out for my well-being."

"There's always an upside," Aly adds. "You might have a rich uncle who has no heirs to leave his millions to, or maybe you're a descendant from royalty."

"You also make a good point." *Geez, my brain feels like mush right now.*

"You'll never get answers if you don't try. Did you know that Jax loves to study history—specifically, family trees?"

"I remember he enjoyed studying his. He likes studying others as well?"

"Oh yeah, he winds up going down these crazy rabbit holes. Like, he'll take a famous military general and find all the lineage connected to them. If he thinks he's on to something, he'll stay up all night trying to put the pieces together. I think it's kind of boring, but it makes him happy." She pauses to lick some icing off her finger. "Anyway, if you're okay with me telling him your story, I can see if he can dig up anything. Of course, if you're not comfortable about him knowing, this conversation will never go past these doors."

"I'm okay with you telling him. Actually, I'd rather you tell him so I don't have to go through it again." I look over at Michelle, who gives me an understanding nod. "Will you tell Carter everything too?"

"Of course!" Michelle says. The more I think about me telling the guys, the more I believe it would be way awkward. Having my friends tell them makes more sense.

"Thanks, you two." I turn to Aly. "I can't imagine Jax finding much. I really don't have much information to give him."

"There are no guarantees without a test, of course." Aly shrugs her shoulders. "Plus, you have a pretty common name, but he's really good at this stuff. You can always let him have at it for a bit and if you decide later you want to do a DNA test, he could probably help you with that too."

"It would be kind of nice to meet someone with a connection to my family." I quickly warm up to the idea. Even if they turn out to be strange, it doesn't mean I have to meet them. "Do you know I don't have any pictures of them? Nothing of my parents or sister. All of that went up in flames."

"None?" Michelle asks. "That's almost hard to believe. Nothing on social media or your phone?"

"No." I hang my head in sadness. "My mom wouldn't let us have any social media accounts—if she caught Mari or me with Facebook or Snapchat, we'd have been grounded for life! And we wouldn't have disappointed her or Dad. We loved them too much."

"Yeah, my parents wouldn't let me or my siblings have any social media accounts." Michelle frowns. "But that's because they were worried we'd do something stupid and ruin the family name."

"I wish my parents had cared." Aly shrugs. "It's fascinating how differently the three of us grew up."

"I had my cell phone with me, but it was only filled with selfies and things that I ate. I was so mad at myself for being so self-centered."

"Sounds like you were a typical sixteen-year-old." Aly reaches across the table and grabs my hand. "Please don't beat yourself up for that."

"Do you really think Jax might be able to trace my history?" The thought is exciting and scary at the same time.

"It's very possible." Aly's eyes light up as she talks about her husband. "I know he won't leave any stone unturned. He's so thorough with everything he does. So very, very thorough."

"Are you still talking about Gabby's family?" Michelle chides as I laugh.

"Hmm? Yes. Oh yes." Aly's face turns a shade of crimson. "Anyway, I'm sure Jax can help find you some information. Best-case scenario, you find some family members, get some answers, and hopefully some photographs."

"And the worst-case scenario?"

"You're stuck with all of us as your family."

22

Alex

It's been several days since I rescued Gabby from her nightmare date. I haven't physically seen her since the morning after everything happened as our schedules have not lined up. True to my word, I told her I'd back off and let her take the reins on whatever is going on between us. Unfortunately, that's a whole lot of nothing because, with the exception of a handful of texts here and there, we've hardly had any communication. I know she needs time to sort out all these new emotions she's got going on, but I miss her.

"Well, this is depressing." I push through the doors of our condo's gym to the sorry sight of Jax lying on a weight bench staring at the ceiling. Across from him, Carter hangs half draped over a stationary bike. "I'm no expert, but I don't think that's how exercise equipment works."

"Leave me alone. I'm tired," Carter grumbles without looking up. He's another one I haven't seen in a few days. His mom caught some sort of virus, so he took time off to help with his younger siblings.

"I'm sure you are. What are you even doing here?" I knew he was coming home today, but I figured he'd be resting. His siblings are much younger than him and are full of energy.

"Aly asked me to babysit this asshole." He points a finger at Jax, who mumbles something inaudible.

"Why would the asshole—I mean Jax—need a babysitter?" I look over at my grumpy friend, who continues to lie forlorn on the weight bench. I haven't seen much of him either, but that's nothing unusual.

"Because Aly is working on some sort of project for the university and Mr. McHandsy over here wouldn't leave her alone to do her job. She texted me and asked if I could keep him busy for bit."

"I was just trying to give her a back rub!" Jax says exasperatedly.

"It's never just a back rub." Carter rolls his eyes.

"Agreed." I take a seat on the weight bench opposite Jax. I'm glad they're both here and that no one else is utilizing the gym at this time. I need to get some things off my chest. "I assume you already know what happened with Gabby?"

"About losing her family?" Jax moves to a sitting position. "Aly told me. Man, that's awful."

"Michelle filled me in on one of our nightly phone calls." Carter steps off the bike and takes a seat next to Jax. "I feel terrible that we didn't know. How has she been doing?"

"I wish I knew. She's been pretty quiet, and I haven't seen her because we've been on opposite schedules." I lean over to rest my arms on my knees. "I'm concerned about her."

"Ah, I wouldn't be too worried. She probably has a lot going on," Carter says in his relaxed surfer guy tone. His voice has the ability to put anyone at ease.

"Aly's been keeping her busy." Jax's dark gray eyes seem to lighten at the mere mention of his wife. "Turns out Gabby has a talent for decorating. In her off time, she helped Aly finish up the nursery, and now their next project is organizing the kitchen."

"That's great!" I'm relieved at Jax's news. "I was worried she might slip into a funk after everything."

"So was Aly," Jax agrees. "She's familiar with the signs of anxiety and depression, so she took it upon herself to help Gabby channel her nervous energy into something positive." He uses air quotes on the last part. "Or...you know, some shit like that. I saw them together the other day at the house and it looked like they were having fun. They were discussing different shades of white, so I got the hell out of there."

"Isn't white just white?" Carter furrows his brows.

"Oh no." Jax smirks. "Apparently, there's ivory, eggshell, antique, and cornsilk."

"What's the difference?" I ask with genuine curiosity.

"There is no difference!" Jax waves his tatted arm. "I got in trouble for saying that, so if any of the girls mention weird-ass colors to you, just go with it. Trust me on this—you don't want a lecture."

"Wow. I never thought I'd see the day you'd be doling out relationship advice." Carter chuckles.

"Speaking of relationships." I look at my two friends. "I told Gabby that I'd back off on pushing her into anything, but these last few days without her have been driving me crazy. Do you think it would be too much to ask her to dinner?"

"Doesn't sound like too much to me." Jax shrugs.

"As long as you don't propose to her over appetizers, I think you should be fine." Carter rubs his chin. "It's not unusual for you two to grab something to eat. Just keep things casual."

"Yeah, I learned my lesson about the proposals." I look down at my feet. "Everything is different now."

"Are you having second thoughts about being with her?" Carter asks.

"It's not that." I shake my head. "My feelings for her are stronger than ever. But now I'm worried that I'll screw things up or say the wrong things. I don't want to scare her off."

"Oh, you'll definitely say the wrong things." Jax snorts.

"Thanks for the vote of confidence."

"Just speaking from experience." Jax stands and grabs a water bottle nearby. "The other day, I told Aly to rest cause her ankles looked big."

"Ouch." Carter winces.

"Yeah, stupid choice of words." Jax points the water bottle at me. "Thankfully, your girl was with us. She agreed with me and got Aly to elevate her legs and drink some water. The swelling went right down."

My girl, I repeat Jax's words in my head. I can't believe that after over a year and a half, my dreams might actually come to fruition.

"I'm happy Gabby was there," Jax continues. "It's nice having a medical professional living right across the hall."

"Don't forget about me," I pipe up. "I know things too." I may not have as much experience as Gabby, but I'm pretty knowledgeable with the basics."

"Yeah, but I don't want you touching Aly."

"Understandable." I can't blame him there.

Jax's phone pings and he scrambles to grab it out of his gym shorts. "Yes!" He pumps a fist in the air. "Aly said she's done working and I can come back now. Time to make good on that backrub." He nearly trips over his own feet as he barrels out of the gym without so much as a goodbye.

"Lucky sonofabitch," Carter, my uncharacteristically quiet roommate, mutters under his breath.

"You okay, buddy?"

"Yeah." Carter scrubs a hand over his face. "I just really need some sleep." He stands and heads out the door looking like his little league team just lost the world championship game.

I can't help but wonder what's going on with my roommate, but I know I won't be able to get anything out of him if he's exhausted. Instead, I pull out my phone and fire off a text to see what Gabby is up to.

23

Gabby

My foot taps nervously as I hover over the printer, waiting for the discharge papers for one of my patients to print.

"What's going on?" Marissa swivels in her seat to look at me.

"Huh?" I press a few buttons, hoping the machine didn't jam.

"You've seemed distracted all day."

"Is it that noticeable?" I worry that I made a mistake or did something wrong.

"No." Marissa shakes her head. "Nothing bad. You've just had your head in the clouds ever since the firefighters stopped in earlier."

Ah yes, the firefighters that volunteer to visit with patients and hand out stuffed animals to the kids. It's so sweet to see a young patient's eyes light up when they see a real firefighter has come to spend time with them. They act like they've been visited by actual superheroes, and in a way, they have been.

Three of the guys from the department showed up today, and of course, Alex was one of them. It was the first time I'd seen him since I poured my heart out to him the other day. The moment we locked eyes, my nerves got the best of me and I dropped a cup of ice I was bringing a patient. He just smiled with those dimples of his and helped me clean it up.

"Grab the papers." Marissa points to the glitchy printer that's spitting out the forms I need.

"Ah, sorry." I pick up the papers and start putting them in order. "When the guys were here earlier, Alex pulled me off to the side and asked me to have dinner with him tonight."

"And…you're not hungry?" Marissa looks at her watch, well aware our shift will be over soon.

"I'm just nervous to go out with him." My coworker blinks at me like I sprouted a third eye, so I decide to elaborate. "We hang out a lot, but I feel like this time, he's thinking it might be a date."

"You lost me." Marissa stands and stretches. "I thought you two have been dating for a while."

"You're kidding." I drop my papers again.

"No." She hands me a stapler. "I've seen you together plenty of times here and around town. Rumor has it that Alex hasn't been with anyone in ages. I think everyone just assumed you two were an item."

"Get out of here." People think Alex and I are already a couple? Good thing no one from work witnessed that awful date with Josh. What would they think then? Thankfully, I have not seen or heard from Dr. Payne since that crazy night. His name doesn't even show up in the hospital database, leading me to believe that there was indeed some type of malpractice suit.

"I'm serious." Marissa places a hand on her hip while she looks me up and down. "Quite frankly, I've been waiting for a wedding invitation."

"Oh my gosh! I'm not. We're not. I-I don't know what we are."

"Well, whatever." Marissa shrugs. "Get your booty out of here and go have a meal with that man. Don't worry about putting a label on whatever good thing you two have got going. Just enjoy it. Some of us would pay to have what you do."

"Thanks." I finish discharging my patient while mulling over Marissa's words. She's right. I need to worry less about putting a label on us. What Alex and I have is special, and even though Aly has done her best to keep me occupied these past few days, I'm really looking forward to spending time with my favorite person tonight.

Once I get home, I enlist my roomie, the fashionista of our group, to help me pick out the perfect outfit for tonight. I want something that's a little nicer than my usual wear but still casual in case Alex is not considering this a date. Basically, I don't want to be under or overdressed.

"Should I go with the purple or the blue?" I hold up two shirts for Michelle to study. I'm still on pins and needles anticipating this evening and can't wait to go out at the same time. Go figure.

"The blue. It reminds me of Alex's eyes." She was elated when I asked her to help me pick out an outfit for tonight. "Are you sure this is a date?"

"I have no idea." I walk into the bathroom but keep the door cracked open so I can talk to my roommate. "He told me he wouldn't push me into anything, but then he asked me out."

"But that's not unusual. You two go out all the time. It could be just as friends."

"Exactly." I walk back out and twirl for Michelle to study my outfit. "When I told Marissa about tonight, she told me that she thought Alex and I have been dating for a while."

"I can see that." Michelle pokes through my jewelry box and hands me a pair of earrings. "Everyone who lives here knows that you two are very good friends, but to someone on the outside? It probably does look like you two are a couple."

"Hello." Alex's voice carries from the hallway.

"I'll be out in a second." I put my earrings in and walk into the living room.

Relief washes over me when I see Alex dressed in his regular outfit of jeans and a SBFD T-shirt. This is normal attire and I can handle it. Okay...I might be a little excited.

"Sorry I didn't invite you along, Peanut." Alex shoves his hands in the back pockets of his jeans while I grab my purse off the hook near the door.

"No worries." Michelle brushes him off. "Carter and I are going to the movies anyway. You two have fun."

"Thanks," we say in unison and make our way toward the elevator. As the door opens, Alex turns to me. "Do you think Carter and Michelle have something going on?"

"Why do you ask?" I push the button for the ground floor. "They always hang out a lot, kind of like us. Oh!" The light bulb in my head turns on.

"Yeah, *oh* is right." Alex smirks as the elevator reaches our floor. "I feel like they've been spending a lot more time together lately. Then a few weeks ago, he mumbled something about being stuck in the friend zone. But I don't know. Forget I said that. I have zero sensibility about these things."

We get to Alex's SUV and, always the gentleman, he opens the passenger door for me. I decide I need to know what this is about. "Is this a date?" I blurt out as I sit down.

"Do you want it to be?" The creases in his dimples begin to show.

"I'm not sure," I say honestly because I'm a ball of utter confusion. The wall I built around my heart is starting to crumble, which excites me and scares me at the same time. "You said you wouldn't push me into anything. Wait!" I gasp as a completely new thought pops into my head. "You're not doing this out of pity because my previous date passed out in his potatoes?"

"What?! Why would you even think that. Unless...have you seen him? If he's bothering you, I'll pun—"

"No, Alex, I've not run into hi—"

"And he's not even said he's sorry? What an—"

"Alex, leave it be. I don't think he even works at the hospital anymore. I'll let you know if there's a problem. But answer me... I need to know your intentions." Finally, he gives me a chance to get a full thought out, but now he has the goofiest grin on his face.

He sits and clicks his seat belt into place. "The truth is, I've missed you. We haven't seen each other in a few days, and I just felt like spending time with one of my closest friends."

"I missed you too." I'm surprised how disappointed I am by the term friends, but that really is all we are right now. "Where are we going?"

"I made reservations for us at The Lighthouse." He keeps a straight face while turning out of the parking lot.

"No!" I gasp and place my hand over my rapidly beating heart. I cannot show my face there again anytime soon...or in this century. The last time I saw that place was the morning after my disaster date when Alex took me to pick up Stinky. Despite being abandoned in the parking lot overnight, my trusty sidekick on wheels started right up and we hightailed it out of there.

"I'm kidding." His shoulders shake with laughter. "I figured we'd have dinner at The Local."

"I can't believe you did that." I try to look annoyed, but I'm excited to go back to my favorite restaurant.

Within twenty minutes, we're settled into a booth with a sampler plate of appetizers between us.

"Are you still planning to come with me next week to my parents' anniversary dinner?" He squeezes a lemon into his water.

"Yup. My days off were approved. Is the itinerary still the same?" We're supposed to drive out on Friday night and come back on Sunday.

"Actually..." He fidgets with his straw. "I was thinking about driving back Saturday night after the party instead of Sunday morning."

"Don't want to spend any extra time with the Joneses?" The change doesn't bother me at all. I'm just along for the ride. And moral support.

"Yes, but there's more to it than that." He hesitates for a moment. "I have an interview on Monday and I want to have enough time to get into the right headspace before it."

"Interview?" My stomach plummets thinking that after all of this, he's planning on moving somewhere else.

"Yeah." He stretches his hand behind his head. "There's a lieutenant position opening and—"

"Here?" I hold on to the side of the table, trying my best not to jump out of my seat. Dear God, please say it's here. I can't imagine him not working in the building next to me. "You're talking about the same department, right?"

"Of course." He gives me a look of confusion. "I passed the test a while ago and it looks like they have it narrowed down to Smitty and me."

"This is fantastic!" I gush. "Alex, you would make an amazing lieutenant!"

"You really think so?" His face lights up. No question, I'm one of his biggest supporters, and he is mine. Alex has had my back since the moment we met...which was when I locked my keys inside Stinky less than twenty-four hours after arriving in my new hometown. Not the most graceful introduction on my part, but that certainly didn't matter to Alex. He's been coming to my rescue since day one.

"Absolutely. I've never seen someone stay so calm under pressure. You're the perfect person to handle that responsibility, and you already have the respect from your coworkers. I'm so happy for you."

"Thank you. But I don't have the job yet." His face flushes at the attention, and I wonder how many times someone has stood in his corner or told him they believe in him. I get out of my seat and scoot into the booth next to his side.

"In case no one has ever said it..." I place my hand on his shoulder. "I'm so proud of you."

"Thanks," he mutters without making eye contact with me. His response confirms my suspicions. How could you *not* be proud of this man?

"Has—"

"I love this song," Alex cuts me off and nudges me out of the booth. "Let's dance while we wait for the rest of our food."

We make our way to the dance floor where other couples have already gathered as a country ballad plays from the jukebox. I'm too short to rest my head near his shoulder, so I opt for his chest instead. No complaints here.

"Mmm." I snuggle in closer while Alex keeps a firm grip around my waist. "Have I ever told you that I love the smell of your cologne?"

"I don't think so."

"This is kind of embarrassing, but I loved when my room flooded and we had to take turns sharing your bed. Your sheets always smelled so amazing." Good heavens, I'm getting comfortable way too fast.

"I enjoyed sharing my bed with you too. I especially liked the night I woke up to find you on top of me."

"You stop it right now." I snap my head up to look at him. "We promised to never talk about that night." There may have been a moment when I woke up to find myself straddling Alex in bed. To this day, I have no memory of the action, only the aftermath when Alex woke me up. I was so embarrassed, I never even told Michelle or Aly about what happened.

"You mean the time you mounted me like I was your noble stallion and we were galloping off into the sunset?"

"I swear, I was asleep. I didn't know what I was doing," I hiss, hoping no one heard him.

He begins to neigh, earning weird looks from couples dancing nearby. I do the first thing that comes to mind. I jump up on my toes, wrap my arms around his neck, and shut him up with a kiss. At first, it's hasty. I've caught him off guard. He takes a step back for better balance but never pulls his lips away from mine. Every nerve in my body flutters as he tightens his grip around my waist with one hand and runs his other hand up my back and into my hair.

"Get a room!" a voice calls from somewhere, startling us both and ending the most epic kiss of my life. Not that I've had many, but I don't need to kiss a million frogs to know I've met a prince.

"Well, that was unexpected." Alex pulls back with a surprised, yet satisfied, smirk.

"It was the only thing I could think of to get you to stop." I pant. My heart is racing at triple speed.

"I thought you wanted to take things slow." Concern washes over his face.

"Wasn't that slow?" I place my hand on my hip, trying to act casual.

"If that's what you consider slow, I'm all for it." He places his hand on the small of my back and guides me to our booth where our dinner is waiting for us.

Reality seeps in as I sit down. Oh my God, I just kissed Alex. Me! I initiated it and I liked it!

"Hey." He reaches across the table and places his hand under my chin. "What's going on in that head of yours?"

"I don't know if I can put it into words." I look into his bright blue eyes. "The more I fall for you, the more I'm scared to lose you."

"I'm not going anywhere."

"But you don't know that. Life is unpredictable." I berate myself for bringing this up again for like the hundredth time, but I can't get it out of my head.

"Gabby, stop. The Earth could get wiped out by a giant meteorite tomorrow. No one knows what will happen to any of us. But you do have a choice. You can live in fear, expecting the worst, or you can live in the moment and enjoy what you have."

"I'm trying to live in the moment." My voice quivers. "But then my nerves get the best of me."

"I know." He runs his thumb over my cheek. "You just have to keep trying, and you know what?"

"What?"

"I'm not giving up on you."

24

Alex

"Okay, we've got Twizzlers, Skittles, Sour Patch Kids, Blow Pops, three different flavors of potato chips, trail mix, mini donuts, Snoballs..." Gabby giddily pokes through a large reusable shopping bag. Today, we're driving out to my parents' anniversary dinner. I told her to grab some snacks for the road while I got gas for our trip, but I think she may have gone overboard.

"Snoballs?"

"What? You've never heard of them? They're little chocolate cakes that have some sort of cream in the middle. Then they're topped with marshmallow and covered in coconut."

"Holy sugar rush! You're going to put us in diabetic comas before we hit the interstate!"

"Don't be so dramatic." She brushes me off. "We'll spread this out over the course of the trip going there and then stock up again on the way back."

"You sound like you have this all planned out." I'm happy she's excited about this little adventure of ours. It feels like we've been getting even closer ever since that epic kiss at The Local. We've run into each other several times this week and she has kissed me every single time. This whole letting-her-call-the-shots thing has turned out to be pretty sexy. It wasn't that I had planned it that way, but all in all, I love watching her confidence grow. I have no doubt that the drive will be the best part of this trip. Hopefully, the family dynamic will go smoothly, but typically that's never the case. One thing is for sure. Having Gabby with me will definitely make it more manageable.

"That's because I do. Seriously, Alex, you're acting like you've never been on a road trip before." I pull out of the gas station while she rummages around in her bag of goodies.

"I've been on road trips before, and I've bought snacks for the occasion. But I didn't expect you to buy out the entire convenience store."

"Then you shouldn't have left me unsupervised," she says with a piece of licorice dangling from her mouth. Chuckling, I pull it out and start snacking on it.

"Okay, now give me the rundown on your family." She settles back in her seat with a bag of trail mix.

I let out a loud sigh. I've been putting off telling Gabby about my family, but there's no time like the present. While she knows some generic information, I've purposely left out the nitty-gritty details—the stuff I tell no one. But since she'll be there with me, meeting everyone, she needs to be prepared. "Well, you're already aware of who my mom and dad are. My mom's name is Elena and she's from a town right outside of Mexico City, and my dad, Bob, is from Vancouver. The British Columbia Vancouver, not the one in Washington."

"Gee. You don't say," she deadpans.

"You'd be amazed at how many people confuse the two. Anyway, you know about their job backgrounds, so I'll skip to my siblings. The oldest is Victoria. She's a production assistant at the news station where my parents work. She's married to Seamus, who's from Ireland. They have five kids. Next comes Roberto."

"As in the Spanish version of your dad's name?" Gabby laughs. "It's still hilarious to think that your dad's name is Bob Jones."

"It's the closest my dad could come to getting a junior." I shrug. "Roberto does the lighting for the TV station. He's married to Roberta and they have one son...Robert."

"Stop!" Gabby giggles, nearly choking on her trail mix. "You're making this up."

"Oh, trust me. I wish I were." I keep my eyes focused on the road ahead. I know if I turn to look at her, I'll start laughing too. What's even worse is that my family doesn't understand why their names are so funny. Sometimes, I feel like I'm the only family member with a sense of humor, which is another reason why I feel like an outsider.

"Okay. Okay." She tries to take a few calming breaths. "Who's next?"

"Lilliana." I can't help but smile at her name. She is, by far, my favorite sibling and I am so eager to introduce her to Gabby. "She's the one who's the psychologist. She's single and doesn't have any kids."

"Aww," Gabby coos. "I guess you're close to her?"

"Yeah. I mean, if there's any sibling I wish I lived near, it's Lilli. We share the same birthday, only ten years apart."

"Wow! Was she mad to share her birthday with her little brother?"

"Not at all. According to my parents, she was so excited for me to be born. She called me her birthday gift. It was like I was her baby. She carried me all over the place, fed me, and played with me. She was the only one who could get me to finish my green beans." I shudder.

"You hate green beans."

"I did back then and I still do, but for some reason, if Lilli asked me to eat them, I'd gobble them up like they were candy. I swear, my sister had some sort of magical powers."

"Is Lilli the reason you always go back home for your birthday?"

"Yeah. I joke and say it's because I'm my parents' favorite. But the truth is, I like to go back and celebrate with my birthday buddy."

"Has she ever come to celebrate with you?"

"She would, but my parents would make a big deal out of it. My family likes to do everything together and since they all live within twenty minutes of each other, it's just easier for me to go there. The Joneses like to stand as a united front. They're not happy that I broke away from the herd." More like I escaped a totalitarian-run household, but I leave it at that. It's probably best to ease Gabby into all of this.

"But you left because you didn't want to be in the spotlight." This was also a huge reason for leaving and something Gabby and I had touched upon. I'm not into the fame and fortune thing, which is something my parents and siblings have a terrible time understanding. I enjoy the anonymity out in Starboard Beach, and I love helping people when I can, but unlike the rest of the Joneses, I don't need any fanfare or special recognition for my good deeds.

"Exactly. They still don't see it that way. They act like I abandoned them." I make the huge mistake of turning my face to look at Gabby, who has traded in her trail mix for some flavor of Blow Pop. While she's innocently enjoying a piece of candy, the sucking sounds she makes can easily be interpreted as something else. *This could be a very long weekend.*

"Do you feel like you abandoned them?"

"What? Oh, yeah. Sometimes," I answer her question as it pulls my mind out of the gutter. "Okay, a lot of times I feel guilty that I left. But a few hours back home usually remind me why and then I'm good again for a while."

"Okay." Gabby senses my discomfort. "Let's get back to the topic at hand. We've already discussed Victoria, Roberto, and Lilliana. Who's next?"

"Next in line is Isabella. She is a math genius and financial advisor just like her husband, Tony. Which reminds me. If one of them corners you and starts talking about stocks and bonds, send me some kind of signal and I'll come rescue you. Trust me on this one: they'll bore you to tears."

"Noted. Who's next?"

"Luis."

"I don't think I've ever heard you mention him." Now she's crunching on the candy, revealing what looks to be some sort of gum in the middle.

"That's probably because the guy is less interesting than watching paint dry."

"Stop!" Gaby giggles. "I'm sure he can't be that bad."

"Luis is an entomologist. *No one* has anything in common with him."

"Wait! Isn't that a person who studies bugs?"

"Oh, he doesn't just study them. He lives for them. His house looks like a laboratory. I'm sure if some sort of ant colony needed a leader, he'd be the next one to fly the Joneses' coup." While she's laughing and trying to blow a bubble now, I pause and reflect on my family for a moment. Man, we're such an odd crew.

I'm usually a mess when I go back to visit my family. With the exception of Lilli, I've always felt like an outsider. I should be feeling vulnerable about letting Gabby see this part of me, but I don't because somehow, she gets me and that's all that matters.

"On second thought, forget what I said about ignoring Isabella and her husband. It's better to get stuck listening to the latest trends in IRAs than getting a lecture on the mating habits of dung beetles."

"Alejandro, I swear, if you're telling me stories to make me look crazy when I meet them, I'm going to be so pissed off at you."

"I'm telling the truth," I say in defense. "Trust me, my life is stranger than fiction."

"Sounds like it," she says, but I know she doesn't fully believe me. I wouldn't believe it either. Except I was born in this family. "Is Luis, the entomologist, married?"

"Yes, to his work."

"Gotcha." Gabby toys around with the air conditioning vent. "Who comes after Luis?"

"Ugh. Angel." I cringe.

"Oh boy. I take it that he doesn't live up to his namesake?"

"To the outside world, yes. But he's hated me since the day I was born. He was the baby of the family until I came along."

"Ah, so he was jealous of you."

"Yeah, but it's not like I did anything to provoke him. I was just, you know, born."

"That's normal with older siblings. I remember feeling jealous toward Mari. Her birthday was in January and with mine in March, it always felt like she got to celebrate first."

"Uhh...you know it doesn't work like that."

"I know that now." She playfully slaps me on the shoulder. "But as a little kid, it always felt like her birthday came first. So what did big brother Angel do to you?"

"When we were little, he told me there were monsters under my bed, my toys always ended up mysteriously broken, or my artwork would have squiggly lines drawn over it. We'd play hide-and-seek and he'd accidently forget I was playing and leave me wherever I was for hours."

"Hours?!"

"I take hide-and-seek very seriously." Lilli stands by her theory that Angel was intimidated of me since I was the baby of the family. His fear of being outshined led to his sinister behavior. "It got worse when we got older. When I was a freshman in high school, he was a senior. He stole every girlfriend I had." I nearly spit out the last sentence.

"That's awful! Did your parents ever intervene?"

"Nope. I could never prove anything. Angel was too smart to leave behind evidence. If my toy broke, it was because I left it out somewhere it didn't belong. My ruined artwork? He slipped holding a marker. The times he forgot to find me during hide-and-seek? Purely accidental. And then later with the girlfriends? Well, why date a freshman when you can date a senior and captain of the football team." Yep. My mom actually said that. Reliving this is making my head hurt.

"That's terrible!" Gabby gasps.

"The only one who ever cared or believed me was Lilli. But her word wasn't enough. Angel had and still has everyone wrapped around his finger."

"I'll be sure to keep my distance."

"Yeah. Please do. He'll try to seek you out. I have no doubt about it. His trophy wife, Camilla, is also an evil villain. It's like they gain extra power by putting other people down."

"Uh-oh. Is she one of your exes that he stole?"

"God no. I would never date a venomous snake like her. She and Angel met in college, but Camilla dropped out once they were married. She stays at home with their three perfect kids in their Pinterest-worthy 8,000-square-foot house. They're so freaking *fake*." Yep, that sums up most of my family...fake. I shake my head in disgust.

"You forgot to mention what he does for a living."

I can't help but roll my eyes as I respond. "He's a criminal defense attorney."

"Sounds like that's the perfect profession for him."

"It is. Just make sure to take whatever he or Camilla says to you with a grain of salt." I reach across the center console to give Gabby's hand a squeeze. Her touch alone does me a world of good as my pulse rate begins to relax. For the first time ever, I'm going into a family event with confidence and I know it's because Gabby has my back.

"I promise," Gabby reassures me and gives my hand a loving squeeze back.

25

Gabby

"Wow! It's bigger than I imagined."

"That's what she said." Alex is right on cue with his retort.

"I should've known better." I sigh. I'm usually wiser at choosing my words and skirting around his sarcasm and innuendos.

"Gotta get it out of my system now, baby girl. We're about to enter the crypt."

"That does not look like a crypt." I point to his childhood house. The three-story brick mansion sits upon a meticulously landscaped hill. Water cascades down from a stone garden fountain that's surrounded by rose bushes of various pinks and reds.

"I hate that fountain. When I was a kid, it always gave me the urge to pee whenever I walked past it," Alex grumbles as we exit the car and walk up to the ornate double doors.

"Do we knock?" I whisper to Alex while taking in the security camera above the entrance.

"No." He snorts. "I have a key." He produces it from his pocket and unlocks the door.

We step inside what feels like a home straight off a movie set. An enormous chandelier hangs in the foyer. The lit crystals make the pristine white tile floor look like it's sparkling. Directly in front of us is a grandiose staircase that could make the one on the Titanic look tiny. I become mesmerized by two large marble statues of elephants that flank each side of the staircase.

"My mom has a thing for elephants," Alex answers before I can ask any questions. "She says they bring good luck."

"I actually think I've heard that before." I turn to him. "But only if their trunks are up."

"That's correct," a feminine voice carries through the room. I pivot to see a petite woman in a blue dress suit. Her dark hair is pulled back into a perfect chignon that shows off a diamond pendant necklace with matching earrings. She exudes class and professionalism, which confuses me a bit because it's well after midnight. At this hour, I'm usually in a sweatshirt and leggings; if I'm not working the night shift, of course. This must be the one and only Elena Jones.

"Hey, Mom." Alex walks over and gives her a hug. It's then I realize how much of a size difference there is between mother and son.

"Mom, this is Gabby. She's *the one* I was telling you about."

I blush at the way he enunciates the words. His mom must pick up on it too because she takes a step back in surprise before introducing herself.

"Hello, Gabby. It's so nice to meet you. Alejandro has never brought someone home with him before... Not that he visits very often." A condescending look washes over her face, but within seconds, she shifts back to being all business.

"It's lovely to meet you as well. I'm so sorry to keep you up. We hit a bunch of traffic on the interstate."

"Oh, you're not keeping me up, dear. I only sleep a handful of hours a night." She turns to her son. "I'm afraid your father has retired to bed already. He had a long day."

"No problem at all." Alex picks up our bags. "We'll let him rest and see him in the morning."

"I doubt it." Elena tsks. "He has to be at the station at four a.m."

"He didn't take tomorrow off?"

"Of course not. The weather doesn't take a day off and neither does he. He'll make a few recordings tomorrow so the station can play those while we're at the hall."

"Hall? I thought you said it was going to be a small gathering at the house with caterers." Suddenly, I'm feeling the panic that Alex is now vocalizing.

"Yes, that was the original plan, but then the food bank contacted us and said they were running low on donations. We decided to make it a charity event and sell tickets."

"You sold tickets to your own anniversary dinner," Alex says flatly.

"It's for a good cause, *mijo.*" Elena's face hardens. "There are people who need our help, and we are fortunate enough to be in a position to support them."

"I know." Alex's shoulders tense as he adds, "I'm proud of the work you do."

"It's so good to have you back home." Elena places a loving hand on her son's forearm, then turns to me. "Gabriella, it was nice to meet you. I need to work on some final preparations for tomorrow and I'm sure you need to get some rest. You can stay in your old bedroom, but the guest house is also available."

"Perfect. We'll stay in the guest house." Alex picks up his bag and escorts me out a side door after we say our goodbyes.

I zip up my hoodie as we make our way through a path lit with small solar lights. It's not terribly cold, but the brief meeting with Elena left me with a chill. I'm not sure what I was expecting, but it wasn't that. Nothing went wrong with our introduction, but still, something just felt off. There's something about the whole atmosphere of this place—it doesn't give off warm and friendly vibes. Maybe I'm just tired from the drive.

"I'm kind of disappointed I don't get to see your old bedroom," I tease as we stop at a house that looks like an exact replica of the main one but on a much smaller scale.

"There's nothing much to see. I took everything with me when I moved out. I only left some clothes in the closet in case I need them."

I can tell meeting with his mother has left a mark, which makes me feel bad too. I want my fun-loving firefighter back, and I fear that this trip is going to be tough on him and I hate that. Alex drops his bags in front of the guest house and punches a code on the keypad next to the door. The lock unclicks and we walk inside.

"Wow." I stop to take in my new surroundings. While the outside looks just like the main house, the inside to this place is much cozier. The place has an open concept with the living room and kitchen area sharing the same space. A dark blue sectional overlooks a beautiful stone fireplace, and built-in bookshelves fill an entire wall on one side. I'm disappointed to see that they're filled with decorations instead of reading materials.

"The master bedroom is to the left and a smaller one is to the right. Both have their own bathrooms. You can have whichever one you like, or we can share." I look at him and my heart flutters at the sound of sharing. Alex and I both had off the last few nights and have spent it cuddling on the couch watching TV. We have fallen asleep together each time and I've never woken up feeling so refreshed. It's not a foreign experience for us to wake up together after a platonic night of rest. Well, except for a few kisses and did I say cuddling? Lots of cuddling.

"It would be nice to share. You know, considering I'm in an unfamiliar place and all." It's a total lie and he knows it. I just want to be close to him. "But just sleeping." I feel the need to add that stipulation, not that we've ever done anything before.

"I know." He holds out his hand and leads me to the master bedroom. "I know you're not ready yet, but I'll happily take what I can get."

I change into a pair of purple pajama bottoms and a tank top while Alex goes for his normal sleepwear of boxer shorts. We slide beneath the fluffy down comforter where he wraps his arms around me and I fall into a sound sleep, feeling that all is right with the world.

***

"What was that?" I sit straight up in bed, clutching the sheet to my chest. I was sleeping so peacefully until it sounded like someone with a chainsaw was breaking through the window. My eyes dart around the room. Everything looks just like it did last night. Alex rolls over and mumbles something.

"What did you say?" I look down at his sleeping frame. The muscles in his arms flex as he adjusts the pillow under his head, clearly unbothered by the racket outside. I run my hand over his strong jawline that's covered with a night's worth of stubble. I've always been attracted to the strong, rugged type, and Alex? It's like he's stepped straight out of my dreams. But dreams don't come true…do they?

"It's just the landscapers." He yawns.

"The landscapers? It's like eight a.m. on a Saturday!" I hop out of bed and peek through the window blinds. There are about a half dozen workers weeding and pruning the already meticulous lawn. A man with a leaf blower clears some clippings from a pathway and I realize that's the sound that startled me.

"Gotta keep up with appearances." Alex sits up in bed and rubs his eyes. "They're here all the time. I'm so used to the noise that I just sleep through it now."

"I don't think I could ever get used to that."

A worker with hedge clippers begins to trim a rose bush directly outside our window. Feeling completely exposed, I make sure to close the blinds tight.

"It's like an invasion of privacy."

"That's nothing." He snorts. "Try having a housekeeper come in to dust your room while you're just trying to live your life as a teenager."

"That had to be rough." Mari and I had our fair share of conflicts while sharing a bedroom, but I can't imagine complete strangers just walking around your house.

"It was," Alex confirms. "The only silver lining was that every employee of the Joneses has to sign a Non-Disclosure Agreement before they can step foot on our property. If they see you do something embarrassing, at least they can't tell anyone."

"I guess that helps a little." I chew on my lower lip, feeling grateful for the simpler life I lived. I climb back in bed to Alex's waiting open arms. He pulls me under the soft down comforter. While we haven't been fully intimate with each other, we're getting closer with stolen kisses and more cuddling. I love that I don't have to make up excuses to touch him anymore. But just when I think I can fully dive into a relationship with him, anxiety rears its ugly little head and tells me that if I do, I'll just end up brokenhearted. It's still mostly fear of losing him in a fire, but the fear of rejection is also nagging at me.

"How'd you sleep?" He places a kiss on my shoulder. His lips linger on my bare skin.

"Great until I thought we were under attack."

"Sorry about that. I should've warned you, but it's just a regular day at the Joneses'. I didn't think about it."

"It's okay. I—"

"Yoo hoo!" a voice from outside cuts me off.

"Lilli!" Alex leaps out of bed. He pulls on a pair of jeans and a T-shirt in record time and springs for the door before I can even get my bearings. I grab a white bathrobe hanging near the closet and wrap it around me before greeting our company.

"Careful, careful. I have hot coffee in my hands." Lilli giggles and places a large brown paper bag and a holder with three to-go cups on the kitchen counter. "Now." She spins around with her arms wide open. "Come here and give me a hug."

Alex pulls her in for the biggest bear hug. He lifts her up and spins her in a circle before gently placing her feet back on the floor.

"I don't think I'll ever get over the fact that my baby brother towers over me." She pulls back from their embrace while I study her features. She's certainly shorter than Alex's six-foot frame, but she's taller than me. Her wavy honey-colored hair hangs just below her shoulders and when she turns to me, I see she shares the same light blue eye color as her brother.

"Hi, you must be Gabby." She gives me a wide smile and a quick yet welcoming hug.

"And you are the famous Lilli." I give her a quick squeeze back. I feel more at ease with her in the two minutes she's been here than the whole meeting with Alex's mom last night.

"Uh-oh, how much has Alex told you?" She gazes lovingly at her brother.

"Not much." I rock on my heels. "While Alex likes to over-share a lot, he's pretty tight-lipped when it comes to his family. I do know that you are one of his favorite people, though."

"I think that's something we both have in common." She nudges me with her elbow.

"Truer words have never been spoken." Alex puts his arms around each of us and squeezes our shoulders. "Now show me what you brought because I'm hungry and whatever is in that bag smells delicious."

"Of course you jump right to the food," Lilli chides. "I didn't know what you would like, so I bought a little of every-thing from a new bakery in town."

"Oh yeah?" Alex grabs a plate from a cabinet and begins putting an assortment of pastries out on display. "Where is it?"

"About a block away from the TV station. Mom and Dad were guests of honor for the grand opening. They helped the owner cut the ribbon with those big scissor-type things."

"Of course they did." Alex rolls his eyes and picks up what looks to be an apple fritter.

"They didn't tell you?" Lilli tilts her head to the side.

"Mom probably mentioned it during one of her phone calls, but I tend to zone out when she starts going on and on about her latest public appearances."

"Did she tell you that the anniversary dinner was moved to Manzanita Manor?" Lilli takes a cup of coffee and blows some steam off the top of it.

"Manzanita Manor?" Alex groans. "She told me they were selling tickets and mentioned a hall, but I didn't think to ask her exactly where it would be held."

"What's Manzanita Manor?" I look between the two siblings.

"Only the most upscale hall in the area." Alex runs an exasperated hand down his face. "I'm sorry, baby girl. I figured we'd lounge around here or I'd show you around town. Now that has to change."

"I'm not following."

"Manzanita Manor is black-tie only. I'm guessing you didn't bring an evening gown with you?" Lilli asks.

"I—" I gasp. I only brought a regular dress for a small gathering. I don't even own anything black-tie worthy. I'm not even sure I know what something like that would look like and it certainly is not in my budget. But the thought of being underdressed feels dreadful.

"*Relájate.* Relax," Lilli says reassuringly. "I figured that was the case. That's why I came over early. I thought we could do a little dress shopping while getting to know each other, and do not worry about the cost. I got you covered."

"Lilli." I gasp. "I can't let you pay for something like that."

"It's no problem." She waves her hand. "Consider it a gift. My brother might be the happy-go-lucky type, but I've never heard a smile in his voice until he met you. That's worth more to me than the cost of a gown. Plus, it will be fun. We can get to know each other better."

"Well..." My eyes shift to Alex as if to ask for reassurance.

"I think you should go," he answers my unspoken question. "I don't want you to feel out of place. Especially with meeting my family...and half the town."

"What about you?" I ask, realizing that he only brought a pair of dress slacks and a button-down shirt.

"I have a tux here in case I ever need it." His eyes glance over to where the main house sits.

"This will be so much fun!" Lilli claps her hands, then turns to her brother. "I promise I'll take great care of her."

"I know you will," he responds appreciatively.

"I guess I better go get dressed." I look down at my robe. I have to admit, I'm kind of excited for this little shopping trip. I never got to go to my prom or anything, so now I'll know what it feels like to get all dolled up.

"Yup!" Lilli grabs her coffee cup and another one for me. "Pick out a pastry and we can eat on the drive over. I know the perfect boutique that will have something to accentuate those amazing curves of yours."

"But nothing too accentuating." Alex gives a lopsided grin. "I prefer to keep those curves all to myself."

"Yeah, yeah." Lilli waves her hand. "We'll meet back here at two to get ready, do our hair and makeup. The limo is coming at four to take us to cocktail hour."

"Cocktail hour?" Alex whines.

"Yes. Once the party got upgraded to a larger event, they added in a cocktail hour."

"Of course they did." Alex's tone deepens and the muscle in his jaw ticks.

"Everything will be okay," Lilli soothes. "And just think, now you get to spend the evening with two of your favorite girls."

26

Alex

I fucking hate bow ties. They remind me of ventriloquist dummies. Although I guess that's not too far off from reality. A good portion of my life has been one big script, so I suppose the look is fitting. The only difference between me and a ventriloquist dummy is that the doll usually says funny things. I'm not allowed to have a sense of humor. Why? Because people could take a joke the wrong way. One sarcastic remark gone wrong could destroy us for life.

Life wasn't always this way. I do remember a happier, carefree time when it was acceptable to be myself. My parents' careers didn't fully take off until after I was born. Up until the age of seven, we lived in a much smaller house, and besides the nuances that come with being the youngest of a large family, our life was pretty normal. My dad would help us kids with homework and Mom would cook dinner. I have fond memories of family picnics at a local park and long drives to the beach.

One day, my mom was asked to endorse some type of hair-care product. With the money made from that side gig, my parents started making investments, which paid off nicely. From there, they made more investments and more money. With their recognition on the rise, other companies started offering endorsement deals for both of my parents. Every successful moment fueled my parents' hunger for more fame and fortune.

Before I knew it, a cook and a nanny replaced my mom making us breakfast and seeing us off to school. A tutor took the place of my dad helping with homework. As their reputations continued to grow, so did their expectations of the kids. The rest of my siblings seemed to handle all the changes well. I did not. I wanted my old life back...a simpler life.

The sound of giggling behind the guest room door pulls me from my melancholy thoughts. Gabby and Lilli came back to the guest house a little over an hour ago with their arms full of bags. They locked themselves in the spare room to do their hair and makeup, claiming that I could not interrupt their girl time. I'm happy they're getting along. If there's one family member I want Gabby to bond with, it's Lilli.

My sister opens the door a crack and pokes her head through. "You're going to lose your mind," she squeals with delight.

"Are you finally done hogging all the time with my girl?" I cross my arms over my chest. Gabby and I haven't officially labeled each other as boyfriend and girlfriend, but it certainly seems like that's what we are to each other. I find it funny that for over the past year and a half, I begged her to date me and now that we're here, I don't care what we are as long as we're together.

"I want to steal her away more often. We had so much fun today." Lilli beams.

"All the more reason to come to Starboard Beach."

"Yes! But only for a visit," she stipulates. I would be over the moon if Lilli moved to Starboard Beach, but with her being ten years older, she's firmly set in her career. Lilli adores her patients, and I know nothing would pull her away from them. Even though she also has differences with our family, she's happy and content here in Elmwood Grove.

My sister opens the door wider and steps out of the room wearing a dark-blue floor-length gown that has some sort of diamond-looking clip in the front. As always, she's the epitome of sophistication.

"Ahem. May I present to you, your date for tonight."

Gabby steps out of the room looking like an angel sent directly from Heaven. My mouth drops open. She could wear a pillowcase and I'd find her attractive. But this? Damn!

"The lovely Ms. Gabriella Ramirez is wearing a high-waisted amethyst gown with a sweetheart neckline and a floor-sweeping hem," my sister says like she's an announcer at a fashion show. "Her classy updo, styled by the magnificent Lilliana Jones, shows off her diamond teardrop earrings and matching necklace. We ran out of time to go shoe shopping, so those are just the heels she brought from home," Lilli adds.

"I feel like Cinderella," Gabby gushes as she lifts the hem of her dress and daintily walks over to me.

"You look gorgeous." I wrap my arms around her waist and pull her in for a hug, careful not to mess with her hair or makeup. I know better than that.

"We had so much fun today." She pulls back from our embrace. Her eyes seem to dance as she talks. "It felt like old times when Mari and I used to go back-to-school shopping. Except this was way more upscale."

"I'm glad you two had a good time."

Gabby has been doing a lot more of that lately—opening up to me about her past. I love that she feels comfortable enough to share her memories with me, and I know it's a positive step to help her through her grief. I enjoy learning about the Ramirez family and I'm happy she grew up surrounded by so much genuine love.

"We really did." She bites down on her lip and keeps her voice low. "I'm worried about how tonight will go. Lilli told me a little more about your family and how you guys grew up. I mean...not much different than what you said, but hearing it from her perspective—I don't know, it just made me more nervous."

"Hey." I place my hand under her chin and lift it so we're eye to eye. "Everything is going to be okay."

Gabby responds with a nod and a smile. I can only hope my words turn out to be true.

27

Gabby

A small orchestra plays a classical number as we make our way through a huge crowd. The lights, sounds, and people send me into sensory overload. It's an unusual feeling for me, but I guess I'm on high alert. During the limo drive to the party, I learned even more about the Jones family, the high expectations they have, and how critical they are of their children's partners. As a girl who grew up in a low-income household and later became an orphan, I know I'm already starting out with several strikes against me.

"I hate this kind of music." Alex leans down and whispers in my ear. "It makes me feel like I'm trapped in an elevator." He tugs on his bow tie. He looks devastatingly handsome and totally uncomfortable at the same time.

I nod in agreement as I take in my surroundings. Guests in designer suits and gowns make small talk as waiters carrying a variety of hors d'oeuvres and champagne weave their way through the crowd. Though I feel like a fish out of water, I'm relieved Lilli took me dress shopping. At least I blend in with the rest of these stuffy people.

"Alex," a nasally voice calls from behind us. We spin around to the sight of a short man with jet-black hair, brown eyes, and glasses too big for his face. Without the eyewear, he could almost pass for the female version of Elena.

"Luis." Alex pastes on a smile as I wrack my brain, trying to remember details about each sibling.

"I didn't know you were coming." Luis pushes up his glasses.

"It's Mom and Dad's anniversary. Why wouldn't I be here?" Alex frowns.

"You don't show up to everything."

"I might not show up to every party or fundraiser, but I do when it counts." Alex's voice takes a bitter tone.

"Hmm, yeah, I guess." Luis turns to me. "Who are you?"

"I'm Gabby. I'm here with Alex." I lean into my date and place my hand affectionally over his chest.

"What's your favorite insect?" Luis's eyes narrow on me like my answer will determine if he approves of me or not.

"Oh! Umm. I don't think anyone has ever asked me that before. I guess ladybugs are nice." My voice lifts at the end, making it sound more like a question than a statement.

"There are over 5,000 different species of ladybugs around the world and around 150 types in the United States alone. Could you be more specific?"

"Uh...the red ones with the black dots?" My hand on Alex's chest begins to vibrate and I know he's silently laughing.

"But that's—" Luis tilts his head to the side, completely baffled.

"Hey! Look! I see Victoria and Seamus. We better go say hi." Alex cuts off his brother as he simultaneously puts both of his hands on my shoulders and leads me farther into the crowd. "The red ones with the black dots?" he says into my ear.

"I may have panicked a bit." I look up at him.

"A bit?" Alex lets out a deep chuckle. "That was adorable."

"He was..." My voice trails off as I try to come up with a word to describe his brother.

"Different?" Alex offers.

"Sure, we can go with that."

"Luis is okay. He's a bit eccentric and certainly doesn't pick up on social cues, but next to Lilli, he's the easiest and least judgmental of the siblings."

"So I should consider that little meeting a warm-up?" I ask as we get closer to a dark-haired woman in an emerald-green form-fitting gown. Standing next to her is a tall, redheaded man who appears to be glued to his phone.

"We're walking on thin ice from here on out. Just a re-minder, Victoria and Seamus are the ones who work at the news station," Alex murmurs out of the corner of his mouth as we approach the couple.

"Got it," I whisper, grateful for the information.

"If you're coming over here on Luis's behalf, I don't want to hear it." Victoria puts her hands up in surrender as we approach. Seamus, her husband, doesn't even bother to look up from his phone.

"Nice to see you too, sis," Alex deadpans. "I wanted to introduce you to my date, Gabby."

"Hi." I give a tiny wave, not sure what to think of this odd interaction.

"Oh. Sorry about that." Victoria shakes her head. "Luis has been hounding me to let him do a reoccurring segment on the importance of sending representatives from every insect species to Mars in the event that humans colonize the planet."

"What?" Alex and I say in unison.

"He insists it will increase our ratings." Victoria rolls her eyes, then scans me from head to toe. "What was your name again?"

"I'm Gabby." I try to offer my warmest smile.

"I've never seen you before." She studies me.

"Oh! This is my first time here." I fumble with a stray piece of my hair. "I live in Starboard Beach, like Alex. Actually, that's how we met. We're—"

"Don't tell me Luis is on that bug segment thing again," a woman with light brunette hair in an updo and hazel eyes interrupts.

"He's called me every day this week." The woman sighs exasperatedly. "I showed him the projected stats. The number of viewers interested in that niche just aren't there. The station is not going to take a gamble on something like that. I'll go talk to him." She turns to leave.

"Wait!" Alex calls out. "Isabella, you didn't meet Gabby."

"Oh." Alex's sister looks at her brother as if she's just realizing he's been standing next to her. "I didn't know you were coming."

"Of course I'd be here," Alex groans. "Why is it so surprising that I showed up for our parents' anniversary?"

"Your attendance rate at these events continues to decrease," Isabella states matter-of-factly. "You attend approximately four percent of family gatherings, so the probability of you showing up today was slim."

"Ah, you must be the math genius." I snap my fingers as I continue to sort out who's who.

"Who are you?" Isabella tilts her head to the side.

"I'm Gab—"

"Gabriella Ramirez of Starboard Beach. She's a registered nurse and our baby brother's date." A man with a predatory look pushes past the two sisters. He grabs my hand and kisses the back of it before I can pull it out of his clutches.

"Cool it, Angel." Alex steps in front of me and stares down his brother. I rub the back of my hand on my dress. I feel like I'm back in kindergarten and he just gave me cooties.

"Relax, baby brother. I was just coming over to introduce myself to your friend here," Angel's voice taunts. "Lilli caught me as soon as Camilla and I walked in and read us the riot act." He holds his hand up like a Boy Scout oath. "I promise to be on my best behavior. After all, this night is for Mom and Dad. Unlike someone else we know, I don't want to disappoint them."

The vibe this guy gives off sends a shiver right down my spine. It's easy to see why Alex isn't a fan of his brother. I'm happy Lilli was looking out for me...wherever she went. Unfortunately, as soon as we entered the building, someone pulled her away and I haven't seen her since. She warned me that would probably happen. Still, it would be comforting to see her kind and familiar face right now.

Wanting a sense of security, I take a step closer to Alex. As if on instinct, he places his arm around my waist.

"So you live in the same town as my brother?" Victoria asks.

"Yes." I perk up a bit. I'm glad for the shift off Angel. "We live next door to each other."

"Isn't that charming?" Angel supplies a snarky retort. "Looks like our brother didn't have to look too far to find a date."

"What the hell is that supposed to mean?" The grip Alex has around my waist tightens.

Before Angel can respond, another member of the Jones family enters the ring.

"Alex!" A man with similar features to Luis's comes up alongside Victoria. It's then I realize Isabella is nowhere to be found. With the size of this crowd, I didn't even see her walk away.

"What do you want, Roberto?" It's still early into the event, yet Alex sounds exhausted from his family already and I can see why.

"Mom and Dad want to see you in the family suite." Roberto points to a hallway on the left.

"I know where it is." Alex's hand glides from my waist to the small of my back. "What do they want?"

"I don't know," Roberto scoffs. "They just told me to find you and bring you back."

"I think they mentioned discussing speeches or something like that," Angel replies, but a gut feeling tells me he's not being truthful. "I already signed up for the first slot."

"I'm sure you did." Alex starts to lead me in the direction of the hallway. "Come on."

"Uh..." Roberto stops us. "Mom and Dad specifically asked for Alex only." His eyes shift to me. "You'll have to stay back."

"No!" Alex goes rigid. "I don't know what's going on, but Gabby is my date and she's coming with me."

"I-it's okay," I stammer. "Besides the quick meeting last night, you haven't seen your mom and dad in a while. I can understand why they want to spend some time with you alone." Plus, Alex's response was louder than intended and we've drawn a crowd of onlookers. The last thing we need is to bring any negative attention our way.

Alex dips down and whispers in my ear, "I feel like I'm feeding you to the wolves if I leave you by yourself." He looks up and scans the room around us. "I'd feel much better if Lilli were around."

"Then I'll walk around and try to find her," I reassure him. "You should probably go. Your brother is looking impatient."

Alex gives one last desperate scan around the room before conceding. "Okay." He swallows. "Text me if something happens and I'll be back as soon as I can—and you!" He points over my shoulder to Angel. "Stay away from her."

"No worries, little brother. I'm running for city commissioner and I just spotted the mayor. So if you'll excuse me." He glides past us and adds, "I need to go shake some hands and rub some elbows."

"Hope the mayor washes his hands and elbows after that meeting," I say under my breath, earning a swoon-worthy grin from my date.

"I'll be as fast as I can." He looks over my shoulder once more. "I don't know where Victoria went, but that's probably for the best anyway. Just concentrate on finding Lilli and hang out with her until I get back."

"You got it." I give him a wink with a confidence I don't feel.

"Alex," Roberto whines.

"Yeah, yeah, I'm coming."

28

Alex

Something doesn't feel right. A knot grows in the pit of my stomach as I get closer to the door of the family suite. Roberto abandoned me once he saw me headed in the right direction. I've been to several events at Manzanita Manor and the family suite is usually my favorite spot in the place. With a quiet sitting area, some tables, and a private bathroom, it's like a little sanctuary. My mom and sisters use it to touch up their makeup. I use it to get a break from the chaos. But this time? Something feels off. I shouldn't have left Gabby.

The door to the suite opens as I approach. Sunlight from a hall window paints the distinct outline of my father standing in the doorway.

"He's right here," my father says over his shoulder, then looks back at me. "I was beginning to think Roberto couldn't find you."

"Well, it's pretty packed down there," I offer, then realize I don't need to defend my brother. For all I know, he's thrown me to the wolves.

"It's been a while." My father gives me a hard glare and extends his hand to shake mine. He's never been a hugger even when life was simpler.

"I've been busy saving lives." My career choice bothers him to no end, but I hope one day he'll realize that even though I don't have a fancy title to my name, I still make a difference. I reach out to return the handshake. Over his shoulder, I spot a woman I don't recognize sitting in a chair across from my mother.

"Alejandro, come on in," my mother says a little too warmly. She should be welcoming her guests and making her usual rounds at the cocktail hour, not hanging out in here.

"Hey, Mom." I give her a hug. "Happy anniversary." I turn to my dad. "And to you too."

My dad mutters a thanks and takes a seat at a table nearby.

"What's going on?" I look between my parents, trying to ignore the elephant in the room.

"I wanted to introduce you to a new family friend." My mother smiles.

As if on cue, the mystery woman stands and saunters over to me. Her heels click on the hardwood floor with every flirtatious step. She's surprisingly tall but still shorter than me. With perfectly styled curls framing her face and makeup that accentuates her high cheekbones and piercing dark eyes, she radiates confidence. Her ruby-colored dress clings to her stick-figure body. The small train attached to it shifts back and forth like a giant red flag waving in the wind.

"Hi. I'm Octavia." The woman shakes my hand with a rapacious look.

"Nice to meet you," I reply kindly, though it's a lie.

"Octavia started working at the station a few months ago," my mother interjects. "She's a field reporter now, but let me tell you, I wouldn't be surprised if she took over my position one day."

"Oh, Elena, you're too kind." Octavia splays a hand to her flat chest, then turns to me. "I just adore your parents. They've taken me under their wing and have taught me so much. You must be very proud."

"Umm...sure." Am I proud of my parents? Yes, they do help out the community, but sometimes I wonder if it's out of altruism or opportunism. Also, what am I doing here? "Well, nice to meet you, but I better get going and find my date." I purposely drop the hint that I'm not available in case that's what this is all about, and I take a step back.

"But you just got here." My mother places a hand on my arm. "I thought you and Octavia could stay a while in here and get to know each other." And that answers my unspoken question. *Yes, that is what this is all about.*

"I already did." I keep my voice stern. "Now I need to get back to Gabby, my date."

"Son." My father stands. "Listen to your mother. Octavia had to cancel an important interview to come here and meet you."

"Look." I hold up a hand, ready to nip this in the bud. "I don't know what's going on but—"

"Octavia, dear." My mother's tone of voice makes me feel like I'm ten and about to be grounded for knocking over and breaking one of her garden statues during a water gun fight with Angel. "Would you mind waiting in the hall for a moment? Bob and I would like to have a little chat with our son."

"Of course." The woman who my parents are undoubtably trying to sic on me obediently leaves.

"Don't screw this up," my mother whisper-hisses as soon as the door closes. "That woman is perfect for you. She is sophisticated and successful. I wasn't exaggerating when I said she'll take over my job one day. She's going to be a star."

I narrow my eyes at my mother. "Is she perfect for me or perfect for you because I don't know if you noticed, but we have two very distinct tastes. To bring someone here when you knew I was bringing Gabby is insulting to me, to Gabby, and to your colleague."

"Alex." Here comes my father's two cents. "The Abby girl—"

"Her name is Gabby," I cut him off. "Gabriella, to be exact, and you haven't even met her."

"I know she's a nurse in that silly beach town you call home." My father's face hardens. "The fact of the matter is your date isn't compatible with our lifestyle. Octavia fits in seamlessly with the family. You can move back here and work on getting a different job..."

"How could you both stoop so low?" My hands shake with anger. "I know you don't like the choices I've made, and I'm sorry I couldn't make you proud. Gabby is one of my best friends and we're working toward something more. I'm not going to screw that up because my parents want me to move back home and date their protégé. I wasn't happy in Elmwood Grove. I stayed longer than I should have, trying to appease everyone."

My parents both stare at me, stunned. I've never stood up for myself like this before.

I back up a step and continue. "I love you both and I wish you the best. Why can't you do the same for me? I've made my choices. I'm happy with who I've become and with the people who support me back in Starboard Beach. You need to accept that and until you do, I don't think there's any more we can say to each other."

"You and that damn town," my mother seethes. The disgust in her voice is palpable. "It's so embarrassing to think that my son doesn't even own his own home but lives in some condo with a roommate. You're going to be thirty years old, Alejandro. Yet you hang out with your condo friends like you're still a kid in a college dorm."

"I choose to live in a condo because I'm not home a lot. Taking on a roommate helps keep my bills low because I never want to ask for a handout. And those friends? They're genuine. They like me for who I am, not who I'm related to."

"You wouldn't have to worry about bills if you had a better job." My father puffs out his chest like he's ready to fight. His choice to argue over money rather than having genuine friends is no surprise.

"I love being a firefighter. Yeah, the salary isn't as glamorous as yours, but the pride I get from helping others is worth more than a large paycheck." With adrenaline soaring through my veins, I begin pacing the room. "You know, it's funny that you say Gabby doesn't 'fit in' because I never felt like I fit into this family either."

"Maybe you didn't try hard enough." My father's face reddens. "For years, I tried to convince myself that you were in some sort of rebellious phase in your life. Yet you've never grown out of it. Think about your future, son. Moving back home will give you everything you need for the rest of your life. Some people would kill for an opportunity like this...to be a member of this family."

"Maybe it's time for you to accept me for who I am." With that, my parents go silent. I've tried to react passively when it comes to my family, but I can't take it anymore. "I think it would be in everyone's best interest if Gabby and I leave. Congratulations on your forty-five years of marriage. I can only hope that one day, I too will celebrate several decades surrounded by people who love me."

"Alex, we love you." My mother's voice quivers and I actually think it's legit this time. "We just—"

"Want what's best for me," I finish the sentence I've heard so many times before. I know deep down they love me. They just have a funny way of showing it. With that, I open the door to a flustered-looking Octavia who I'm sure was trying to eavesdrop.

"Oh. Hi!" She pretends to smooth out her dress. "Is everything okay?"

"I apologize for my parents bringing you here under false pretenses. I already have someone special in my life and I need to go find her."

"Are you sure?" Octavia bats her eyelashes.

Even if I had never met Gabby, I wouldn't be attracted to a woman like her. *Even more proof that my parents don't know me at all.*

"I'm very sure." Now more than ever. I turn and race down the hallway. I can only hope Gabby found Lilli and that she's faring better than me.

As I make my getaway, I hear my mother's voice in the background. "Octavia, dear, I'm so sorry about that. I should've realized my youngest isn't ready to grow up. But that's neither here nor there. Have I told you about my son Luis?"

29

Gabby

I can do this; I repeat the mantra in my head. I just need to find Lilli and everything will be fine. I'll tell her how I met most of the family, we'll laugh about my stupid ladybug comment to Luis, and we'll stick together for the rest of the cocktail hour.

"Champagne?" A waiter practically shoves the flute in my face.

"Sure." I'm not a fan of the bubbly stuff, but maybe this will help me look like I fit in better.

As I walk around on a mission to find Lilli, I pick up tidbits of conversations here and there. One couple just came back from a cruise, another is putting an addition onto their house, and someone's grandkid just got into an Ivy League University. Everyone's conversations seem phony. Their tone of voice and body language does not resemble a causal exchange amongst friends or even acquaintances. It's like everyone is bragging or trying to outdo one another. All of which is making me feel extremely uncomfortable.

Continuing to meander through the crowd of pretentious guests, I spot Victoria up ahead. While she's not the Jones I was looking for, I can at least ask her if she's seen Lilli. I pick up my pace to catch up with her. I almost make it when a tall, redheaded man looking at his phone knocks into me. My heel turns as I try to maintain balance. I manage to hold on to the champagne flute, but the liquid inside goes flying right onto…

"My dress!" Victoria shrieks at a decibel I didn't know was humanly possible. "You ruined it!" If looks could kill, I'd be dead five times over.

"I'm so sorry." I gasp. "It was an accident." I point to the redhead who I realize is Seamus. "He bumped into me."

"Oh, so now you're going to put the blame on my husband?! I can't believe your audacity! I'm so happy my parents are introducing Alex to Octavia right now. At least she knows what it takes to belong here."

My head spins at Victoria's words. I knew I wouldn't fit in, but they're introducing him to someone else? A wave of nausea hits me. Technically, Alex and I aren't officially anything, but would he choose someone his parents approve of?

It hurts to think that they went to such lengths to make me feel unwelcome, especially without even getting to know me. Well, all except for Lilli. Normally, I wouldn't care what others think of me, especially if I were back home surrounded by my friends. But being here, amongst all this wealth and arrogance, is making me crumble.

"Move along, folks. Nothing to see here!" a familiar voice chimes in. Lilli makes her way up to her sister and stops. "Go fix your makeup, Vic, your mascara looks a little runny. I'll handle this one."

Victoria turns on her heels and stomps in the direction of the bathroom. Seamus, still not paying attention, spins and bumps into a waiter carrying a tray full of shrimp. The little crustaceans scatter around the floor. Guests jump back as if the shellfish will come back to life and attack them.

"Oh, this just keeps getting better and better." Lilli breaks out into a mischievous grin.

"I'm so sorry." I grasp onto Lilli's arm, trying my hardest not to fall apart.

"Oh, honey. I'm not talking about you. I'm talking about my brother-in-law and his phone obsession. Trust me, no one is going to remember a little champagne spill after this." She points to the floor as three waiters frantically clean up the shrimp.

"Victoria said your parents are introducing Alex to someone."

"I know." Lilli grimaces. "I mean, I didn't know, but I overheard Roberto telling Isabella and I started looking for you. I'm so sorry we got separated."

"There you are." Alex steps around a waiter. A look of relief washes over his face when he spots Lilli with me. "We need to leave."

"What on earth is going on here?" a man's voice bellows throughout the crowd.

"Shit." Lilli stands on her toes to look over the mass of guests. "That's our dad. You guys better get out of here before he catches up. Even though none of this was your fault, he'll put his own spin on it and make you feel guilty."

"She's not wrong." Alex frowns.

"Go ahead and take the limo we came in. I'll catch a ride back home with Luis." Lilli pulls us in for a double hug and before I know it, we're back on the road to Starboard Beach.

***

The mountainous landscape passes by in a blur as I keep my focus out the passenger side window. I look at the time on my phone and realize it was less than twenty-four hours ago that we were on the same road, just headed in the opposite direction. What a crazy twenty-four hours it has been. We heeded Lilli's advice and took the limo back to Alex's parents' place where we changed out of our formal wear, packed up our belongings, and hit the road. Alex was silent during our time in the limousine and also as we gathered up our stuff from the guest house. I figured he'd be more talkative once we got in his car, but we've been driving for about an hour and he hasn't spoken a word. Well...I guess that goes both ways because I haven't said anything either. I've been debating if I should bring up the events of the night or open with a lighter topic and work our way up to the harder stuff.

"Did you know that Scotland's national animal is the unicorn?"

"What?" He turns to look at me.

"I had a patient last week—a little girl with a nasty case of pneumonia. Anyway, she was obsessed with unicorns and told me that."

"What the hell does that have to do with anything?"

"Nothing really. It's just better than sitting here in silence." I cross my arms over my chest and glare at him. Unfortunately, my body language doesn't work because he keeps his eyes on the road. I know he's trying to keep us safe while driving, but we can't ignore what happened back in Elmwood Grove and apparently, that's what he's doing.

"I'm going to stop at the next exit and fuel up," he says flatly. "It's the last one for the next fifty miles, if you need to use the bathroom or anything..."

"Perfect. I'm starving." Besides the one little stuffed mushroom and mini crab cake I had at the cocktail hour, I haven't eaten anything since lunch with Lilli. I begin making a mental list of junk food I'll purchase at the rest stop because this night certainly calls for all things sweet, salty, and bad for you.

A few minutes later, Alex pulls up to the gas station pump and I hightail it into the convenience store. I choose an assortment of snacks and do a little victory dance when I come across the display of Alex's favorite brand of beef jerky. I'm not sure if he's eaten anything since breakfast. Maybe all we need is some food in us to get a conversation rolling.

My hope deflates as soon I settle back in the SUV and take in Alex's stiff demeanor. Even worse, he rejects my offering of beef jerky or any other snack, for that matter. We're about twenty minutes back into our journey and I can't take it anymore.

"Okay, clearly, you're upset about what went down tonight and I get that. But do we have to drive back the rest of the way like this? I can't stand the silent treatment anymore."

"I'm not giving you the silent treatment." He takes his eyes off the road for a second and gives me a confused look.

"Well, you could've fooled me because you've been as cold as ice ever since the limo drive back. I'm sorry the party turned out to be a disaster and I'm sorry I didn't live up to your family's expectations—"

"What?!" He turns the steering wheel a hard right. I grab onto the oh-shit handle above me as the SUV skips across the shoulder and up onto a grassy area. He shifts into park roughly. We both jolt forward, and the seat belt locks around my chest.

"What the hell are you doing?" I try to catch my breath while unbuckling the seat belt.

"Are you serious?! You think I'm upset because you didn't live up to my parents' expectations? What on earth would make you think that?" He too unbuckles his tightened seat belt and shifts sideways to face me.

"Well, at first, I thought you were mad at your parents, but you've been so standoffish, so I started wondering if you were disappointed in me. Maybe I could've acted more sophisticated or something. I don't know. I'm not sure what I could've done differently. They didn't really give me a chance."

"Man, I'm screwing this up." He lets out a long sigh and scrubs a hand down his face. "God, Gabby. I don't think I could ever be disappointed with you. I'm embarrassed. Embarrassed about this weekend, my weird family, just everything. Why would you want to be with someone who has a family like mine?"

"What? Because I know you're not like that. Your family doesn't define who you are. You can't choose who you're related to, and I'm certainly not going to hold that against you. Alex, I love who you are. You're the guy who's been there for me every step of the way. I want to be that for you, too." I'm not sure if he heard me or not because his face still looks tortured as he continues talking.

"My parents have always voiced their opinion about my life choices, but up until tonight, they never tried to take matters into their own hands. I can't help but think that maybe there's some truth to what they've been saying." He stares out into the distance. "Maybe I do have an issue with growing up."

Oh. My. God. Where is this coming from? What on earth did they say to him?

"No. No. No." I grab his face and force him to look at me. I'm so pissed that those pretentious people are making him doubt himself. "*No dejes que te afecten.* Don't you dare let their words get into your head. They may have known you all your life, but they don't know who you truly are. I know the real Alejandro Jones. The one who knows what he wants and is not afraid to go after it. The one who'll drop everything to help a stranger in need. The one who has the ability to make everyone feel like they're the most precious gift on Earth."

"Stop, you're giving me a big head." His mouth hangs open as the innuendo he didn't intend to make registers. We both begin to laugh, thank God. The hard lines around his face soften and the man I adore starts to come back from over the edge.

"You know what?" I take a breath and realize I can turn my anger into something else. "I'm not mad at your family. I feel sorry for them because they're missing out on an opportunity to know someone as amazing as you."

My life has improved so much since Alex has entered it. How could I have possibly denied my feelings for him for so long? Of course, as soon as I think that, harsh reality slaps me in the face as we both turn our heads to the sound of a fire engine screaming down the highway. We watch in silence as it whizzes by and disappears around a bend. *That's why. I can't lose him.*

"Stop that." He senses my sadness, reaches across the center console, and pulls me in for a hug.

"I'm trying to get past my fear." I squeeze him like he'll fade away if I let go.

"For what it's worth, I think you're making fantastic progress." He places a kiss on my head. "Take all the time you need. I'm not going anywhere."

We spend the rest of the ride home playfully arguing over music and sharing way too many snacks. I get him to try his first Snoball and am highly insulted when he says he isn't impressed. We discuss the party and some of the ostentatious things I overheard while I was searching for Lilli. Alex opens up about the short meeting with his parents and how turned off he was by Octavia. My heart soars when he reassures me that I'm the only woman for him. I trust this man with everything. The more quality time I spend with Alex, the more I can't imagine my life without him.

We pass the sign for Starboard Beach's city limits, and disappointment settles in. I don't want this night to end.

"Hey, Alex? My eyes focus on the muscles in his forearms as he navigates his way around a particularly winding road. I never paid attention to things like that until I started reading romance novels. Yup, I get the appeal now.

"Yeah, baby girl?"

"Since we didn't plan on coming back until tomorrow and it looks like a nice night, do you think maybe instead of going home we can go count stars?"

"You're not sick of me yet?" The corners of his mouth turn up and I realize I make him happy just as much as he makes me.

"Not at all. I'm enjoying all this extra time with you." I look at him and smile. "You'll have to thank Carter once we get home. I think your plan is working."

30

Alex

"This is the craziest thing I've ever done." Gabby studies the information card from the pocket of the airline seat while the flight attendant goes over her spiel. This is the first time she's been on a plane and her nerves are getting the best of her.

The last few weeks have been a whirlwind. It all started when Jax came barreling through my bedroom door around four o'clock in the morning, scaring Gabby and me half to death. I thought he was an intruder and took a swing. Fortunately for Jax, I was groggy when I took the swing and he missed out on sporting a black eye for a week. Unfortunately, my fist landed right in his shoulder. Specifically, the bad one with his war wound. There was a lot of shouting and before we knew it, the entire 3rd East crew was running into my bedroom.

Luckily, Gabby was wearing pajamas and I had my boxers on. While we've been sleeping together, we're still not *sleeping* together. We've been sharing my bed ever since the night we spent visiting my family. It just felt right. Am I sporting the worst case of blue balls in modern history? Yes. Yes, I am. But I promised Gabby we'd take things slow and I'd let her take the lead. I love having her next to me and I plan to keep it that way.

Anyway, back to Jax interrupting my beauty sleep. After a few weeks of dead ends, he discovered an aunt of Gabby's. It took about ten days to make contact with her, and after some initial shock, she agreed to talk with Gabby if she came to New York. Which brings us back to our current situation.

"You think this is crazier than leaving your hometown and driving a clunker of a car over a thousand miles to start a new life?"

"Stinky is not a clunker." She splays her hand over her chest as if I just insulted the Queen of England.

"No, but I got you to take your mind off what we're doing." I give her a wink and settle into the too tight seat. "Damn, we should've flown first class."

"Did you see how crazy expensive those tickets were?"

"Do you see how my muscular physique does not fit comfortably in this seat?" I retort. "How am I supposed to deal with this for the next sixish hours?"

"You can take a nap," Gabby suggests.

"Are you going to let me sleep?"

"Probably not." The airplane's engine roars to life, and she pulls my hand into a death grip.

"Relax, the plane is just taxiing to the runway. We're not taking off yet." I dig into my pocket and hand her a piece of gum. "Here, chew on this. It can help with the air pressure when we take off."

"Can we go over our plans once more? I need something to distract me from thinking about how this tin can is about to hurl us into space." She pops the gum into her mouth.

"Now who's being dramatic?" I roll my eyes, then start to go over our itinerary. We're spending less than forty-eight hours total in New York. Neither of us could get much time off from work and the traveling alone eats up most of our time. "We'll get into the hotel late tonight. I think it's best to order room service because we'll probably be exhausted, and with the time change, we're going to lose three hours of sleep."

"Deal. Although I can't imagine I'll be able to sleep tonight." Her grip tightens on my hand as we begin our ascent.

"We'll meet Lucia tomorrow morning at her house in the Bronx." I project my voice over the sound of the engine. "How long we spend there will determine how much time we have left to explore the city."

"I really hope we get to see Times Square. Mari and I always dreamed of visiting it. We wanted to see if it looked just like it does on TV. We also wanted to see the big tree at Rockefeller Center."

"It's a little too early to have the tree out just yet."

"I know, but maybe we can at least see where it goes."

"Sure," I agree. *I will take her wherever she wants.*

The plane levels out at 35,000 feet and Gabby begins to relax in her seat.

"Wow!" She stretches over me to look out the window. "We're in the clouds."

"Yup. Do you want to switch seats with me?"

"Yes!" She excitedly nods. Gabby insisted on taking the middle seat. She was petrified that the window would pop out or something. I figured she'd enjoy the flight once the initial shock wore off, and it looks like my prediction is right.

"Do you think this is what Heaven looks like?" she asks dreamily while continuing to stare out the window.

"I'm not sure. But I certainly wouldn't be upset with this view all the time."

"Me neither."

I turn in my seat and hook my arm around the top part of her chest, drawing her back to my front so she can continue gazing at the heavenly sky. "They're okay, baby girl. I have no doubt they're watching over you."

31

Gabby

"This is it." I point upward to a set of windows. Lucia said she lived in an apartment above a deli. I have spoken with my long-lost aunt for a grand total of about fifteen minutes. I'm just grateful she agreed to talk to me at all. I understand her hesitancy. I kind of appeared out of nowhere claiming that I was her niece. She made it very clear that she would not provide any information unless I met her face-to-face. I suppose she figured I must be serious if I was willing to make a cross-country trip.

"It looks like the stairs are on the side of the building." I walk over to the alley and begin my assent up the concrete steps.

"Man, I don't think I could live like this." Alex follows behind me.

"Why? Because your childhood home is the size of a mini mall?" It's funny how I have yet to meet my aunt and I'm already feeling defensive of her. I'm sure my nerves are also getting the best of me. After we arrived at our hotel last night, we ordered room service. I could barely eat because my stomach felt like it had been knotted. Between the noise of the city nightlife and my fears about my meeting today, I got maybe three hours of solid sleep.

"What? No! You know I'm not like that. I was saying I don't think I could live over a deli. I'd be hungry all the time." He stops and takes in a deep breath. "Tell me you don't smell a pastrami on rye with a dill pickle on the side."

"Alex!" I begin to laugh, and my nerves start to calm.

"I'm not joking," he says as we reach the last set of stairs. "I bet I'd be their best customer if I lived here."

His words fall by the wayside as we reach a light blue door with a white screen door in front of it. The mailbox attached to the siding reads, "312."

"It didn't dawn on me until now that we have the same home numbers." I'll take that as a good sign. The uneasiness in my stomach settles even more. "Here we go." I press the doorbell.

"Coming!" a woman's muffled voice combined with a dog barking comes from inside. A moment later, a chain lock rattles and the door eases open.

"Oh my!" The woman gasps and pulls me into a hug. From my periphery, I see a large German shepherd come up beside me. He takes a sniff of my shoes, then does the same to Alex. The dog looks friendly, but I refrain from making any sudden movements just in case. Alex does the same.

"Rex. Kennel," Lucia says as she loosens our embrace. Rex obediently leaves to presumably go lie in his crate. She turns her attention back to me as soon as Rex is quiet. "He's my security guard. He can immediately tell whether someone is here for good or has ill intentions. That's why I wanted you to come to my house. I trust his intuition. If you had been an imposter, he would've eaten you."

"Really?" Alex pipes up from behind me.

"I would've called him off before he did any damage. I'm getting too old to be scrubbing blood out of the carpet."

"I like her." Alex leans down and whispers in my ear. The feeling is mutual, and I immediately take a step closer to the woman who bears a resemblance to my father. Wearing gray slacks and a soft pink sweater, she appears younger than I expected. Her dark hair is pulled into a low bun. It's her eyes that captivate me the most. She has the same deep brown eyes as my dad, and for a moment, I feel like I'm looking right at him.

"I didn't think it was true. I couldn't believe it when I received the message." She lovingly runs a hand through my hair. "I feel like I'm standing in front of your mother."

"Y-you knew my mom?" I gasp as fresh tears rise to the surface. I feel so connected to this woman, though we've just met.

"I did. I have so much to tell you."

"So you're okay with talking to us? I mean, uh...Gabby?" Alex asks. On our way over, we came up with a plan. If I felt comfortable with Lucia, Alex would make himself scarce for a bit to give us a chance to talk. He figured he'd go check out the local firehouses as some of them are deemed historic landmarks. I could text him when I felt ready, or he'd eventually mosey his way back over when he was finished.

"You must be Alex." Lucia sizes him up. She's got quite the height difference on me, but nothing compared to him. "Gabby said she was bringing a male friend, but I never imagined you'd be this handsome."

"Oh, now I really like you." He walks over to my aunt and gives her a hug.

"Come on in." She ushers us into a cozy living room. I immediately notice a wall covered entirely in bookshelves and the plushest reading chair I've ever seen. To the side are more bookshelves and Rex relaxing in his crate. Milk-glass vases filled with silk flowers and ornate picture frames with various inspirational quotes are perfectly tucked within every nook and cranny. The space exudes pure femininity, and I love it.

"I only have the one chair in here to sit, but there's more room in the kitchen. It's only Rex and me here. I never married or had any kids. I was too busy looking after my parents. They were both ill for quite some time," Lucia explains as I drool over the serene space.

"It's perfect." I walk over to admire some of the books up close. "I'm a reader too."

"So was your mother, but I think I'll say you inherited that from me." She winks.

"I didn't expect you to say you knew her too." I have so much hope for this visit now.

"I have a lot to tell you. I didn't want to do it over the phone. It's too impersonal. Plus, I wanted Rex to check you out. Not that I needed him to. One look at you and I just knew."

At the sound of Rex's name, the well-behaved dog pops out from his kennel in the corner and makes a beeline for Alex.

"This guy is so cool." Alex kneels down to show Rex some affection. "I always wanted a dog."

"It's just about the time I take him for a walk. Would you like to take him for me? That would give Gabby and me a chance to chat."

"Sure!" Alex replies way too enthusiastically, then stops and turns to me. "I mean...if you're okay with me leaving now."

"Go on." I make a shooing motion with my hand. I love how protective he is of me without being overbearing. Even though I've just met my aunt, I feel completely comfortable being alone with her.

"I was thinking about checking out the old firehouses around here. Is it okay if I take Rex too?" Alex asks with adorable pleading eyes.

"Of course! It's a beautiful day. Take your time and have fun exploring the area." Lucia hands the leash over to Alex, who looks like he just received the best Christmas present of his life. "Don't worry about getting lost. Just tell Rex you're ready to go home and he'll lead the way."

"Really?" Alex's eyes widen with excitement.

"Si," Lucia confirms. "He's more reliable than any GPS out there."

"Come on, Rex. Show me your stomping grounds!" He leads the dog out the door and then turns to me. "Just text me if you need anything, okay?"

"Thanks, Alex." I give him a quick wave and watch him exit. I'm not sure who is happier to be going on a walk, him or Rex.

Lucia shuts the screen door fully, then turns and studies me thoughtfully. "How about we head into the kitchen to have some tea?"

"That sounds like a fabulous idea," I agree and let her lead me into a small galley-style kitchen.

"You can take a seat over there." She points to a bistro table near a small window that overlooks the deli. I take a seat and peer outside to see Alex strutting down the street with Rex proudly leading the way.

"It's funny," Lucia says, looking over my shoulder at Alex and her faithful companion. "Even though they are human and canine, they give off the same energy: friendly, loving, and protective."

I wholeheartedly agree. Alex has been my rock through my healing, and I know now that I could never have taken that step without him. Even after we returned home from his parents' anniversary dinner, after he was mocked and challenged by a family that should only want the best for him, Alex shoved that all aside to focus on me and my needs. Do I sound like a girl in love? Yeah. I do.

"Did you know about me? Did you ever meet me?" I blurt out. As much as I enjoy thinking about Alex, I can't handle the suspense any longer.

"I knew about you, but sadly, we never met until today." She walks to her stove, picks up a blue ceramic kettle, and places it on a burner. "Besides our parents, it was just Miguel and me. There was a six-year age gap between us, but it didn't make a difference. He was the best big brother a girl could ask for."

"He was an amazing father." I can already feel the hot tears prickling behind my eyes.

"I have no doubt. He'd watch me after school until our parents came home from work. He never complained about being stuck with his little sister. To be honest, I think he enjoyed the company as much I did. He used to make up silly card games, would participate in the tea parties I created for my dolls, and made the best grilled cheese sandwiches."

"Oh my gosh! I loved his grilled cheeses," I gush. "He was a sous chef and could make the most magnificent meals, but whenever he asked me what I wanted to eat, I'd always request a grilled cheese."

"My brother loved to cook. I'm so pleased he found a job that I have no doubt he loved. I'm also happy you got to enjoy his grilled cheeses just like I did. I've tried to recreate them over the years, but I can never get it just right." She brings over a small tin of butter cookies and takes the seat opposite me.

"Me neither! One day, I insisted that I watch him from start to finish. I was convinced he had some sort of secret trick or ingredient."

"Did you find out?" Lucia leans in enthusiastically.

"Everything was completely normal. When I told him that he must've snuck something in when I blinked, he told me that all he did was add love."

"That sounds so much like Miguel." She sighs wistfully.

"D-do you know why my mom and dad ran away?" I stammer, feeling the mood in the air change. It's somber, but I need to know this.

"I was only twelve when he left home. It was devastating. I cried for weeks, but I understood." The kettle begins to whistle, and Lucia stands to move it off the burner. "Your mom and dad met in middle school. I was so young when they got together that I really don't remember a time without Caterina in my life."

"I guess you knew her pretty well. At least until you were twelve."

"Oh yes, I adored your mother. She didn't have any siblings and said I was the sister she always wanted. Miguel and Caterina never treated me like a third wheel or a pesky little sister. They'd take me along with them to the movies or to relax at the neighborhood park on a warm day. They had such a beautiful love...so pure. Even from a young age, I could see it."

Lucia pours us both a cup of tea and sits back down.

"What happened?" I wrap my hand around the warm teacup.

"Your grandmother, Caterina's mother, passed away at a young age, leaving your grandfather to raise your mom on his own. Your grandfather's name was King. I don't know if that was his real name or his street name. My parents tried hard to shield me from him. To this day, I'm not sure what he did for a living, but I know he had a gambling problem and would take his grievances out on Caterina when things didn't go his way. He was a very harsh man."

"My mom never talked about her past. I had no idea she had such a rough upbringing or that she lost her own mother." A pit forms in my stomach. I hope to God Michelle isn't right and there is no crime or Witness Protection Program order. After Jax gathered all the information he could of my family tree, it looked pretty basic—except he could only find details on my dad's side of the family. There was nothing concrete on my mom's.

"Miguel tried so hard to protect her. I know there were a few times he jumped in front of her to take the brunt of King's anger. They had plans to wed as soon as they graduated high school, but Caterina didn't turn eighteen until that August. Until then, she was still under her father's control."

"Their anniversary was a few days after Mom's birthday. I never really thought about why they chose that date. I was just a kid and happy to have two celebration cakes in the same week." I smile thinking how that one week in August was always a favorite of mine and Mari's. We would make homemade decorations, cards, and presents. No matter how terrible they looked, my parents always acted like they won the lottery. "I'd say everything worked out for them, but it couldn't have if they left home."

"No." Lucia winces and takes a sip of her tea. "Things did not go as planned."

"Why? What happened?"

"Immediately after your parents graduated high school, they found out they were expecting. It was a surprise, but they were excited. Everyone knew they'd be together forever. For some reason, Caterina insisted on telling her father without Miguel by her side. I think she was worried her father would go after him. As you can imagine, King didn't handle the news well."

A somber silence falls between us as I absorb what Lucia has told me.

"I remember the sounds of the sirens a few blocks away." She hangs her head. "We knew. We all knew it was Caterina. My parents, Miguel, and I couldn't get to the hospital fast enough. It was touch and go for a while. It was a miracle the baby survived. Do you need me to stop?"

"No." I wipe the tears streaming down my face. "I need to hear this."

"*Entiendo.* I understand." Lucia nods. "When the police came to take Caterina's statement, they took my parents aside and told them they believed King intended to kill her. As you can imagine, he was no stranger to the local law enforcement. Thankfully, some neighbors heard the screams and intervened. We knew King would never be in jail for long. He had too many connections on the outside."

I make a mental note to ask her about these connections, but I don't want to interrupt Lucia in her story. I have to know everything.

"That's why they ran away?" I manage to squeak.

"*Si.* According to witnesses, King repeatedly told Caterina that she brought shame upon their family and that he'd right her wrong. It was all about control with that horrid man. Everyone knew it would only be a matter of time before he was released and attacked her again. My parents adored Caterina. They couldn't bear to see anything happen to her or their unborn grandchild. So that night, they took out most of their savings, handed it to Miguel, and told him to take Caterina and drive for as long as they could. The farther away they got the better."

"Did they contact you after they got away?" My body shakes with a combination of sadness and anger.

"Not for a while." Lucia stands and places a warm hand on my shoulder. "No one could run the risk of King getting wind of where they were. It was also a way to protect our family. He couldn't extract secrets from us if we didn't know where they were either."

"The baby..." I trail off as I try to do the math. My brain is too scrambled to think straight. "Was I the baby?"

Lucia reaches over for a kitchen towel. She kneels before me and begins wiping away my tears. "Yes, *mi sobrina*. They left so you could live."

32

Gabby

"**M**an, this dog is the best!" Alex's voice echoes from the living room. He walks into the kitchen, unclips Rex's leash, and hands it to Lucia. "He took me down this side street. I didn't understand what he was up to, but then, I kid you not, there was this gang of pigeons trying to bully a squirrel. I didn't even know squirrels lived in the city. But anyway, the squirrel was holding on to a bagel for dear life. With one menacing growl, Rex scared those winged rats off. You should've seen all the loose feathers floating in the air as they tried to fly away. This guy is a hero right here and oof—"

I jump up into Alex's arms, unintentionally knocking the wind out of him. As soon as I feel the comfort of his body flush against mine, I lose what little control I have left and cry into his chest. I'm so sick of crying, but I guess that's what happens when you bottle up your emotions for over a decade.

"Hey." He gently strokes my back. "Don't be sad. The squirrel got to eat his lunch."

My sobs turn into laughter at the ridiculousness of what he just said. Behind me, I hear the sound of Lucia trying to compose herself. Then Alex's chest begins to vibrate.

"You're such a goof." I pull away from him.

"But I got ya to stop crying." He winks.

"That you did," I agree, feeling lighter than I did before.

"I figured things would be tense when I got back, but the story of the pigeons is true. This guy is a superhero." He reaches down to pat the top of Rex's head.

"I have no doubt about it." Lucia smiles and hangs the leash on a hook. Rex lies down in his crate as if he's worn out from his heroic efforts.

Alex excitedly recants his adventures of exploring the neighborhood and visiting the local firehouses. He met one guy who was a fourth-generation firefighter and worked at the same firehouse his great-grandfather did. "It's like they were born with it in their blood, but I'm babbling on. Do you need more time? Should I go wander around some more?"

"No. It's all good, Alex. My aunt has filled me in on everything and you won't believe it when I tell you."

As we move into the kitchen, I reiterate what Lucia told me about my parents. My heart melts as he listens intently to my story. He's invested and wants to know my history.

"Your parents sound like amazing people," he says in awe when I finish.

"They really were." I slide my seat up closer to him and rest my head on his shoulder.

"I do have one question, though." Alex turns to Lucia. "You said you knew Gabby existed. How did you know that if they never came back?"

"Ah!" Lucia taps her head. "We were so emotional I forgot about that part. Hold on a moment."

She leaves the kitchen. A moment later, she reemerges with a metal lockbox and places it on the table. After opening it, she pulls out an old envelope and hands it to me.

Inside is a single photograph of an infant in a lilac onesie with a full head of curly black hair. I've seen similar pictures to know this is me. Besides, Mari came out bald. I flip it over to read the caption on the back, 'Gabriella is happy and healthy. We are so in love with her.' I let my finger trace my father's handwriting. It's been so long since I've seen it.

"Alex." I gasp. "Look! This is me as a baby." I practically shove it in his face.

"Aww." He pulls it away from his eyes to study it. "You were cute. I guess your love of purple started young, eh?"

"Oh yeah, I drove my parents nuts. I had this lavender overall set that I insisted on wearing all the time. My poor mother had to handwash it in the sink because waiting until laundry day to wear it again was unbearable."

"They never wrote letters." Lucia hands me the next envelope. "Only a single picture with a sentence or two on the back. There was never a return address, and all the envelopes were postmarked from different areas of the Southwest. We knew they did it that way to keep you safe. When the letters stopped coming, we knew something had to have happened."

"Oh my!" My heart sputters as I look at the next picture. It's of me, sitting between my parents. A birthday cake with a number one candle is displayed before us.

"It hurt so much when they left, but seeing their bright smiles in the pictures they sent gave my parents reassurance that they did the right thing."

"Do you know what happened to King?" Alex asks as I pass the photo on to him and grab the next envelope.

"Sadly, he outlived Miguel and Caterina. From what I heard, he went to live in a state-run nursing home and passed away about four years ago. That man burned a lot of bridges during his life. It's not like he had people chomping at the bit to take care of him."

"So he was never involved in anything nefarious? His name's not, like, on a list or something?" Alex asks. Leave it to my protector to get down to business. Though I have to admit, thanks to Michelle's theories, those thoughts crossed my mind as well. I hope I'm not in any danger by revealing myself.

"Oh no. You mean like the mob?" Alex nods at Lucia's question and she smiles and answers, "No, no. He was the last of his family line here in the States. Caterina's family was small, but for some reason, I recall there might be some family back in Mexico—but honestly, dear, I don't know that for a fact and may be speaking out of turn." Interesting. I'll have to let Jax know that. See if he can find out anything more. But for right now? I'm content with what I know.

I continue thumbing through the pictures, feeling joy return to my heart. I thought seeing my family again might open up more wounds, but instead, it makes me feel closer to them, to Lucia, and to Alex, who's enjoying this experience with me.

"Oh, it's Mari!" I gasp when I pull out the next picture of my two-year-old self holding my baby sister. The caption of the back reads, "Marisol was born right before Gabriella turned two. They are going to be the best of friends!"

"Look at that," Alex says, leaning over my shoulder and reading the caption. "You were best friends."

"It's so good to see them all again." I hug the picture against my heart with a renewed surge of energy. I feel so alive.

"I have had these pictures for a long time. I think maybe it's time they go to a new owner." Lucia reaches across the table and pats my hand. I'd told Lucia all about the fire. That I wasn't there, as well as my self-imposed guilt. As expected, she scolded me and told me they're in a better place, and I totally agree. Knowing I have an aunt here with me makes all the difference in the world. Not to mention a man who's proven he'd do anything for me. I feel like I'm floating on cloud nine.

"Do you mean it? I can have them?" I scoop up the rest of the contents from the box. "I'll make copies so you can have them too."

"I can scan them to make a digital file. That way you'll never have to worry about losing them," Alex offers.

"That's a great idea," Lucia agrees, clapping her hands with joy.

"I just noticed something..." I continue to flip through the envelopes. "I can't speak for the first few years because I was too little to remember, but these postmarks—the location and dates—are from the road trips we used to take."

"Sounds like your parents were very efficient. They found a way to safely contact their family while making memories with you and Mari." Alex thumbs through some more pictures I hand him. "I wish I could've met them."

"Me too. My parents and Mari would've adored you, but..." I trail off as realization hits. "We would have never known each other."

"Hmm?" Alex looks up at me.

"If my family were still alive and well, I would've never left Phoenix."

"Meaning we wouldn't have met," he finishes my thought.

"It sounds to me like fate brought you two together." Lucia looks between us.

Alex puts his arm around me and pulls me close. "I hate that in order for us to meet, you had to endure a horrific tragedy."

"Me too." I thread my hand through his. "But I couldn't have asked for a better person to bring me out of my darkness."

33

Alex

“That is the worst rendition of 'Twinkle Twinkle Little Star' I've ever heard.” Gabby doubles over with laughter while I huff and puff from jumping all over the Big Piano at FAO Schwarz. After our visit with Lucia, we decided to explore the city the rest of the afternoon. It's no easy feat since we're scheduled to fly back tonight, but we're trying to make the most of our time here.

“It looked so easy when Tom Hanks did it in the movie.” I thought for sure I'd be a maestro.

“That's 'cause Tom Hanks is a legend.”

“And I'm not?” I place my hand over my heart, pretending to be offended.

“Maybe not Tom Hanks level.” She wraps her arms around my neck and kisses me on the cheek. “But you'll always be a legend to me.”

“Aww, how sweet. Now it's your turn.”

“What?” She takes a step back, letting go from our embrace.

"Come on. If I can make a fool of myself, so can you." I playfully smack her butt, inching her closer to the keyboard on the floor.

"Oh, fine." She steps over to the piano and tests out a few keys before jumping fully onto the instrument. Then she breaks out a perfect rendition of "Chopsticks."

"No! Uh-uh! You can't be serious!" I say a little too loudly. "How did you do that? It was perfect. You must've cheated somehow."

"All right, you got me." She steps off the giant keyboard, earning a few claps from the crowd surrounding us. She takes a small bow. "I have one of these I keep hidden under my bed. I've been practicing it every night just in case this moment ever happened."

"You are such a smart-ass." I give her a quick kiss.

Gabby looks up at me with a smile that reaches from ear to ear. The golden flecks in her brown eyes look brighter than ever. I've noticed a lightness to her ever since the day she told me about losing her family. But after meeting Lucia? It's like she's floating on air.

Something behind me catches her eye and she pushes on my shoulders to spin me around. "Look!" She points to a wall of stuffed dinosaurs.

"Do you see something you want to get for baby J.J.?" I scan the stuffed animals, not sure what made her so excited.

"No, well, yes, of course I'll pick something up for him, but look to the left." She takes my hand and points to a display of hybrid dinosaurs.

"No way!" I grab her hand and zigzag through the crowd to get closer to the shelves. I pick up a bananasaurus rex that looks similar to the one I gifted Gabby, only this one has a little tiara on it.

"Look!" Gabby squeals and holds up the tiniest tuxedo I've ever seen. "They sell clothes too. We have to get my bananasaurus rex a girlfriend."

A half hour later, we leave the toy store with a stuffed bear for baby J.J. and a girl bananasaurus rex with two sets of seasonal wardrobes so the dinos can coordinate for the holidays. My girl hates receiving flowers, but give her a tiny Santa hat for a bananasaurus rex and she'll look at you like you hung the moon.

"Where to next, milady?" We push through the doors and back out onto West 49th Street with our bags full of ridiculousness. There's a chill in the air, but for the most part, the weather is mild for this time of year.

"I know we don't have too much time left." She bounces on her feet. "And I know it's not the most glamorous thing, but I've always wondered what New York pizza tastes like. You know, the real stuff, not like the places back home that claim it's authentic."

I scoop her up and give her a little spin. "We're in a place that has every type of food imaginable within walking distance and you want pizza. I adore you for that." I bend to place her feet back on the ground.

"Wait! Don't put me down just yet." She throws her arms around my neck. "I like this height. We're at the same level."

"You want to know what it's like to be as tall as me?"

"No. I want to kiss you without standing on my toes."

I press my lips against hers, expecting something quick, but she tightens her grip around my neck and draws me in closer. We've kissed before, but something about this time is different. Her body vibrates with a delicate moan when she parts her lips and lets my tongue explore her mouth. She melts into me and I realize she's finally letting herself savor being in the moment.

"I love you, Alex. I have for a while. I was just too afraid to admit it." She reaches out and fidgets with the zipper of my jacket. "It's like I've had tunnel vision and I'm finally starting to see the light. I've been too focused on the fear of losing you to realize I'd be even more devastated if something happened to you and I never had the chance to tell you how I feel. I understand if you're not ready to say it back, but I needed you to know."

"You think I'm not ready?" My smile is so wide, my face could crack. "I've only been holding out because I didn't want to scare you off. You've been through so much and things between us have been going so well. This"—I point my finger at her then back to me—"is real and I'm living for every moment of us together. I love you too, baby girl."

Things are finally coming together. Gabby has been through so much, and again, her strength astounds me. No question meeting her aunt has freed something within her, but there's more. These last weeks, after returning from the chaos of my parents' party, Gabby and I have become inseparable. We've even had a few more sleepovers under the stars, and that's when we have our most intimate conversations. I'm so proud of her for stepping outside her comfort zone and actually thinking about a future.

"We have a lot of things to look forward to." I grab her hand and head in the direction the sales attendant at the store swore had the best pizza. As we make our way through the endless sea of people, I can't help but wonder how lucky I am to have found the perfect person for me.

"Is that it up ahead?" Gabby stops to point at a tiny pizzeria wedged between a barber shop and a place to buy lottery tickets. "It looks like a little hole-in-the-wall."

"Yup." I walk a few steps and open the door for her. The smell of pizza crust and tomato sauce hits us full force. "The ones that don't look like much usually have the best stuff."

We head to the register and place our order for pizza and some drinks. Our food is put on the counter before I finish paying.

"That's enormous!" I exclaim when I see our dinner.

"That's what she said." Gabby winks and takes her slice.

"I'm a bad influence on you, aren't I?" I follow her to a table near the window.

"I'd say more like a positive one." Gabby sits down and takes a large bite out of her pizza. Her eyes turn into huge saucers. "Oh my God, Alex, you need to try this now!"

I happily oblige. "Wow! Now I get the hype. If we had a place like this back home, I'd be there every day." I hold up my slice of pizza and watch the grease from the cheese drip onto my paper plate.

"This is so good. We have to plan another trip out here so we can spend more time. Maybe we can come back out around Christmas so we can see Rockefeller Center when it's decorated." She pauses to take a sip of her soda. "But I also want to come out when it's warmer to see Central Park. Oh! And I've always wanted to see a show on Broadway and—"

"Do all the touristy things?"

"Exactly." She takes another bite of her pizza and does a little happy dance in her seat. Excitement radiates off her and I can't help but think how beautiful she looks right now.

"I like that you're thinking about the future."

"I'm not just thinking about it. I'm looking forward to it. For the first time in my life, I know who I am. Do you know what that feels like?"

"As a matter of fact, I do. Because every time I'm with you, I feel free to be myself." My phone vibrates with a reminder from the airline that we only have a few hours to check in. "We better get back to the hotel. We might be able to get an hour or two of sleep before we have to get to the airport." Our flight is a redeye back home. The difference in prices was huge, and since we couldn't make a longer stay out of this trip, we didn't want to spend a ton of money on transportation. Next time, though, we're going to take one hell of a vacation.

We make our way back to the hotel hand in hand. It's the most natural feeling in the world, and I'm honored to have this beautiful woman walk beside me.

"I think I'm going to take a shower." I pull off my shirt once we get inside our room. "It might help me relax enough to get some sleep."

"Okay." She nods and chews on her bottom lip. I find it odd since she only does that when she's nervous, and she certainly seems content right now. *She's probably just anxious about the flight back home.*

I start up the shower and grab the miniature-sized body-wash and shampoo. I lose track of time while standing under the showerhead that mimics a warm rainfall. I also make a mental note to myself to see if Jax could install one of these things in my bathroom.

"Alex!" I hear the bathroom door open and immediately go on alert, hoping all is okay. But something about her tone sounds all too familiar.

"Do not tell me I have to sing to your bashful bladder again." I look up at the ceiling and shake my head. *God, I love this woman.*

"No." The shower curtain pulls back slightly to reveal Gabby's silky smooth bare shoulders. A white towel is wrapped around her torso. "I was thinking I could join you?"

"Always." I grab her hand to help her into the shower. The towel around her floats to the floor. I gently bring her under the spray. When she kisses me, I realize she's intending more. I continue to let her take that lead because the last thing I want to do is screw things up. This woman is mine. I've known it from day one. And she'll be mine for now, for tomorrow, for years to come.

Forever and always.

34

Gabby

I can't believe the most amazing day is coming to an end. I'm so thankful for everything that has happened, and Alex has made it all come true. When Jax gave me the ancestry information he'd researched, in record time nonetheless, I didn't know what to do. It was Alex who got us the tickets and prodded me to contact Lucia, and thank God he did. Meeting her and learning about my family pushed all my fears away. Now I'm excited for one thing: my future.

The sound of the shower turns on and my mind instantly flashes back to the day I saw Alex naked in his bathroom. Those toned muscles and blue eyes of his are captivating. It's so easy to want him physically. But it's that heart of gold that makes me weak. He's the best thing that has ever happened to me.

"Alex!" I open the bathroom door and blink as steam hits me in the face.

"Do not tell me I have to sing to your bashful bladder again." I can practically see his eyes roll.

"No." I pull back the curtain to one of the most gorgeous sights. Suds drip down his chiseled chest, over his abs, and down his Adonis belt where his penis grows harder by the second. "I was thinking I could join you?" My heart beats rapidly with the need to touch him.

"Always." He offers his hand to help me in. I let the towel around me fall to the floor.

As soon as I'm fully inside the shower, I lean forward to wrap my arms around his shoulders, but he gently nudges me back. "Not yet. I want to savor this moment." His eyes scan me from head to toe and back again. The way he takes me in is ravenous.

"Like what you see?" I've never felt so beautiful, so powerful.

"You're perfect." He pulls me in by my waist and crashes his lips to mine. The feel of his hard build against me is addicting. I let him explore every inch of my body as my hands roam freely over everywhere I've wanted to touch him but have denied myself. We're messy and chaotic, almost as if we're making up for lost time. I don't want this moment to end, but the water temperature of the shower starts to turn frigid.

"I've taken too many cold showers lately." Alex reluctantly pulls back, turns off the shower, and hands me a towel.

"I'm not ready for this to end." I pant, realizing I haven't stopped to breathe much. He also grabs a towel and makes quick work of drying himself.

"I didn't say this had to end, baby girl." He flashes his dimples, and I brace myself at the mischievous look. In one smooth swoop, he lifts me up over his shoulder and carries me fireman style to the bed. "We just need to relocate to somewhere warmer, that's all."

Pulling back the comforter, I snuggle into the welcomed warmth of the bed while Alex lies down beside me. "Now, where were we?" I climb on top of him.

"Well, before the shower rudely interrupted us, I believe we were doing something like this." His hands glide up the back of my thighs, and I let out a moan when he teases my entrance.

"I don't think I can take this much longer." My hand roams down his solid chest. I don't know how long we spent in the shower, but I'm ready to burst. "I need more."

"Tell me what you want, baby girl." He presses a finger inside me. It helps relieve some pressure, but not all of it.

"You." I push back further on his hand. "I need all of you."

"If you're ready and that's what you want..." His voice trails off. "Crap! I forgot a condom." He jumps off the bed and starts digging through his suitcase.

"Umm." I bite down on my bottom lip. "I'm on the pill."

He freezes and quirks up an eyebrow.

"Just to regulate my period. I haven't been with anyone in...well...in a really long time. I'm clean. If you are too and comfortable with everything..."

"Since I've met you, I've been with no one." He saunters back over to me, and I welcome the return of his body next to mine. His arms cage me in, and he presses his lips to my bare shoulder. "This would be a first for me. I'm clean too and I've always used a condom. I do like the idea of nothing between us." He traces more kisses from my shoulder down my side. "You sure about this?"

"Mm-hmm." I hum as I wrap my hand around his hard length and guide him inside me. "You already have my heart. Now I want you to have my body."

35

Alex

My phone pings with a message from our Uber driver letting me know that he's about ten minutes away from our hotel. I'm glad I scheduled it earlier in the day because I'm sure I wouldn't have remembered to do it later considering the last few hours of pure, unadulterated bliss Gabby and I have been indulging in.

Yesterday, Gabby and I took our love to an even higher level. I have no doubt that letting her lead the way with the physical aspect of our relationship contributed to the magical night we shared. She was more than ready and surprisingly not shy. We spent the few hours we had exploring each other's desires. I can't wait to get home so we can continue to learn more.

"Hey, sleepyhead," I whisper in her ear. "We need to get our stuff and go downstairs. Our ride will be here soon."

"I don't want to go." She rolls over and nuzzles into my chest. "Can't we just stay here and live on love? I don't want this to end."

"We could." I start to play with her hair. "But love doesn't pay the bills, and with the prices out here, we'd be broke in like a week."

"Hmph. Why are you acting all responsible?" She sits up and throws the comforter off her. Even grumpy, she's the most beautiful woman I've ever laid eyes on.

"Because someone has got to, and clearly, you're coming down from a high, so you're not thinking rationally." I reluctantly get out of bed and grab my clothes from the suitcase.

"I'm not coming down from a high." She looks confused but starts to get dressed.

"I mean a pleasure high—a sex high. Last night, I satisfied all your wants and needs. Naturally, I've worn you out." I place my hand over my heart. "It took a lot out of me too, but I'd sacrifice my body all over again just to hear you moan in pleasure and scream my name."

"Oh God." Gabby looks up at the ceiling while simultaneously rolling her eyes.

"Yes, you said that last night. Several times I might add and—" My phone buzzes. "Shit! Our driver says if we're not down in five minutes, he's leaving."

"Ack!" Gabby starts throwing everything in her suitcase while I finish dressing. Thankfully, we packed fairly light since our stay was so short...too short. We need to do this again.

We make it down to the lobby with not a minute left to spare. I apologize to the ticked-off-looking driver, or maybe that's just his face, and promise to tip extra for his patience. After catching our breaths from the panic of almost missing our ride, we settle into the back seat of the Mazda CX-30 that will take us to LaGuardia.

"Part of me doesn't want this to end, but I'm also looking forward to going home," Gabby says while watching the city scenery pass by.

"Same," I agree. "This is a cool place to visit, but I don't think I could live out here. It's too busy for me."

"I'm used to urban life, but even this is too much for me. I didn't realize how quiet and peaceful Starboard Beach is until we came out here." She pauses to reflect for a moment. "It gives me greater appreciation for our little beach town."

"So you're okay with living in a smaller place?" I furrow my brow. "I've always worried that you would get bored with it or move back to Arizona, especially because it's warmer."

"I do miss the warmer weather, but I can't imagine living anywhere else. Home is where my people are. It just so happens that those people live in colder temperatures."

"It's not always cold," I remind her. "Our summers can be pretty perfect."

"This is true." She nods, then her eyes light up. "Did I tell you I invited Lucia to come out this summer?"

"You didn't. But I think that's great. Is she taking you up on the offer?"

"She said she's always wanted to visit the Pacific Northwest and now she has a reason to. We're also going to try for monthly FaceTime chats. Originally, it was weekly, but with my schedule changing so much, once a month is more realistic. Oh! And we're going to start our own little book club, you know, like choose the same book to read each month and talk about it. We have a lot of similar interests."

"I'm so happy you two hit it off." I reach over and thread Gabby's hand through mine. "And that you were able to get some pictures too."

"It's one of the best gifts I've ever received. I can't wait to get back and frame some of them. That way I'll always have my family with me."

"They're still with you, baby girl. Even if you can't physically see them, I have no doubt they're still around watching over you." And I wholeheartedly believe their love has helped guide her through her life. Others in her situation might've given up by now, but Gabby kept pushing through. She made a life for herself. She still cares. She still loves.

I reach over, place a kiss on her temple, and feel a vibration in her coat. She pulls her phone out of her pocket.

"It's Aly." A wide grin spreads across her face. "While you were in the bathroom at the pizza place, I sent the girls a few pictures Lucia sent me."

"I'm sure they got a kick out of that."

"Mm-hmm. Aly loved my baby pictures. She said she needs one from you so she can put both our pictures through an app that will predict what our future children will look like."

"She's really excited we got together, huh?"

"Oh please, she told me she wants us to have babies so they can grow up together."

"Did you tell her we already started practicing?"

"I did not." Gabby's face flushes.

"That's okay." I put my arms around her shoulders. "I'm sure once you get back, you'll tell the girls all about how I kept you up all night meeting—no exceeding, all your expectations."

"That's exactly what I'll tell them." She leans into me, and before I know it, she's sound asleep.

Unfortunately, I have to wake up the love of my life about fifteen minutes later because we arrive at the airport. The short nap gives her just enough energy to get through security and to our gate. I'm pretty sure she falls asleep before our plane takes off. I must've fallen asleep as well because the next thing I remember is the flight attendant waking us up to deboard.

It's good to be home.

36

Alex

"How is it possible to die of starvation on Thanksgiving Day?"

"You know there are so many things wrong with that sentence." Gabby points a turkey baster at me.

Okay, so it's not the real Thanksgiving and I might've had some cereal for breakfast, but the smell coming from our oven is making my mouth water. Last year, everyone spent Thanksgiving differently. Well, almost everyone. Michelle took Aly home with her to be her emotional support person, Jax and Carter each went back to their childhood homes, while Gabby and I both worked. I always volunteer to work the holidays so those with families can take the day off.

This year is similar to last year. Gabby and I are both working; Jax, Carter, and Michelle are still going home to their families; only this time, Aly is spending the holiday with her in-laws instead. Since we're not going to be together again this year, the girls collectively decide to hold a Friendsgiving two weeks before the actual holiday.

"Damn, it smells good in here." Carter walks through the door and takes a large whiff of the turkey roasting in our oven. Our kitchen was dedicated to cooking the bird. Aly is working on the side dishes at her and Jax's place, and Michelle is baking up all the sweet desserts next door.

"What the hell happened to you? You look like the ghost of Christmas past. Did something explode over there?" I study my roommate, who's covered in flour from head to toe. "Don't tell me the pumpkin pie is all over the kitchen. I'll eat that stuff straight off the floor and cabinets if I have to!"

"Alex!" Gabby puts a hand on her hip. "You're being ridiculous."

"I'm not. Have you tried Michelle's pumpkin pie? I'm telling you right now, if something happened to it, I'll bring over a can of whipped cream and eat it wherever it splattered on the walls."

"Nothing exploded." Carters rolls his eyes. "All the desserts are safe. I need to take a quick shower." He heads to his bedroom without another word.

"Weird." Gabby looks at me. "What do you think that was all about?"

"Beats the hell out of me." I shrug. "One minute those two are best friends and the next there's some crazy tension going on between them."

"Hmm." She walks over to me and places her arms around my neck. "Sounds kind of like how we were."

"Nope." I lean down and kiss her on the head. "The difference between you and me and Carter and Michelle is that I was always clear about my feelings for you. Carter has his head up his ass, and I don't know what's going on with Peanut."

"I don't either." She frowns. "I've tried talking to her, but she's pretty tight-lipped when it comes to her love life. Between you and me, I don't think she's ever had a boyfriend."

"Everybody decent?" Aly cracks open our door to call in.

"Come on in, Legs."

"Will you stop calling her that?" Jax appears behind Aly like a dark shadow.

"Why? I've been calling her Legs since the day we met."

"Yeah, but we're married now. It sounds weird."

"I don't mind it at all." Aly walks toward the kitchen and looks through the oven window at the turkey. "It's looking good!"

"Will you step away from the oven?" Jax huffs. "You're too close."

"Gabby, will you please tell my husband that I'm perfectly safe staying on the outside of the oven?"

"Umm...yeah. She's fine, Jax." Gabby covers her mouth to hide a smirk.

"I just don't want her to get overheated," Jax tries to reason.

"He's been driving me nuts all morning. He insisted that he help with the cooking."

"That doesn't sound so bad. I helped Gabby with the turkey." I try to back up Jax.

"You were making the turkey dance while I was adding the seasoning," Gabby deadpans.

"Where there's fun, there's flavor." I earn a collective eye roll from everyone.

"Jax wouldn't let me touch any sharp objects." Aly shoots daggers over at her husband.

"They were getting too close to your belly."

"Are you saying my belly is too big?"

"No! I'm saying you're pregnant and... I'm not going to win this argument, am I?" Jax runs a frustrated hand over his face.

"Nope," the rest of us say in unison.

"What brings you over here anyway?" I ask, hoping to change the mood in the room, though I know there's no true animosity between the power couple standing before me. Even with their banter, they still look at each other like the other one hung the moon.

Aly pivots on her heels to face me. "So you know we'll be moving into our new house once J.J. is here, and that time is coming up soon. I started getting sad about not seeing you guys every day."

"Aww, don't worry about that. You'll only be a twenty-minute drive away. We'll come over all the time."

"No, you won't," Jax grumbles under his breath.

"What was that?" I cuff my hand to my ear. I know damn well what he said and just for that, I'm going to make up every excuse to show up and annoy the shit out of him.

"I said that sounds great." Jax pastes on a fake smile.

"Anyway," Aly says, ignoring her husband, "I was wondering if I could have a little memento to bring with me."

"Did you have something in mind?" I ask, not sure where this is going. By the way Jax's face is twisted and turning all sorts of red, I can tell he's not happy about whatever Aly is going to request.

"Your Mr. February towel," Aly states flatly.

"You mean the one Alex gave to me?" Gabby laughs.

About two years ago, I had my Mr. February picture from the calendar printed on a beach towel. I gave it to Gabby as a present shortly after she moved in. Fast forward a few months later and Aly used the towel to prank Jax at the pool.

"I'm surprised you're okay with this." I look at my grumpy friend.

"Gotta pick and choose my battles," he grits through his teeth.

"I wanted to ask you both if it's okay since it was a gift. I can have another made up for you. It's just that the original one holds sentimental value."

"Aly, if it will make you happy, I'm fine with it." Gabby gives her blessing.

"I'm fine with it too, and actually…" I run off to my room and come back a moment later with a padded envelope. I hand it to Gabby. "I was going to wait until Christmas to give this to you, but you can have it now to replace the one Aly's taking."

Gabby reaches into the bag and pulls out a new towel with an updated picture printed on it. "I didn't know you had the photo shoot already," she says, opening up the folded fabric.

"It was rescheduled a few weeks ago when you were working all weekend. I wanted it to be a surprise."

Gabby's hand traces over the picture of me posing shirtless in front of a firetruck. A bouquet of roses is in one hand and a box of Valentine's Day chocolates is in the other.

"You got February again?" Jax gives a sarcastic smirk. He's heard me vent about it being the shortest month of the year.

"I think I'm being typecast." I hang my head.

"I like it." Gabby continues looking at the towel. "I have to admit, it's fun saying that I'm dating a guy from a hot firefighter calendar, but I also like that you're only on display for twenty-eight days."

"Getting a little possessive of me, huh?" I walk over to my girl and wrap my arms around her waist. I'm so in love with this woman, I can barely contain myself.

"Maybe a little bit, Lieutenant Jones," she says with a sultry voice and pulls me in for a kiss. I found out about a week ago that I'll take over lieutenant duties come the first of the year. I think Gabby was more excited to hear the news than I was. She's been referring to me as Lieutenant Jones ever since then.

Gabby insisted I call my family with the news. Fortunately, they were at some charity event and couldn't talk for long, but they told me what they thought and it was as expected. Which is fine. I know now I'll never gain their approval, and I've made peace with that. The only person I care about pleasing is the one who's currently trying to climb me like a tree.

"And on that note, we're leaving," Jax says as the door clicks shut and I continue to kiss the hell out of my girl.

37

Gabby

"We're going to be eating leftovers for days," Jax says, staring at the enormous spread of food. Every flat surface has some type of dish or dessert on it.

"I wish Travis had taken us up on the offer to join us." Aly passes a basket of dinner rolls over to Michelle.

"He's still not comfortable in some social settings." Jax scoops some mashed potatoes on his plate. "I'll bring him some food tomorrow."

"Maybe he'll be with us next year." I try to look on the bright side. Up until a year ago, Travis was only used to hanging out with Jax, Carter, and sometimes Alex. Then Aly moved in and changed the dynamic...for the better, of course. But still, I'm sure it's been a lot for him.

"Speaking of next year..." Aly reaches for the cranberry sauce. "I thought it would be fun to host Friendsgiving at our place."

"That sounds like a great idea." Michelle perks up. "Maybe we can take turns hosting at different places every year."

"Like you'll be around much longer?" Carter grumbles.

"I'll still be here next year and possibly the year after. It's not like I'm just breezing through my classes," she hisses at him, making everyone around the table tense.

That's when it hits me. Everyone else is a permanent resident of Starboard Beach, but Michelle is only here until she finishes law school. Once she graduates, she's slated to work for her family's firm back in Northern California. My heart sinks at the thought of losing what we have. Alex reaches under the table to squeeze my hand. When I look up at him, he winks as if silently telling me that everything will be all right.

"Speaking of your new house..." Michelle blatantly changes the subject. "How are the renovations coming?"

"Great." Relief washes over Aly's face at the new topic. "Everything is move-in ready. Well, except Jax's office."

"Is that the room that had all the mirrors in it?" Michelle asks.

"Yup." Jax looks at me. "Your doctor friend really did a number on that one. We spent so much time trying to salvage it, but ended up ripping it down to the studs." Alex gladly did the honors of telling the guys all about my date from hell and us dropping Josh off at his house and discovering the similar mirrored decorations in his bedroom. We still don't really know whether the home Jax and Aly are moving into had ever been Josh's, but they like to tease the heck out of me anyway.

"He was not my friend," I deadpan.

"Whatever happened to that guy, anyway?" Carter asks.

"There was a rumor going around the hospital that he was let go. No one has seen or heard from him. It's almost like he just vanished."

"He skipped town." Alex pours some gravy over his turkey. "Not only was he a shitty doctor—pun intended—but he's wanted for tax evasion."

Everyone stops eating and stares at Alex. I'm dumbfounded that he never thought to mention this before. Then again, I'd asked him to never breathe Josh's name again.

"What?" He looks at all of us. "I'm friendly with some of the cops. In related news, the house he was living in is going on the market soon."

"Pass." Jax puts his hands up, earning a laugh from everyone, then looks at Alex. "Unless you want to volunteer to remove all those mirrors again."

"No, thanks," Alex replies. "Once was enough."

"I might be interested in it...or something like that," Carter nonchalantly says while buttering a dinner roll.

"What? Why?" Alex is completely taken aback. "Are you looking to leave me?"

"Uh, yeah, with you and Gabby together, I'm kind of like a third wheel."

"Oh, Carter." A pang of guilt hits me. I've been unofficially staying with Alex for a while now. We all get along so well, it didn't occur to me that he was feeling left out. "I'm sorry. I didn't mean to make you feel unwelcome in your own home."

"It's fine, Gabby. It's just kind of the natural order of things. It's time for me to get my own place."

"I've already told you..." Michelle glares at Carter. "I have plenty of space here and I have no intentions of taking on any new roommates."

"And I told you that I don't want any handouts," Carter practically spits out.

"I have a solution." Everyone swings their head to look at Jax. "We haven't decided whether to sell or sublet our condo, so if you want to rent it out for the time being, you can."

"Oh, I love the idea," Aly gushes. "I've gotten so attached to our place, but knowing someone I care about would be living in it makes me feel better already. Plus, it even has an office for all your work stuff."

"I have always wanted an office." Carter leans back in his chair. "And I know you did some quality upgrades."

"The best. Plus, you get the view of the woods and awesome neighbors." Aly goes in to seal the deal.

"All right, you got me." Carter holds his hands up in surrender, then looks at Jax and Aly. "I guess we'll go over the details later?"

"Yup." Jax takes an enormous helping of Aly's sweet potato casserole. "We'll talk over all the boring stuff then."

The rest of the night continues like nothing is changing at all. Aly tells Carter and Michelle how she's the proud new owner of Alex's Mr. February towel. The guys discuss an upcoming convention for home renovators, and at some point, we each talk about our favorite childhood Christmas. We eat a ton, laugh a lot, then eat some more.

This is what I love about my life. This is my family.

38

Gabby

Lights flicker overhead as thunder roars like a hungry lion protecting its pride. My mom used to tell me that the sound of thunder was angels bowling. If that's the case tonight, they're having one hell of a party.

"Good thing the hospital upgraded their generator a few years ago." Marissa looks up at the ceiling. "It sounds like it's going to come right through the roof."

I nod in agreement. I'm so grateful that Alex is at home tonight. I'd be worried sick thinking that he was working out in this weather. Not that I want anyone to risk their life out there, but I'm still coming to terms with the fact that my boyfriend has a dangerous job. If I'm being honest, I don't think I'll ever be fully okay with it.

Looking at my watch, I realize it's just about time to check on one of my patients. The latest Taylor Swift song plays behind the curtain to Room 402. I peek in and smile. There lies a fourteen-year-old girl who has mysteriously started having seizures. Thankfully, all the tests we've run have come back normal, but there's only so much we can do at our small community hospital. She's going to have to see a pediatric specialist for her condition.

"Hi, Brianna. I have good news. There's an opening up at Children's. We're working on getting you transported there now." I look around the empty space by her bed. "Did you kick your parents out?"

"I told them to go get something to eat in the cafeteria," she says with her eyes glued to her phone. Her honey-brown hair lies atop her head in a messy bun. A pink hoodie hides the hospital gown underneath. I wonder if she's trying to make a fashion statement or needs another blanket.

"Are you cold?"

"No," she says with all the defiance of a young teenager. Oh, I don't miss those years.

"Well, I need to get your vitals, so can you put your phone down for a minute?"

My patient rolls her eyes but does as I ask. I grab my thermometer and place it near her forehead.

"Ninety-eight point six. Perfect." I place the thermometer in the pocket of my scrubs.

"Then why am I still here?" Brianna whines. "There's a school dance tonight. All my friends are there, and I'm stuck in this stupid hospital bed."

"You know why," I say gently. I remember all too well being her age. "Hopefully, this is just a temporary thing and you'll be back hanging out with your friends soon."

"My parents won't leave me alone. They keep staring at me like I'm going to disappear or something."

"They love you." I have her remove the sleeve of her hoodie to take her blood pressure. "I know they seem to be hovering, but they're worried. They want the best for you. Can you give them a little slack?"

"Maybe," she grumbles and looks away from me.

"You know, I was around your age when I lost my parents."

"You were?" She turns her head to look at me with wide eyes. Thanks to the support of Alex and the rest of my friends, I'm strong enough to talk about my experience now. Maybe I can help others by sharing my story.

"Yes, and my little sister too." I drag a chair next to her bedside. Thankfully, she's my only patient for the night.

"What happened?"

"They passed away in a fire. I didn't have any other family, so I had to live in a group home until I was old enough to leave. I know right now your parents seem like the lamest people in the world, but I'd give anything to have my mom yelling at my sister and me to clean our room." I sit in the chair, reminiscing about my childhood. "Oh, and the dad jokes. My dad had the worst dad jokes ever."

"Mine does too!" Brianna laughs. "I hate it whenever I say I'm hungry and he's like, 'Hi, Hungry. I'm Dad!'"

"Yup, mine said that one too."

"I'm sorry about your family." Brianna's shoulders slump. "I guess I've been kinda mean to them."

"It's okay. I—" A commotion from the hallway has both of us turning our attention to the door.

"Sir, you need to leave!" I hear the panic in Marissa's tone. Something crashes and scatters to the floor.

"I have a right to see my daughter!" a deep, angry voice bellows.

"Oh no!" Brianna gasps. "That's my dad!"

"Your dad? But I thought—"

"Tim is my stepdad. Greg is my biological dad. He's supposed to be in rehab."

"Brianna!" Greg's voice becomes louder. Another crash. He's getting closer. Someone yells for security.

Scanning the room, I contemplate how to keep us safe. Patient rooms don't lock from the inside and there's not enough time to barricade us in.

"Brianna, I need you to go into the bathroom. Take the shower chair and try to barricade yourself inside." I begin helping her out of the bed. "No matter what I say, do not come out until you hear a cop tell you it's okay. Do you understand?"

Her face pales, but she agrees and stands. Her body trembles as I usher her into the bathroom. As soon as I hear the door click shut, I turn around to meet a set of angry gray eyes that are glassy and bloodshot. Brianna's biological father towers over me. His dirty, ragged clothes hang off his slender frame, and greasy black hair droops in front of his face. He looks and smells like he hasn't bathed in days.

"I just want to visit my daughter. I went to the house and some neighbor said they saw an ambulance take her." His speech is barely comprehendible. "Nobody told me."

He pushes me up against the door with such force, my head makes a loud thud when it connects with the steel frame. My ears begin to ring and I feel a warm trickle of blood down the back of my neck. At least I'm still standing upright when I look up to face my aggressor. If I can stall him for just a few more seconds, security will get here and everything will be okay.

"Hi. Your name is Greg, right?" My voice sounds like I'm in a tunnel. More yelling comes from down the hallway. *Help will be here any moment.* "Brianna had to use the bathroom. She'll be right out."

"I will see her now," Greg growls.

"And you will. In just a—"

"I said now!"

A sharp pain sears through my abdomen and my vision blurs before everything fades to black.

39

Alex

"Man, this storm is brutal." Carter stares out the window just as another flash of lightning illuminates the sky. It's not often we get rough storms out here, and this one seems to be a doozy.

"Yeah, I'm glad I'm not working tonight." Gabby is at work, but thankfully, she got there before the worst of it hit. I know she's safe.

"I think I'm gonna go down to the gym and blow off some steam. You want to come too?" He grabs his sneakers from the pile of shoes next to our front door and begins lacing them.

The phrase "blowing off steam" and "Carter" is an unusual pairing. My roommate is the calm, cool, and collected one of our bunch, but lately, he's been getting agitated about every little thing. I should go with him to see what's up, but I'm not the Dear Abby kind of guy, and I know he won't talk until he's ready.

"Nah, tonight is the perfect night to work on a project of mine." I rub my hands together.

"A project?"

"Yup! Hold on a sec!" I run into my bedroom and pull out the black velvet box that's hidden in my sock drawer. I can barely contain my excitement when I come back out to show my friend the secret I've been keeping.

"Dude—" Carter's eyes widen the minute he notices the box in my hand. "Is that what I think it is?"

"Yup." I flick open the lid to reveal a white gold diamond and amethyst engagement ring. I contemplated taking Aly or Michelle to help, but neither of them was around. It turned out I didn't need their input because the moment I walked into the jewelry store and saw the ring with Gabby's favorite color in it, I knew it was the one.

"Damn, man! I don't know much about jewelry, but that looks like it was made for Gabby."

"I know, right? I'm so excited to give it to her, but I'm not sure how to propose."

"You mean you don't want to do it the same way you've done it the last thousand times?"

"Exactly! This is serious business. This time, I'm coming equipped with sparkly things." I hold the box back to admire my selection. I can't wait to give it to her. Our relationship might still be new, but I think it's safe to say we're in this for the long haul. If we can handle everything we've already been through, we can handle whatever life throws at us. "I thought I'd scroll through YouTube and get some ideas for a proposal."

"I'm also not an expert on that, but my guess is to avoid anything in public. Gabby's not the type that wants a lot of attention drawn to her."

"Yeah, I already figured that. I'm thinking about placing the ring somewhere she might not think of and having a quiet dinner at home, or something like that."

"Well, let me know if you need help with anything." He claps me on the back.

There's the Carter I know.

Once my roommate heads downstairs to the gym, I plop down on the couch with my phone in one hand and the ring in the other. Angry thunder rattles our windows as I scroll through countless proposal ideas.

"Hey!" Aly pops her head in through the door. "Are you, umm...busy?"

"Not really." I study Aly's features as she walks through the doorway. It's not like her to come over to our place, and something about her seems...different. "Everything okay, Legs?"

"Yeah, umm...kinda." Her eyes immediately home in on my left hand, and her energy switches back to regular bubbly Aly. "Oh my God! Is that—"

"Shh!" I cut her off, though no one is around to hear us. I jump up and meet her near the doorway, holding the ring box out for her to see.

"Oh, Alex!" she gushes. "This is beati—ohhh." She grabs onto my bicep and digs her nails into my skin. That's when I realize she has her other arm wrapped around her belly.

"Shit, Legs! Are you in labor?"

"I don't know," she says after taking a deep breath, her grip loosening. "I thought it was Braxton Hicks contractions like all those other times, but then my water broke and—"

"Your water broke?!" I shout.

"I didn't mean for it to break! It just happened." Aly's voice cracks and a few tears stream down her face.

"I'm sorry. I didn't mean to yell at you. You just caught me off guard. Where's Jax?" I look behind her as if he'll magically appear.

"Travis's truck got stuck in the mud. Jax went to help. I told him to wait out the storm at Travis's because I didn't want him driving in this weather. I'd be a stressed-out mess." She stops to take some slow, deep breaths. "That was before my water broke and the contractions got stronger. I tried calling him, but it's going straight to voicemail."

Shit. Travis is the one who lives in the log cabin out in the woods where Gabby and I count stars. Cell service can be finicky out there. With this rain and wind, I wouldn't be surprised if it's completely knocked out.

"Is Michelle around?" I could call Carter for help, but if he's in the gym, he has the music cranked up to full blast and won't hear my call. Plus, he has a weak stomach.

"She had a study group at the library." She doubles over in pain. "Oww! It's getting worse!"

"I need to call nine-one-one. I don't think it's safe to drive you to the hospital."

"I already called. There are lots of accidents and trees down blocking the roads. They said it could be a while before they get here."

I curse to myself. I know this is a scary situation and the last thing I need is for her to panic even more. I take a breath and center myself, knowing what I have to do. I am a paramedic, certified and all. I can do this. Actually, I've done this before.

"I need you to find a comfortable place—the couch, the floor, wherever you want. I'm going to grab some towels and my medical kit. I have news for you, Legs."

"B-bad news?" She pants in pain.

"No bad news, only good news," I tell her confidently. "This is not the first time I've delivered a baby."

"God, I was hoping you'd say that." Aly's shoulders visibly relax as she awkwardly sits down on the couch.

"I've delivered two babies before, which makes this number three and that just happens to be my lucky number."

I run into my room, put the ring box back in my drawer, and grab some towels and my medical kit. I come back out to see Aly resting comfortably on the couch. I think just knowing she's not alone has put her at ease. I kneel down in front of my friend and take her hands in mine.

"Everything is going to be okay. We got this, Legs."

***

"I can't believe he's here." Aly cradles her healthy baby boy while sitting upright in her hospital bed. I'm glad she finally has a chance to rest.

Things got pretty crazy for a while. Aly's contractions became steadier and stronger. Before we knew it, she needed to push. Jax and the paramedics arrived just as the baby made his grand entrance. The look of panic, realization, and elation that crossed over Jax's face in that moment is something that will be engrained in my memory forever. Also, I'm never going to let anyone forget that I helped bring baby J.J. into the world.

"You know, Jaxon Junior is nice and all, but have you considered changing his name to Alejandro? It has a nice ring to it."

"You're never going to drop this, are you?" Jax groans.

"Nope." I rock on my heels and turn toward Carter, who's been quietly sitting in the corner. "How ya holdin' up there, buddy?"

"I've been better." He rests his head up against the wall, still looking a little green around the gills. Did I mention my roommate is a class-A wimp?

"I'm sorry you had to see all that." Aly winces.

"I just wish neither of you saw that part of my wife," Jax grumbles.

"It's okay." Aly puts a reassuring hand on Jax. "Alex was strictly professional, and I don't think Carter saw much before he blacked out."

"Please, let's just never bring this up again," Carter moans. Unfortunately for him, he showed up shortly before Jax and the paramedics did. It was right at the height of Aly's labor and to say he saw more than he bargained for is an understatement. The poor guy passed out in the doorway, and Jax had to step over him to get to Aly.

Once Aly and J.J. were taken care of, I helped Carter try to pull himself together. I fired off a text to Michelle and Gabby, hopped in the shower, grabbed my still-stunned roommate, and headed for the hospital.

My phone pings in my pocket with a text message from Michelle. "The road by the library has cleared and Peanut is on her way. Gabby hasn't read the message yet, but she's still working. I'm going to run up to Peds and let her know the good news."

I leave my friends to go tell Gabby my epic story. She's going to be so excited, yet disappointed she missed J.J.'s birth.

I feel the change in energy before the elevator doors to the pediatric unit fully part. Cops line the hallway and medical equipment is scattered all over the floor. A woman cries in a chair while a man has his arm around her shoulder, trying to comfort her. The place looks like a tornado went through it, and Gabby is nowhere to be found. My heart sinks into my stomach.

"Alex!" a voice calls from behind me. I spin around to see Marissa, the charge nurse. Her hair is a mess and mascara streaks down her face, but worst of all, her scrubs are covered in blood.

"Marissa, what the hell happened?!"

"Th-there was an altercation," she stammers. "Security was called, but they didn't get here in time. Gab-Gabby tried to protect a patient and was attacked. She—"

I don't bother listening to whatever Marissa has to say. I'm already bolting down the stairwell to the Emergency Department. The fact that someone was violent toward the woman I love, the woman who wouldn't hurt a fly, makes me damn near feral. I have to see her. I have to know she's okay. I can't lose her.

I throw open the door to the Emergency Department, running so fast that I nearly skid when I spot Dr. Cody, one of the attending physicians. His face grows solemn as soon as he sees me approach.

"Where is she?" I demand.

"I'm so sorry, Alex. She was taken upstairs for emergency surgery."

40

Gabby

Sunlight peeks through the curtain and pierces my eyes. I turn my head from the offending light. My body feels heavy, like I've been buried in weighted blankets. I can't stand weighted blankets. I remember Michelle saying she thinks they are the best invention ever, but I don't like the feeling of being held down. I blink my eyes open to move the troublesome blanket but realize that only a light sheet is covering me. It's my own body that feels like lead.

I wiggle my toes in an attempt to wake up my feet. A tickly, tingly sensation shoots up my legs. I wiggle my fingers next. My one hand moves freely, but my other hand is stuck. With the energy of a sloth, I lift my head up a bit to see what's trapping my hand. Another hand. Another hand is holding my hand through the rails of the bed. A hospital bed. I'm in the hospital all the time but not as the patient. I don't need to follow the hand up to its owner because I'd know that hand anywhere.

Alex is sleeping in a chair next to me with his feet propped up on another. The usual stubble on his face is much fuller. I wonder how long I've been here, how long he's been here, and who the hell put in these IVs?

"Al—" I try to call his name, but my mouth and throat are a dry, sandy mess. I try to say his name again to no avail. I resort to wiggling my fingers that remain under his heavy palm. He shifts at the feeling but doesn't wake. I move my fingers in a scratching motion. That seems to do the trick. His eyes flicker open. We stare at each other for a moment before he leaps from his chair.

"Oh my God, you're awake!" He cradles my head and places kisses all over me. He pulls back and sees the confusion written all over my face. "Do you know where you are? Do you remember what happened? Oh God! Do you know who I am? Wait a second!" He runs over to a table and comes back with a cup of water. Hallelujah!

With a shaky hand, I take a small testing sip. I can feel every drop of the cool liquid absorb into my body. I take a larger sip and then another. Alex watches me with wide eyes.

"Do you...umm...do you remember anything?" he asks.

I swallow another sip of water and test my voice. "I-I don't know. What am I doing here? Was I in an accident or something?"

"You were attacked trying to protect one of your patients." His face falls. It's then I notice the dark circles under his red, puffy eyes.

"Brianna." A blurry memory comes to the forefront of my mind and I wince as searing pain rips through my torso.

"Where does it hurt?" Alex grabs the nurse call button and presses it.

"Here." My voice sounds gravelly as I wave my hand over my middle section. "Where's Brianna? Is she okay?"

"Thanks to you, she is. She said you used your body to block her from her father. You have a lot of severe bruising and—"

He pauses to take a deep, shaky breath. "He stabbed you." Tears begin to streak down his face. He uses the hem of his shirt to wipe his bloodshot eyes. "I could've lost you."

"Alex." I hold out my hand to grasp his. My heart sinks, looking at the agony written all over his face. "You would've done the same thing. I don't regret what I did. She was so scared."

"I just wish I were there to protect you." He brings my hand up to his lips.

"Did someone press the call button?" a familiar voice calls from behind the curtain.

"Yeah, Emily, she's awake." Alex doesn't take his eyes off me.

A young nurse with dark eyes and a long braid down to her waist walks in. Her rose-colored scrubs look like they were tailored to her body, and the metal stem of the stethoscope around her neck catches in the sunlight. I don't know Emily well, but I've heard several doctors sing her praises about the attention she gives to her patients. I smile, realizing that my care team was most likely handpicked.

"It's nice to see you awake." Emily checks my IV.

"Please tell me what happened." I look at my nurse. "I know if I ask him, he'll try to sugarcoat everything."

Alex harumphs in his seat while Emily takes over my care. I know he doesn't want to worry me, but not knowing will make it worse.

"You're in good shape, all things considered. You were stabbed in the abdomen. We had trouble controlling the bleeding, so you were sent for an exploratory laparotomy. Thankfully, the attacker missed all your vital organs. We're running antibiotics in case of infection. You have a few compression fractures to your spine. You'll be making a fashion statement with that back brace for a few weeks."

"Ugh." I lean my head back. That's also why I feel like I'm being held down. "He slammed me up against the door. What happened to him...the...um...father?"

"Greg," Alex answers with his lips pursed tight. "He was taken into custody before I got a chance to beat the bastard's ass. They're holding him on assault charges, violation of a restraining order, and a laundry list of other things."

I reach out to touch Alex's face and am surprised by the amount of stubble. "How long ago did this happen?"

"Two days," Alex answers. "You've been asleep for most of the time. You'd stir every now and then, but the pain meds kept knocking you back out."

"And this guy has not left your side." Emily gives a wink only I can see. My heart melts knowing this loving man has stuck with me. Not that I'd expect anything less. I have never once doubted his love for me.

"The guys at the station are taking turns covering for me. They knew I wouldn't be in the right frame of mind to work." Alex's phone pings. "Peanut is looking for updates. According to Carter, she's been stress-baking twenty-four seven."

"Tell her I'm fine and she can come visit anytime, but please don't bring anything to eat." I fight back the pain in my lower half and adjust myself in the bed. I love her food, but I don't see myself indulging in anything anytime soon.

"Will do." He nods and types something into his phone.

"Aly must be a worried mess." I can't imagine how she took the news, between her anxiety and her heightened emotions during pregnancy.

"Legs is doing well. She's pretty distracted right now." Alex's face twists into an odd smirk.

"Oh?" I say, confused, and then it hits me. "Oh my God! Did she have the baby?"

I try to shift in my hospital bed with a surge of adrenaline. I don't know where she is, but I want to be there for her.

"It happened the night you were attacked." Alex stands to fluff my pillow. "She went into labor during the storm and had the baby at home. Well...our home. On the couch, specifically."

"Wait. Don't tell me you delivered J.J." I gasp.

"All nine pounds, two ounces of him." Alex puffs out his chest.

"Are they here?" I can't believe I missed two days of baby snuggles.

"I think they're getting discharged today."

"More like right now," Aly's voice sounds from the doorway. A nurse pushes her wheelchair while Jax walks beside them, holding a baby carrier.

"No. Way!" I fight through the pain to sit up straighter. I already want to rip this back brace off me.

"Hold on, let me help you." Alex puts his arms under mine and lifts me a bit.

"I insisted that you meet our newest family member before we left." Aly lifts up from her chair to give me a hug. "I'm so happy you're okay," she says into my ear. "I wanted to come up and visit you, but I wasn't allowed to leave maternity. Alex did a great job giving us updates, though."

"I'm so sorry I missed J.J.'s birth," I tell my friend as she pulls away from our embrace.

"Everything worked out." She sits back in the wheelchair. "You should've seen Alex take charge of the situation. I knew we were in good hands."

"Can we not talk about that part?" Jax mumbles as he gently unbuckles his newborn son from his carrier.

"Let me guess. Alex wants you to name J.J. after him now." I try to stifle a laugh. I know it will hurt like hell if I do, but it feels so good to be surrounded by many of the people I love.

"Of course he does." Jax rolls his eyes and moves closer to me. "Would you like to hold him?" He looks down at his baby boy.

I'm so excited, I can barely get the words out, so I opt to nod vigorously. Alex grabs a pillow to help steady me, and Jax places the most peaceful-looking baby into my arms.

"He's so perfect," I gush, taking in his chubby cheeks and button nose.

It's at that moment I realize that I want the type of life Jax and Aly have. Heck, I always wanted to get married and start a family of my own. The only thing holding me back was fear. I look up at Alex, who watches me with all the adoration in the world, and I know he's thinking what I'm thinking.

The next time he proposes will be the last time. I want to spend the rest of my life with this man.

41

Alex

"Get your butt back in bed," I order Gabby. She responds by sticking her tongue out at me. "Oh, real mature." I try to hide my smile. It's been a few weeks since the attack, and Gabby is recovering beautifully under my care. She has officially moved in with me, and Carter has moved into Jax and Aly's old place for the time being. It's like we played musical condos or something.

"Dr. Johnson did not confine me to bedrest. She even told me it's good to move around."

"Yes, but that was before you pulled your stitches from trying to reorganize the closet." I place my arms across my chest.

"But I'm so bored," she whines. I've heard nurses make the worst patients and now I see why. Trying to get this girl to relax is like trying to herd kittens.

"We're going out later," I remind her. Jax and Aly are having everyone over for dinner tonight. Gabby thinks it's a housewarming party, but that's just a ruse.

"That's still hours away." She pouts.

"I'll tell you what. I might have something to keep you occupied until then, but you need to go back to bed."

Gabby gives me a look and I realize it sounds like I'm propositioning her for sex.

"It's not what you think." I bark out a laugh. "Now get back to bed."

Once she returns to our bedroom, I grab the gift box off the top of the fridge. Having a short girlfriend has its benefits. It's been hidden up there for a week and she still hasn't noticed.

"What is that?" Her eyes home in on the gift box. Michelle helped with the wrapping, so it looks extra fancy. It's wrapped in sparkly purple paper and topped with a silver bow to match the colors of the other gift I have for her.

"Open it and find out." I sit beside her on the edge of the bed.

Gabby begins tearing through the package like a kid on Christmas morning. Her eyes light up when she sees what's inside the box.

"You got me an embosser?" Her voice lifts with excitement.

"Yup. Now you can personalize all your books." I grab one of the many books from her nightstand and hand it to her. "Want to try it out?"

"Yes!" She opens the book to the title page and presses down on the handle. When she pulls it away, she runs a finger over the stamped design and reads the custom text. "From the Library of Gabriella Jones."

Confused, she continues to examine the imprint while I pull a second box out of my pocket and get on one knee. I study her face as she puts it all together.

"Now I know this is not the first time I've asked you, and I realize you never took me seriously all those other times." It dawns on me that I never prepared a formal speech, so I decide to just say what's on my heart. "My family was right about something. I've always been afraid to grow up, but that's because I associated aging with becoming more like them. I think that's why I've been so drawn to you. From day one, you've never asked me to change who I am."

"That's because I love who you are." Her voice quivers as she wipes away a few stray tears from her beaming face.

"And I love who you are. I know you miss your family, and I wish I could've met your parents because they created such an amazing woman. What do you think about starting a little family of our own?"

I open the ring box. "Gabriella, will you make me the most ridiculously happy man on the face of this Earth and marry me?"

"Yes!" She throws her arms around me, nearly knocking us both to the ground. Her embosser and book fly off the bed, but I keep a grip on the ring box and my future wife.

Once we both get into an upright position, I place the ring on her trembling hand while she squeals with delight.

"For someone who didn't want to get into a relationship, you seem pretty excited right now," I tease.

"We're really getting married." She holds out her hand to admire her ring. I'm elated to know I picked the perfect one.

"Yes, we are." My face hurts from smiling so hard.

"When?" She takes her focus off the ring to look at me.

"Whenever you feel like you're ready." I shrug, not really caring about the details. As long as we're together, I don't mind. "It can be in ten minutes or ten years."

"Well, I can definitely say that ten minutes is out of the question. I'm not getting married with these bruises all over me."

A lump forms in my throat at the realization of how I could have lost her just a few short weeks ago. On top of the main injuries, Gabby sustained severe bruising when she was pushed up against the door. The dark black and blue coloring all over her back has since switched to purples and yellows, but it's still going to be a while before all traces of the assault are gone.

"And ten years is way too long," she continues, pulling me out of my thoughts. "Maybe a year?"

"A year sounds great." I don't know much about weddings, but I know planning can take time.

"On second thought." She nibbles on her bottom lip. "A year would put us in the winter. I'd rather get married in warmer weather."

"Then we can wait until the following summer." I wrap my arm around her shoulders and place a kiss on her head.

"Perfect!" She clasps her hands, then gasps. "We can get married on the beach! Would your family be okay with that? I also don't want anything too big."

"Don't worry about them," I reassure her. "It's not their day, it's ours." I already plan on telling them that they're not allowed to attend the wedding if they plan on showing up with a camera crew and attitudes.

"We can invite Lucia, and—oh my gosh, I have to tell the girls!" She grabs her phone from her nightstand, but then catches the look on my face.

"Do they know already?" She raises a brow.

"So you know that housewarming party we're supposed to go to? It's actually an engagement party for us."

"No. Way. What if I said no?"

"Then we would be having a really awkward dinner."

42

Gabby

"Wow! It looks like a winter wonderland." My jaw drops as we pull up to Jax and Aly's house that's outlined in twinkly white lights. The white wraparound porch is adorned with garland consisting of holly leaves and red berries. A life-size gingerbread village display takes up the majority of the front lawn.

Christmas is only a week away and I'm still not quite sure what we're doing for the holiday. Alex already told his family that he would not be visiting this year, stating that I was not in any condition to travel and he wasn't going to leave my side. His parents were horrified when they learned about the attack. They wished me well, but it only gave them more fuel to promote moving back to Elmwood Grove. Because now, in their eyes, Starboard Beach must not be a safe place to live.

As for me, I've always felt safe and at home here. The attack could've happened anywhere. I'm thankful the response time was quick and I have the best support a girl could ask for. I know I'm going to be okay.

The door to Jax and Aly's new home nearly flies off the hinges as two of my closest friends stampede down the driveway toward me. I freeze and squeeze my eyes closed, bracing for impact, but it doesn't come. Instead, I open my eyes to Aly and Michelle scanning Alex and me intently.

"She has gloves on," Michelle whispers loudly out of the corner of her mouth. "Do you think he did it?"

"They both look happy...and Alex is smiling." Aly playfully pokes him in the chest. He's clearly amused by their behavior.

"Doesn't count." Michelle shakes her head. "Alex is always smiling."

"Good point," Aly agrees and looks down at my hand again. "Why are you wearing gloves?"

"I should be asking you why you're wearing a tank top out here in the frozen tundra." I cross my arms over my chest. It's below freezing and there's a fresh coating of snow on the ground. Just looking at her gives me chills.

"My hormones are still all wacky. I keep getting hot flashes."

"Post-partum hot flashes," I inform her. "That should go away once your hormone levels go back to normal.

"Yes, yes. That's what my doctor said too." Aly jumps impatiently from foot to foot. "Now take off those gloves. Do we have something to celebrate or what?"

I look up at Alex, who gives me a goofy grin of approval. I hold up my hand and pull off the glove like a magician pulling a rabbit out of a hat. The girls scream and shower me with hugs the moment they spot the ring sparkling on my finger.

"Whoa! Whoa!" Alex gently pulls Aly and Michelle away from me. "Remember, Gabby is still experiencing some soreness and—oof!" The girls tackle him to the ground, and I dissolve into a fit of giggles. It hurts a little to laugh, but it's worth it.

Carter and Jax stroll out the door and take in the situation. "What do you think, Jax?" Carter says. "Should we help him?"

"I think"—Jax kneels down and packs some snow into his hand—"that's a great idea."

"Run!" Aly yells as a snowball pelts Alex in the leg. He quickly goes on the defense and begins creating his own arsenal. Carter pitches a snowball but ends up accidently hitting Jax, which results in a full-on war amongst the guys.

"Come on!" Michelle laughs as she and Aly usher me away from the craziness and into the warmth of the house.

"Oh, Aly—you did such a beautiful job!" I gush as soon as we enter the living room. A grandiose Christmas tree with presents stuffed underneath stands in the corner, and little snowmen and gingerbread decorations are tastefully tucked onto shelves throughout the room. Above the fireplace mantel hangs a banner that says, "Congratulations, Alex and Gabby!"

"We are so happy for you." Aly pulls me into a hug. I feel another set of arms around my back and I know it's Michelle trying to get in on all the love.

"Now let's get a better look at that ring." Michelle grabs my hand and begins asking me a million questions about the proposal. My friends listen intently as the guys make their way back into the house and hang their wet coats and other winter stuff to dry.

"I almost forgot," Aly pipes up once I finish my story. "We have a ton of food in the kitchen. We set it up buffet style so everyone can just get what they want."

"I call first dibs on those lemon bars Michelle was making," Alex yells.

"Don't hoard them, Alex," Michelle calls out. "Because it's a special day, I made a separate batch just for you to take home."

"Woohoo! Thanks, Peanut!" Alex gives her a quick hug, then looks at me. "Do you want me to get you anything?"

"Maybe just something to drink. I could really go for some baby snuggles right now. Is J.J. in his room?" I ask Aly. She has brought him over several times for some cuddle sessions and I have no doubt cozying up with that sweet little baby has helped with my recovery. I'm grateful that he's still in the newborn stage so I can easily hold him. I should be fully healed by the time he starts to get all wiggly.

"He's in the nursery with the best and most unexpected helper ever." Aly beams. "Go take a look."

Soft lullaby music plays as I walk down the hallway to J.J.'s bedroom. My heart melts when I peek in and see Travis in a rocking chair with a red bundle lying on his chest. A sleeping Gus rests in front of the crib.

"Hey," I whisper, not wanting to startle the sleeping baby.

Travis turns to me with a serene look on his face. "Come on in, Gabby. You won't disturb us. If this kid can sleep through Gus's snoring, he can sleep through anything."

"Gus does sleep quite loudly," I agree. As I get farther in the room, I realize J.J.'s onesie is actually a little Santa suit. "Wow! Even the baby didn't escape the Christmas decorations." I sit down on the ottoman in front of the rocker.

"I'd say this was all Aly's doing, but I know for a fact Jax bought this outfit." Travis looks down at my hand. "Congratulations."

"Thank you." Even if J.J. can sleep through loud noises, I keep my voice light.

"How are you feeling?" he asks, and I know he's referring to my recovery and not my recent engagement. It's sweet that he's concerned.

"I'm good, all things considered. I, uh...I've been dealing with some nightmares."

"That's to be expected." Travis nods. "The nightmares should decrease over time, but if you feel like you need extra help, I can give you a list of some counselors that specialize in PTSD."

"Thanks. I've actually been doing phone sessions with a psychologist. I think it's been helping." I fidget with the ring on my finger. "Aly said you've been a great help."

J.J. makes a small cooing sound, and Travis gently pats his back.

"Aly said you've been a great help."

"I enjoy coming over and hanging out with this guy. He doesn't cry when he looks at me." Travis visibly swallows a lump in his throat. "But I know newborns don't have the clearest of sight."

"He can't see far away things, but he can see enough. Babies are very intuitive. J.J. knows he's safe with you." My heart breaks for the wounded warrior in front of me.

"Aly keeps trying to reassure me that J.J. will be fine because I've been with him since day one."

"And she's right. All J.J. will ever see when he looks at your face is love."

A horrible odor cuts through the air, ruining our heart-to-heart moment.

"Oh God, is that smell coming from the baby or Gus?" I look between the two possible offenders.

"That is definitely the baby." Travis stands with J.J. comfortably in his arms. "Come on, Jax owes me a favor since I was the one who climbed up on the roof to hang the lights."

"Really? I didn't know Jax has a fear of heights." I follow Travis into the hallway.

"He doesn't. He has a fear of geese and several of them flew overhead just as he was climbing the ladder."

"Oh." I bite down on my lower lip, trying not to laugh.

"Don't worry about laughing. I still give him shit about it to this day." Travis spots Jax across the room and heads over to make a special delivery.

"There you are." Alex hands me a mug of hot chocolate. "Did you get your baby snuggles in?"

"Not yet." I take a sip of the chocolaty goodness. "I will once he gets all cleaned up."

"Oh God! I think it's a blowout!" Jax runs past us in a panic with his son in his arms.

"Do you think that will be us one day?" Alex leans down and whispers in my ear. "The, uh...having a baby thing, not the dirty diaper thing."

"I knew what you meant." I laugh. "And definitely, but I'd like to just take some time for me and you first."

"Sooo you mean you want to focus on the present and not worry about the future?"

"Exactly." I stand on my toes to give my fiancé a kiss. "Thank you for not giving up on me."

43

Epilogue

ALEX, SIX MONTHS LATER

"We are gathered here today to celebrate the life and untimely death of Stinky the car." I dramatically pause to acknowledge the small audience gathered in the parking lot.

We knew Stinky's time was coming to an end, but we didn't realize how soon until this morning when we received word that the entire transmission and electrical system called it quits. Gabby became emotional when the local mechanic offered to have it towed to the junkyard. I knew we needed to have a formal goodbye. Thankfully, Michelle, Aly, Jax, and Carter were able to make it to the lot just in time to give Stinky a proper send-off.

"I remember the first day I encountered Stinky. It's a day forever etched in my mind because that's the day I met my future wife. As I'm sure you all know, Gabby locked her keys inside Stinky and in a magnanimous act of sheer heroism, I braved the hurricane-force rain and winds to—"

"Wait a minute," my bride-to-be interrupts. "Yeah, it was a nasty day outside, but it was by no means hurricane level."

"Woman." I narrow my eyes at her. "Let me tell my story. You'll get your chance in a minute." I turn back to the crowd. "As I was saying, my altruistic actions saved Gabriella from the bear and—"

"All right." Carter walks up and places his hand on my shoulder. "I think we've heard enough and I'm sure the tow truck driver here has another job to get to. So how about you say goodbye and we move on to someone else."

"Fine." I roll my eyes and turn toward Stinky, who is already hooked up to the back of the flatbed. "Thank you, Stinky, for the fond memories and for bringing the best person in my life safely to me." I pull out a pine tree air freshener and toss it into the rolled-down driver's side window.

"Who's next?" Carter looks at the crowd. "Michelle? Or do you need to be somewhere that's not here?" Thankfully, she ignores his dig as Aly raises her hand.

"I'll go." Aly takes her place in front of the tow truck. "I was the last of the group to meet Stinky, but I grew fond of him in the short time I knew him. Whenever I think of Stinky, I'll be reminded of all our trips to The Local and the times we'd sneak out to Whips even though we told Alex we were picking Michelle up from her late-night study group."

"Wait! What?" I shoot a look at Gabby, who pretends to be distracted by a bird in a nearby tree.

Aly says her goodbyes, takes an air freshener, and tosses it through the window. She turns to her husband. "Jax, would you like to say something?"

"I'm good, sweetheart." Jax waves his hand while bouncing his son in his arms. With his dark hair and gray eyes, baby J.J. and his father look so much alike. I've been wanting to take some face paint and draw a sleeve of tattoos on J.J.'s arm.

I think it would look so cool. Jax is not a fan, but Aly has softened up to the idea. She's been mushy with everything lately since she and Jax found out that baby Parker #2 is on the way.

"I guess I'll go next," Michelle pipes up, giving Carter the evil eye and taking the spot Aly just abandoned. "I always got a little excited when I pulled into the parking lot and saw Stinky there. It meant that my roommate and friend was home. I love the times we spent together, but I never really did care for the smell, and I still stand by my theory that Stinky was a delivery car for a cheap Italian restaurant and—"

"Thank you, Michelle," Carter says, handing her an air freshener. Oh. My. God. These two! They've been on-again, off-again for months now, and Gabby and I can't seem to get a peep out of our friend. And we're dying to know what's up!

"But I wasn't finished," Michelle argues.

"Yes, you were," Carter mumbles under his breath and motions for Michelle to finish up.

"Thanks for the memories, Stinky." She flings the air freshener. It bounces off the rim of the window but lands safely inside the vehicle.

"I guess I'll go next." Carter takes the invisible stage. "To an outsider, Stinky was a bit of a nuisance, considering the keyed entry, the perpetual smell, and the annoying smoke that came from the exhaust pipe."

"Hey!" Gabby looks at Carter. "The smoke was only a recent thing."

"Yeah, well, I got stuck behind you like five times on Ensign Street during the last few weeks," Carter hisses. He looks like he's about to elaborate but decides against it. "Rest in peace, Stinky." He too takes an air fresher and tosses it through Stinky's window.

"I guess it's my turn." Gabby hesitantly takes a step toward the flatbed. "Stinky has seen me through so many times in my life. From living on my own while in nursing school to starting my career and eventually moving a thousand miles away to Starboard Beach. Throughout most of those years, Stinky was the only consistent part of my life. I think that's why it's so hard to let go. But over the course of the past two years, my family has grown. I have grown and I know I'm going to be okay.

"Goodbye, Stinky. Thank you for doing your job and safely bringing me to the next chapter in my life." She takes an air freshener and tosses it through the window. "May you rest peacefully in that big junkyard in the sky."

44

Bonus Epilogue

GABBY, 5 YEARS LATER

"What in the world are you doing?" I call to my crazy husband as he walks past our reading nook for the umpteenth time. It's my favorite spot in the house. Alex and I moved out of the condos shortly after we were married. Our home is one of Jax and Travis's flips. I knew I had to have it from the moment Aly showed me a picture of the cozy-looking cottage. It came with everything I wanted: a place for my books, a large backyard for gardening, and our own washer and dryer.

Our six-month-old daughter Maya sits on my lap while drooling over her favorite book, The Very Hungry Caterpillar. Her face lights up when Alex finally stops and pokes his head in. She's a daddy's girl through and through.

"I'm just making sure everything is perfect." He adjusts a large duffle bag strap on his shoulder. A blanket is draped over his head, and Maya's favorite stuffed penguin is tucked under his other arm.

"It looks like you're bringing the whole nursery with us." I scan him as Maya spots her penguin and puts her arms out, desperately trying to reach it.

"You can never be too prepared." Alex drops the blanket and bag on the floor to quickly hand our daughter her lovey. She grabs it and immediately starts chewing on the beak. Those poor teeth are coming in fast and furious. It's led to some rough nights, but we've been taking it all in stride. Just a few years ago, this was everything we wished for.

Alex and I decided to start a family about a year after we were married. We, of all people, should have known that life never goes the way you expect it. Still, we were shocked month after month when those little pregnancy tests kept coming back negative. It was painful, especially watching Aly seemingly become pregnant every time she looked at Jax.

Then one night on our annual trip to New York to visit Lucia, I became ill. I thought it was something I ate, but Alex insisted on running over to a local pharmacy and purchasing a test. Lo and behold, two pink lines finally appeared.

"You know, we don't have to go tonight. We can wait until Maya gets a little older."

"But the weather is perfect." Alex's smile falls. "Have you even looked outside? There's not a cloud in the sky. Plus, I already dropped Bear off at Jax and Aly's."

Bear is our German shepherd that Alex insisted we adopt. He was sure the dog would make a great sidekick for him. But Bear chose me as his person instead. It's not that Bear doesn't like Alex. It's just that he prefers me and I love it. He's also a fantastic and gentle playmate for Maya.

"I haven't." I take in the sight of my husband, who still gives me butterflies. Much to Miss Ruby's delight, Alex's muscles have only grown bigger as evidenced by the sleeves of his shirt wrapped tight around his upper arms. Once we found out we were having a baby, he increased his upper body workouts, stating that he wanted to ensure he could carry Maya anywhere and everywhere. Sometimes, I worry if she'll ever learn to walk.

"Well, if the weather is good..." My voice trails off as I hold our daughter up for Alex to take.

"Hello, *mi princesa,*" Alex coos while adjusting Maya in his arms. "We're going to take you somewhere special. It's a place where Mommy and Daddy have been going since before we were an item." He pauses. "Now that I think of it, it's probably where you were conceived."

"Alex! That's not appropriate!" I hiss and stand from my chair. Although...he's probably not wrong.

"She has the right to know how she got here," he states matter-of-factly, and because he knows how much they affect me, he flashes his dimples.

"What am I going to do with you?" I groan and throw my hands up in the air.

"I can list several things you can do with me, but *that* would be inappropriate considering our audience."

Our daughter just looks at us with a gummy grin. We have yet to determine her eye color as it changes depending on what she's wearing. Sometimes, they have a bluish hue like her dad's and sometimes they look brown like mine. With the little fuzz she has on her head, we've determined she'll probably have dark hair, although right now, she resembles Mari as a baby. She's absolutely adorable, and I can't believe she's ours.

"Let's just get going." I grab the duffle bag and blanket Alex placed on the floor and head to our vehicle. I opted for another small sedan after Stinky bit the dust, but I recently traded that in for a minivan. I thought it would be overkill with having just one baby, but I do enjoy the fact that it can hold a ton of supplies. Plus, it's a pretty smooth ride.

We even took the minivan back to Elmwood Grove to visit the Joneses. While I'm still not their biggest fan, we all manage to stay cordial for the few visits we make each year. We want our daughter to know who her grandparents and extended family are even if we do keep them at a distance. Lilli, of course, is the exception. She was even in the delivery room when Maya was born.

I hate to admit that it took me far too long to realize that you don't need to share blood to be a family. And boy, do we have quite the family out here in Starboard Beach. Even Ms. Ruby has adopted Maya as her grandchild...or maybe that's great-grandchild since she just had her ninety-third birthday. Her neighbors threw her a huge block party complete with food trucks and bouncy houses for the kids. It felt like half the town came out to celebrate with her. I can't wait to do it again next year.

There's no shortage of love out here in Starboard Beach, and although I sometimes like to reminisce over my past, I try my best to live in the present and look forward to the future.

"She's all buckled in and ready to go," Alex says, slipping into the driver's seat.

"It really is a beautiful and clear night." I keep my eyes focused on the sky as I take my seat on the passenger side.

"See? What did I tell ya? It's perfect." He clicks his seat belt into place and calls out behind him, "Okay, baby girl. It's time you get to experience counting the stars."

Acknowledgements

A huge thank you to Sue Grimshaw (Edits by Sue). Because of your prompts and confidence in me, this book did not turn out to be a novella with a large plot hole in the middle.

Erica Russikoff (Erica Edits)- Thank you for your patience with me as I continue to learn the ins and outs of writing fiction. I'm so happy we were able to work together again.

Emily A. Lawrence (Lawrence Editing)- I am so impressed with your knowledge and love that you take such great care to ensure my work is polished.

Thank you to Kari March (Kari March Designs) for creating a gorgeous cover that blends so well with book one.

Kelly, my alpha reader, I don't know what I'd do without your positivity and encouragement.

Holly, my beta reader. If I can get your stamp of approval, I know everything will turn out great.

Sarah, my sensitivity reader. Thank you for graciously volunteering and offering your input. I truly appreciate it!

To my mother-in-law, Diana, and my brother-in-law, Eddie, who are both registered nurses, thank you for helping me ensure Gabby's parts were accurate.

To the original Stinky, my brother-in-law's '82 Chevy Citation; thanks for the inspiration!

A heartfelt thank you to all my friends, family, and readers for your support and words of encouragement.

About the author

Tracy is a former teacher turned homeschooling mom of three amazing kids. She resides in her home state of New Jersey; however, thanks to her husband's military career, she has also lived in the Southeast and Pacific Northwest. She is a lover of coffee, chocolate, vanilla seltzer, and the Oxford comma. She often writes at her kitchen table with her rescue dog at her feet. For news and updates on future projects, please go to tracymcjames.com or visit on the following pages:

 facebook.com/TracyMcJamesAuthor

 instagram.com/tracymcjamesbooks

 pinterest.com/authortracymcjames

 twitter.com/@tracymcjames